TOR&THE IMMORTALS

Heather,
I hope you
enjoy the book!
Your friend
Paul. Duffé

PAUL DUFFÉ

Paul Duffè

Special thanks to Sonya D., Elizabeth Copley, Ryan Schinneller for the cover art and technical assistance, Kevin L. Sneed for the internal art, and especially Tor.

Prelude

"Confound this wretched fog!" grumbled the portly house servant as he stood under a flickering gas lamp that was barely illuminating the foggy street corner.

"The bloody bastards probably changed their minds," he again mumbled out loud noticeably agitated looking at his pocket watch.

The time was 1:05am and the damp night air was chilling him to his bones. Deciding to wait no longer, the servant snapped the watch closed and stormed off across the street in the direction of his employer's extravagant town home. Midway across he heard the faint sound of footsteps approaching. "Who's there?" he demanded. "I say, who's there?" he said again almost in a panic.

As the sound of his voice faded into the night, three fashionably dressed men suddenly emerged from the fog almost right before his eyes.

"It's about bloody time you got here," the servant snapped expressing his irritation. "If my master was to return home early and find me out here at this Godforsaken hour, he'd be sure to release me from my employment," the servant said nervously looking from side to side.

"You are being paid and paid well for your service," said the taller of the three men as he stepped forward to confront the shorter-portly servant. Though his features were mostly obscured by the darkness, his aristocratic tone suggested he was a man of considerable stature.

"Well, be that as it may, I was beginning to think that maybe you had changed your mind," the servant added with a twisted and halfcocked smile.

Ignoring the sarcasm, the tall man looked up at the many barely visible outlines of elegant townhomes surrounding the square, "Which one is it?" he asked with a harsh commanding tone.

"It's this one sir," the servant said pointing to the large three story building in front of them.

Grosvenor Square was one of London's more elite residential neighborhoods. Here, the who's who of London society resided when in the city for the season.

"Where does he keep it?" the tall man asked looking up through the thick fog at the barely visible building.

"On the third floor, in a locked room at the top of the stairs. You will need this," the servant added as he pulled a key from his breast pocket.

"He keeps the door locked?" asked the tall man.

"Yes, locked up tight at all times. The staff are forbidden to enter that room."

"And you are sure he will go to the room this night?"

"Aye sir, he will come tonight. That I'm sure. Every time he goes to that part of town, he returns somewhat out of sorts and goes straight to the room. He spends hours up there. Sometimes we hear yelling, shouting, laughing and even crying. It's bloody peculiar if you ask me. A man of his stature should not be carrying on in such a way. Bloody peculiar," the servant again repeated.

"I did not ask for your opinion," said the tall man with a dismissive tone. "Tell me, does he have anything else in that room?"

"No sir. Only the painting."

"About this painting, how long has he had it?"

"Many years sir. I was a young man when his artist friend presented it to him. You know the one, the bloke who went missing all those years ago. The portrait briefly hung in the master's study until one day he suddenly covered it and had it moved to the room on the third floor. We believe that was the day he made his deal with the Devil," the servant added.

"Deal with the Devil? What deal?" demanded the tall man fixing the servant with a withering stare.

"Why sir, surely you've heard the stories about my master's deal? You know, how he sold his soul to Lucifer himself in order to always stay youthful?"

"Ridiculous" hissed the tall man.

"No sir, it is not. That was nearly 30 years ago and as you can see, I've aged considerably but not my master. He still looks as he did the day I began my employment. Take my word for it sir, I know! I've seen things. No one who has done all he has can remain untouched by time. His youthful innocence only conceals a much darker-no, not darker, evil. Yes evil is the word for it. Evil inner monster. He's an abomination that's what he is!"

"Enough of this nonsense." the tall man said interrupting the servant and turning to address the other two men who had accompanied him. "Tonight gentlemen, we will end this." Neither spoke but nodded in agreement.

"When will he return?" the tall man asked facing the servant.

"Just before dawn."

"And you are sure he will go to the room this night?"

"Yes, I'm sure. Like clockwork," the servant added with a smug halfcocked smile.

"Good. Stay out of sight until we return. Is that clear? He must suspect nothing."

"Yes sir. Whatever you say sir. But when do I get the rest of my money?"

"You will be paid when we return," the tall man responded. He turned to face the servant, "Do not disappoint me. For if you do, I can assure you you will not live to regret it." As the tall man spoke his eyes flashed with a brilliant yet frightening yellow green glow.

"Yes, Gov." the servant stuttered, "I...I'll be waiting as you say sir."

Then the tall man nodded to the others and all three disappeared into the fog as they climbed the stairs to the townhouse.

"Society people, what a pompous ass. I'll wait here all right. With what you're paying me, I'll be here all night." the servant muttered to himself as he too disappeared into the fog.

# # #

At precisely 4:45 in the morning, the three men were alerted to the sound of a carriage racing along the avenue. As it drew closer, they heard the frantic clattering of horse hooves on the deserted cobblestone streets. Looking down from the third story window, the tall man saw a carriage emerge from the fog and come to an abrupt stop in front of the townhouse. Seconds later he heard the front door burst open and footsteps running up the stairs.

"This is it gentlemen, conceal yourselves," he whispered. On his instructions, the three men disappeared into the shadows of the room.

Moments later the door burst open. From the doorway all that was visible in the darkened room was the covered painting that was partly illuminated by the dim light flooding in from the hallway. From the shadows the men watched as a fashionably dressed hysterical young man ran in and frantically pulled the cover off the painting. Frozen in place, the young man had a look of unspeakable horror on his face. The image he saw looking back at him was hideous. He could see every sin and unspeakable vile and evil act he had ever committed starring back from a grotesque, but familiar face.

The young man clutched at his hair and began to scream. Catching the sight of a knife laying on the window ledge, he grabbed it and then plunged the knife into the painting. Upon doing so he felt a sharp pain in his back then fell to the floor in agony.

Hearing the screaming from the street, the servant stared in the direction of the third floor window and noticed the fog was glowing a strange yellow-green color. "May God have mercy on his soul," muttered the servant. He looked down and stepped back into the shadows.

Moments later the three men returned to the street.

"How'd it go Gov?" The servant asked the tall man.

"You will never speak of this night. Do you understand?" the tall man said avoiding direct eye contact. "Never again," he repeated under his breath.

"Yes, yes. Sure Gov. Whatever you say. Just pay me the rest of what you owe me and you can count on my silence," the servant said, casually dismissing the warning.

"Never Again!" the tall man hissed as he abruptly looked up and locked his eyes directly on to the servant's while simultaneously grabbing him by his neck and pulling the stunned man to within inches of his face.

The servant's face was locked in a mask of frozen horror. The tall man's eyes were ablaze with a frightening yellow-green glow. The servant felt the life draining from his body and was helpless to do anything about it. Those terrifying eyes were the last thing he saw as darkness closed in.

Slowly closing his eyes, the tall man released the servant letting his lifeless body fall to the ground in a crumpled mass.

Turning in the direction of the other two men he said, "We shall never speak of this night again gentlemen." The three men disappeared into the fog.

PART ONE

Chapter 1
Jacksonville Florida
Present Day

Another goddamn Doctors appointment the man thought to himself as he sat in the waiting room of his doctor's office. He had had so many appointments over the past six months he figured he should be use to the waiting by now. But, he wasn't. Ryan Anderson was one of the youngest and most successful advertising executives in the southeastern United States. His time was valuable and he was not a man who waited for anything. And, once again he had no choice. For the past six months his health had been rapidly deteriorating and no one knew why. Marked by a considerable loss of energy matched by an equally alarming loss of weight, Ryan felt like he was slowly wasting away.

What the hell is going on with me? he thought for the millionth time as he sat waiting. *Am I going to die? Why me? I've got the best health insurance money can buy! What is the fucking problem! Why can't they find what's wrong with me and fix it! Goddamn doctors are milking my insurance company while I wither away! What kind of treatment is this?* He worked himself into a rage. *They better find something this time! Six months of testing and still nothing! Today better be different!* He sat simmering in his mounting frustration.

"Mr. Anderson, the doctor will see you now," said a kind faced heavy set nurse. She smiled while trying to hide her shock at seeing his appearance. Use to the routine, Ryan followed her as she led him to a scale. "Let's get your weight," she said. Giving her an annoyed look, he complied.

"Another 6 pounds. I wish I knew your secret Mr. Anderson. I could stand to lose a few pounds myself," the nurse joked trying to make light of the situation.

"Unless the doctor has an answer, I might be taking this secret to my grave," Ryan snarled. He abruptly stepped off the scale. He was in no mood to joke. She showed him to a private waiting room.

After waiting only a few minutes there was a knock on the door. Ryan's doctor entered carrying a thick file. He tried to hide his surprise at Ryan's physical appearance as he reached to shake his hand. "How are you doing today?" he asked.

Ryan rolled his eyes. "The same," he said. "Please tell me you found an answer in that pile of paperwork you carried in, Dr. Green."

Dr. Green shook his head noticeably frustrated then sat down in a chair across from Ryan and exhaled a long sigh. Looking directly at Ryan, Dr. Green tried to remain professional.

"I wish I had the answer Ryan. God knows I do, but I'm sorry, I don't. I cannot find anything physically wrong with you." he said. His desperation briefly showed through his stoic professional mannerisms.

The doctor's compassion was of no comfort. Unable to contain his aggravation, Ryan momentarily lost control and slammed his hands down on the examining table. "Damn it, Doctor! This has been going on for over six months! What the fuck is the problem? I'm wasting away here! What's happening to me?" Ryan demanded. He was desperate. "What's happening to me?" he asked again as he bowed his head. He didn't have the energy to carry on, his outburst drained him. All he could do was put his hands to his face and lower his head in disappointment.

"Don't give up, Ryan," Dr. Green said. He put his hand on Ryan's shoulder to try and comfort him momentarily losing his professionalism and taking on more of a fatherly role. "I understand your frustration, really I do. But so far our tests haven't found anything. Everything comes back normal," Dr. Green said. His composure had returned.

"Normal? Does this look normal?" Ryan asked as he stood up and lifted his shirt. He was practically just skin and bones. "If I suck in what's left of my gut my pants will drop to the floor. I've lost over 70 pounds in the last six months. I can't afford to lose any more!"

"I know Ryan. I'm also concerned. Please be patient. We will get to the bottom of this I can assure you of that," Dr. Green said with genuine concern in his voice.

"I only hope there's something of me left by the time you have your answers." Ryan shook his head and sat back down on the examining table. "Can you at least give me something for the pain? Every time I eat I feel like someone punched me in the stomach," he said rubbing his abdomen with his right hand.

"Of course Ryan." Dr. Green wrote out a prescription and handed it to him. "In the meantime, I'd like you to do another round of tests."

"Great, more tests. Can't wait."

"I can't fix you until I know what's broken."

Dr. Green paused. Then with obvious hesitation, he continued.

"I'd like to refer your case to some of my colleagues. I think the more minds we have working on this the sooner we'll get answers." He took a deep breath and again hesitated before continuing. "Because to be totally honest with you, I have no idea what's wrong. I'm completely stumped." Dr. Green's eyes showed he was telling the truth. Next to Ryan, he was the most concerned.

Reading his expression Ryan actually felt sorry for the man. Disappointed he managed a partial smile and said, "Do what you have to. I trust you," he added lightly squeezing the doctor's shoulder before getting off the examining table.

As Ryan was leaving Dr. Greens office he couldn't help but be discouraged. He'd lost count of how many times he'd been to see him over the past six months. It all started in mid-July when he began having severe stomach pain. At first he thought it was his appendix or an ulcer and immediately saw his family doctor, Dr. Green. But everything checked out okay. Over the next several weeks the pain grew worse. After numerous tests, his doctor was baffled and referred him to specialist after specialist. But months later and now under the care of yet another "specialist" there was still no change. If anything, his condition was only getting worse. Much worse.

Ryan was on a total liquid diet. No solids. Even the slightest solid food threw his stomach into a convulsive fit. And now, even liquids were beginning to cause him extreme discomfort. Desperate and hardly consuming anything, he was again at his doctor's office and again given no answers, only sent for more tests. "How can everything be normal when I feel like this? There has to be something wrong!" Ryan said to himself out loud as he exited the building where his doctor's office was located. Discouraged, he decided not to go to work and drove home instead.

# # #

Dr. Green sat in his office thumbing through Ryan's file. "What the hell am I missing?" he said out loud. "The answer has to be here somewhere." Shaking his head, he examined the numerous test results.

A few minutes later an intern walked in.

"Was that Mr. Anderson again?" he asked.

"Yes, I'm afraid so," Dr. Green said. He leaned back and exhaled a long sigh visibly expressing his frustration.

"What's wrong with him?" the intern ask, taking a seat across from Dr. Green.

"I don't know, Frank. I honestly just don't know," the doctor said. He sat up and removed his glasses. "Ryan's been coming to me for months now and only seems to be getting worse."

"Could it be psychological?"

"I guess. But I doubt it. I've known Ryan for many years and he's always been healthy. That's the most puzzling part of all this. I don't think the guy has ever been sick a day in his life. Until six months ago, I'd only see him for routine checkups and at our gym. He's always been in exceptional condition. But, now I just don't know. Nothing makes sense. To tell you the truth Frank, I honestly don't know what's wrong with the man. He's practically starving to death and there's nothing I can do to stop it."

Chapter 2

The next morning as Ryan was getting ready for work, he caught a glimpse of himself in the full-length mirror in his bedroom.

Damn! Is that really me? He looked like a concentration camp victim he thought as he examined the image looking back at him from the mirror. He was startled by how bony he looked. His ribs were showing through his skin. His sunken eyes and thin face so shocked him that he momentarily felt a sense of panic and fear. His physical appearance was especially alarming since he had always made such an effort to keep it up. As a teenager, Ryan found comfort in working out and pushing himself to his physical limits. He especially liked taking part in various physical activities. Some of this had a lot to do with boredom, but, mostly Ryan liked rigorous physical challenges and pushing his body to its limits. His natural athletic build went a long way in helping him achieve his goals. He enjoyed showing off his physique and more importantly taking care of himself. His efforts did not go unnoticed by beautiful women either. Fortunately, he had the looks to compliment his body, and as he matured into a handsome young man, he learned the value of having both.

Because of his physical attributes, he proved to be good in most sporting activities especially swimming and soccer. Ryan was competitive by nature and enjoyed receiving recognition for his successes. By participating in various sporting events and competitions, he often got the attention and acceptance he could not get at home.

Unfortunately, Ryan's childhood was one of sadness and tragedy. He knew nothing of his real parents, but he did know he was adopted when he was just a baby. When he was five he lost his adoptive parents in a plane accident. Not having any other children, Ryan was the sole beneficiary to a large fortune.

Ryan's father owned a wide variety of businesses and his mother had inherited a considerable fortune from her family. Upon their death, Ryan became the responsibility of William Blake, acting CEO of his parent's financial empire. Knowing Ryan would one day be of age to access his trust, Mr. Blake made it a priority to get Ryan the best education money could buy. After years of private schools and college abroad, Ryan returned home a well-educated young man.

Though he excelled academically, physical activities were his primary means of satisfying his competitive nature and showing off. Exploiting his athletic abilities through competitive sporting activities allowed him to receive recognition for his successes and accomplishments. His coaches, his friends and teammates were his family, the only family he knew.

Though Mr. Blake made it a point to see that Ryan got the best education he could, he was not a loving man, never expressing emotion or giving praise. He was always very serious with Ryan. Over time, Ryan learned to accept this. He bore no ill will toward Mr. Blake. After all, he was grateful to have all that he did. Ryan respected Mr. Blake and understood that their relationship would always be distant. For this reason most of all, Ryan sought to earn the attention and acceptance of those around him and he did this by pushing himself and excelling in everything he did, physical and academic.

By the time Ryan graduated from college and was of age to take control of his inheritance, he instead opted to postpone accepting any money from his trust. He left Mr. Blake in charge of his assets and decided to try and make it on his own. When he announced his plans, he felt for the first time in his life that Mr. Blake was actually proud of him. Blake accepted Ryan's decision and assured him that all would be there for him when he was ready.

Within five years Ryan had become one of the city's top advertising executives by making partner at age 26. He liked working with people and his natural competitive nature made the advertising industry a perfect fit for him. Though he always knew he could have large sums of money available to him with just a phone call, Ryan resisted the urge. Until the onset of his unexplained illness, he had done very well. For fun he even got involved with a promising local band that was becoming popular throughout the city.

Disturbed by the image in the mirror, he quickly turned away and shook his head in bewilderment. Looking at his newly acquired black and white cat, Tor, laying on his bed cleaning himself Ryan said, "Well, at least I still have you buddy. You don't care what I look like as long as I feed you do you boy?" Ryan joked. He patted Tor's head before continuing with his morning routine.

Tor was a great comfort to Ryan. If not for him, Ryan firmly believed he would have been dead months ago. In a strange kind of way, Ryan felt a sort of soothing comfort when around Tor. The mysterious pain in his stomach always seemed to ease up in the cats presence. Unfortunately, the relief was only temporary. Eventually, Ryan would have to leave Tor and the pain always returned.

Standing in the shower while letting the hot water refresh and awaken his senses, he briefly thought about the last time he had sex. The mystery pain in his stomach and lack of energy only seemed to be getting worse. Every day he was noticing some new kind of pain. Sexually, he had no drive or desire. Over the past 6 months along with his energy, his sex drive had dropped significantly. No longer working out or doing any kind of exercising, he barely had enough energy to drag himself into work each morning. Sex was the last thing on his mind these days. This was disturbing in itself, especially since he had spent most of his young adult life in its constant pursuit. At least he found some comfort in knowing that he did not have AIDS. Having been tested for everything numerous times he knew it was nothing sexual, anyway. But still, he was growing more and more concerned daily.

As he got out of the shower and dried off, he again couldn't help but notice how scrawny he looked in the bathroom mirror. He thought to himself that he hoped it wasn't too windy outside today or he might get blown away.

Chapter 3
Dr. Alistair Wolchek

Arriving at the office every morning had also become uncomfortable for Ryan. His firm occupied the 20th floor of the Adams building downtown. From the time the elevator doors opened, he knew he was on display. He could feel the looks as he made the walk through the department to his office. His physical appearance made it impossible to hide that something wasn't wrong. For the time being, his co-workers were doing their best to pretend as if everything was normal. They still greeted him warmly while hiding behind fake smiles and pleasantries. Ryan was aware of the office gossip about his health. He knew he was the subject of whispered conversations that always ended abruptly when he walked by. Most days he would get to the office early so he could avoid the morning greetings. It was the looks and fakeness he wanted to avoid. The fake concern and the questions. How are you? Are you OK? How are you feeling today? He could see the truth in their faces. It was like everyone was a mirror trying to hide what he already knew and he hated it! For someone who was used to being the object of attention and interest, now he just wanted to be invisible. Get to work, do what he had to do and leave ASAP was the daily routine. That is, when he did go into work.

For the time being, Ryan's job was secure. At present, he was a full partner and the top earner in his firm. He specialized in image consulting, mostly for large corporations looking to be viewed as more people and/or environmentally friendly, as well as for prominent and elected officials who wanted to "shine up" their public images. Politicians were especially lucrative. Even if Ryan couldn't stand the individual he enjoyed the challenge. Mentally, he was still as sharp as ever. And to his benefit, his reputation preceded him. This allowed him the luxury of using the phone to meet most of his client's needs. In the advertising arena, this was a luxury few in his position could claim. This kind of work typically required a considerable amount of "flesh pressing". Ryan was fortunate in that he had put together one of the best creative teams in the southeastern United States. Ryan knew he could count on his people to perform their jobs well. Though he still was involved with creating strategies, he left the public work to his subordinates. Knowing how important image was in this industry, Ryan was concerned about the message his image would send to existing or new clients. This was difficult for him since this was the part of the business he enjoyed the most.

For now the plan was to keep his clients at phone's length and lean on his team as much as possible. Occasionally he had to meet clients for various unavoidable reasons and wondered how comfortable they were working with a man who looked as if he already had one foot in the grave.

A secondary concern was the firm itself. More and more Ryan found himself wondering if he should just quit and live on his inheritance until he died. But the answer was always the same. No. He needed to work and the social interaction. What he did was rewarding, even addictive to some extent. He would try and stick it out as long as he could.

For the time being his position was secure. But competition outside his team by other partners was fierce and they were always looking for that one opportunity or weakness to exploit. At present, Ryan was the top earner, but there were many more right behind him waiting for their shot. Hungry to prove themselves and he was aware of this. After all, it's how the game is played and to some extent he even respected it. But for now, he was not ready to step aside, not yet anyway. Unfortunately, his health was working hard against him. The more time he took to deal with his health issues, the more opportunities he created for his enemies to position themselves to strike. Some had even offered to take over his team under the guise of "just helping out." For the present, Ryan still had control, but even he was beginning to wonder for how much longer. Working required a considerable amount of energy-energy he did not have. Many believed it was just a matter of time. Most felt Ryan was on his way out.

As he was walking to his office he casually nodded to two of his more attractive female coworkers. Temporarily interrupting their conversation, they smiled and said good morning. After he passed, one of the women said to the other,

"I heard he was out again yesterday."

"Yes. Another doctor's appointment."

"Is it serious?"

"I don't know. He's not talking about it. But have you noticed how much weight he's lost?"

"Yeah." Then suddenly realizing something the one lady exclaimed, "Oh my God!"

"What?"

"Do you think it's...well, you know, AIDS?"

"Oh my God! I hope not. But, well...he has been around."

"I think he's been with every woman on this floor. Present company included."

"Do you think we should get tested?"

"Couldn't hurt."

"Damn! I hope it's nothing serious. He's a good lay!"

"Lisa! I'm shocked! What would your husband say?"

# # #

Later that morning one of the firms junior partners stopped by to visit with Ryan in his office.

"Knock, knock, knock, hey buddy. Just stopping by to check on your party plans for New Years. Are you going to make it to Ronda's party? If it's anything like last year, it should be a blast!"

Surprised by the question, Ryan thought to himself, "Yeah sure. I'll be there. I'll even bring the band and we'll kick it all night like we did last year. What a fucking stupid question. Do I look like I'm in any condition to party you ass kissing little bitch!" Instead Ryan remained calm and with a halfcocked smile looked up from his paperwork and said, "I think I'm going to pass Stan. Maybe next year."

Stan Cooper was probably one of the most concerned about Ryan's health. By his own reasoning, Stan believed he would have the most to gain if Ryan had to step aside. Though Stan did show a minor amount of creative talent, mostly he benefited by latching on to the efforts of others. In Ryan's opinion, Stan was a complete waste of company resources and only had his job because of a family connection to a very senior partner. Ryan could not fire him, but he didn't have to work with him. Nor would Ryan let him latch on to any of his or his teams projects. Stan however, saw Ryan's illness as the perfect chance to weasel his way into taking over Ryan's team and Stan had already began laying the ground work at higher levels to do just that.

He took a seat across from Ryan. "You know man, I don't want to pry, but I'm worried about you. When's the last time you got laid? Are you Okay? I mean health wise. Everything cool?" he asked. His face registered an almost believable show of concern.

Amused by his performance, Ryan was again temped to say, "Have patience Stan. I'll be dead soon enough and then all my accounts will be yours to fuck up." But again he forced a smile and said, "Thanks for your concern but the doctor says everything is checking out okay. It's just a bug or something."

"Well, that's good news," Stan said. He stood up and forced a big toothy smile. Continuing to act relieved he added, "We can't let anything happen to you Ryan. We all know you're the number one man around here."

Ryan rolled his eyes and faked humility. "Thanks Stan. And don't have too much fun at Ronda's New Year's Eve party."

As Stan walked out of his office Ryan couldn't help but laugh. *Stan should get an award for that performance. His concern almost sounded genuine,* Ryan thought to himself as he laughed out loud.

Interrupting Ryan's mental critique of Stan's performance, Ryan's assistant, Cindy, buzzed in and said, "Ryan, I have a call for you on line one."

"Who is it?"

"He says he's a doctor. He has a very pronounced English accent. Do you want me to take a message?"

"That's okay, I'll take it. Thanks." He picked up the phone.

"Ryan Anderson here, how can I help you?"

"Mr. Anderson? My name is Dr. Alistair Wolchek. We haven't met but I know your doctor."

Ryan hesitated. "My doctor?"

"Yes. Dr. Green? He said you gave him permission to seek outside assistance with your case."

"Oh yes, of course. Sorry. I forgot. How can I help you?"

"Hopefully I can help you Mr. Anderson. I've been reviewing your case and would like to examine you myself."

"Great, more tests. Wonderful. Sure Doctor. Just tell me where and when," Ryan said, with a clearly disappointed tone.

"I understand your frustration Mr. Anderson. And I promise not to take much of your time."

Ryan realized he was rude to the man. "Sorry Doctor. I didn't mean to sound ungrateful. I'm just frustrated by this whole thing. I do apologize and would be thankful for any help you can give me."

"No need to apologize. I understand your frustration. I'm going to be in the U.S. next week. Can I call you to set up a meeting?"

"The U.S.? May I ask where you're coming from Doctor?"

"London. I have some business over there next week so I thought if it was convenient, I could see you then."

Surprised and noticeably hopeful, Ryan said, "Sure Doctor. That's fine with me. Just call with the time and place and I'll be there."

"Thank you Mr. Anderson for your time. I look forward to meeting you."

"As do I Doctor. As do I."

# # #

Looking up from his desk, Dr. Wolchek focused his gaze on a distant portrait hanging on his office wall. "So we finally meet," he said out loud. Settling back in his chair and closing his eyes he continued, "May God have mercy on your soul young man."

"May God have mercy on whose soul Alistair?" The question came from a distinguished looking gentleman standing in the doctor's office doorway.

Momentarily startled, the doctor quickly regained his composure and stood from behind his desk "Oh just a case in America," he responded trying to make light of the matter.

"Are you sure of his condition?"

"I don't know for sure. You know as well as I do that these symptoms can be from a number of other causes. But he seems to fit the profile. After a physical examination next week I will know for sure."

"Is he of interest to the Society?"

"Possibly," but then with hesitation Alistair added "He's young."

"How young?"

"Late twenties. But he's a professional and by all accounts very financially secure."

The distinguished man was irritated with Alistair. "You know the young ones always give us problems," he said.

He turned and faced the same portrait Alistair was looking at. "Just remember the code of the Society my friend. Evaluate and report your findings. If it turns out that he is one of our kind then his future will be decided by the full counsel," the gentleman said. He turned back and gave Alistair a stern look.

"Of course I will! I know the code!" The doctor responded throwing the pen he was holding down on the desk.

"I know you do, old friend," the distinguished gentleman said. He smiled a dark and twisted smile. "I know you do." He nodded as he exited the room.

Chapter 4

Wednesday afternoon the following week, Cindy informed Ryan that Dr. Wolchek was on the line.

Eager to take the call, Ryan immediately answered.

"Dr. Wolchek, it's good to hear your voice. I was beginning to think you changed your mind about coming."

"Oh no, Mr. Anderson. Not at all. My prior business delayed me a little longer than I expected."

Unable to restrain his hopeful enthusiasm, Ryan asked, "So when would you like to meet Doctor?"

"As soon as possible if you don't mind. I'm only going to be in town for a short while. I have to return to London sooner than I planned."

"I'm sorry to hear that," Ryan said frowning as he looked out his office window.

"I'm afraid so. I'm staying at the Belmont by the airport. Room 308. Can we meet at 8:00 this evening?"

"I'll see you then."

"Good by Mr. Anderson."

As Ryan hung up the phone he thought it was strange to be meeting in a hotel room, but quickly dismissed it. The pain had become constant and the new pain medication was doing nothing for him. His energy had been steadily declining and now Ryan was practically forcing himself to drink his liquid foods. The quality of his life had degraded so much that he found himself contemplating ending his life with alarming frequency. He often thought if given the choice of continuing to live this way or die, he would choose death. As it was now, he had no life. Not anymore. Maybe for that reason most of all, going to meet a stranger in a hotel did not bother him. *Hell, if I'm being set up, good,* Ryan thought to himself. He'd finally be out of his misery.

# # #

At 8:00 Ryan was standing in front of room 308. A strange feeling settled over him as he stood in the deserted hallway. On the one hand, he felt in a weird unsettling way that this was going to be it; the end of the line. If this doctor could not diagnose his problem then it may be time to take matters into his own hands. On the other hand, if he was being set up, then good. Hopefully, it would be over quick. Either way, he felt he had nothing to lose so he knocked on the door.

When the door opened, Ryan was greeted warmly by a professional looking middle aged man, in his early fifties and by all accounts in remarkably good health. He was wearing dark glasses that immediately got Ryan's attention.

"Mr. Anderson I presume?"

"Please Doctor, call me Ryan."

"Dr. Alistair Wolchek. Nice to meet you." He shook Ryan's hand.

Carefully studying Ryan's face, Dr. Wolchek thought to himself, how remarkable. Ryan looks just like the portrait that hung in his office. The resemblance is unbelievable.

"Remarkable!" Dr. Wolchek said, but this time out loud.

"Remarkable is not exactly how I would describe myself Doctor. At least not these days," Ryan said. He lifted his arms and looked down at his scrawny frame.

Dr. Wolchek quickly regained his composure. "I'm sorry, Ryan. You just look like someone I knew a long time ago. Please come in." He smiled and motioned for Ryan to enter the room.

After a brief physical examination, Dr. Wolchek directed Ryan to a chair. "I would like to ask you some questions," he said.

Ryan took a seat in one of the two chairs that accompanied a small table by a large window. Dr. Wolchek retrieved a pen and pad from his brief case and took a seat in the other chair.

"So tell me Ryan, when did you first start experiencing these symptoms?"

Thinking back for a second Ryan replied, "Six and a half months ago. It was a Sunday morning to be exact."

"How are you so sure of the exact time of onset?" Dr. Wolchek asked surprised.

"Believe me Doctor, I remember. Ever since that morning nothing has been the same."

"Very interesting Ryan. Tell me about the previous day or days. Did anything unusual occur before that Sunday morning that you can recall?

Rubbing his chin and thinking back Ryan said, "Something did happen now that I think about it. It was so strange. I hit a small owl with my car the night before when I was returning home after a show"

"A show?"

"Yes, I'm a part time singer in a band. I was anyway. Not doing a lot of singing these days." Ryan tried to joke, as he gestured to himself.

"Are you any good?" Dr. Wolchek asked with surprise in his voice.

"I think so. We'd developed a fairly large local following. People seemed to like us," Ryan said, exhaling a long sigh and looking down at the floor.

"An owl you say?" Dr. Wolchek asked with noticeable interest as he sat up in his chair.

"It was very late. I was on my way home from a show. Probably about a mile or two from my house when out of nowhere I saw a gray streak fly in front of my car. I heard a dull thump and looked up in the rear-view mirror and saw a small clump of feathers rolling in a gutter. I felt bad for the critter so I turned around and went back to check on the little guy. If it was injured I was going to take it to an animal shelter the next morning. I'm a sucker for an animal in distress. I know it's terrible but I'd practically break my back for some poor animal before I'd lift a finger for some lazy piece of shit human. Sorry Doctor. That's just me," Ryan said, shrugging his shoulders.

"No need to apologize, I can relate believe me. But please continue."

"I parked my car, got out and walked along the road in the general area until I found him."

"Found what?" Dr. Wolchek asked excitedly.

"The owl. A little fellow, too. He looked okay but one of his wings was sagging a little. He didn't seem scared or anything so I slowly reached down and picked him up. As I was pulling him toward me he clamped down with both feet on my left ring finger with such force I felt like I had slammed my finger in a car door. But I didn't panic. Instead I sucked up the pain and got back in the car to take him home and deal with him in the morning. Let me tell you Doc, for just having been hit by a car this little guy had some major strength. On the drive back he never let up on his grip. I felt like my finger was going to be squeezed right off. Strange though," Ryan said. He hesitated.

"What?" Dr. Wolchek asked.

"On the drive back the little guy never seemed frightened. All the way home he was calm and just leaned against my stomach and looked around the car. Every so often he looked up at me as I drove. When I got home, I parked the car in my driveway instead of the garage in case he decided it was time to go. This way he had a clear exit. This decision turned out to be a good thing because when I got out he calmly checked his wings by extending them one at a time. Then, just as calm as can be, he looked up at me and flew off. It was strange. Though I was happy that he was okay, I was even happier to have him off my finger."

"Did the owl cut you or draw blood or cause any kind of physical damage?" the doctor asked with a hint of excitement in his voice.

"No. Not that I noticed anyway."

"Very interesting," Dr. Wolchek said as he quickly scribbled several notes on his pad.

"But there was something else that still puzzles me about that night, Doctor."

"And what was that?"

"Well, I know I hit the owl around 2:30 in the morning. And it only took about 10 minutes for me to get home after picking him up. I remember parking in the driveway and looking at the car's clock. I distinctly remember the display showing 2:41. I'm certain of this time. The problem is, I don't know what happened next."

"What do you mean?" Dr. Wolchek asked, a little confused.

"That's just it Doc. I remember getting out and the owl flying away. I went inside and remember feeling exhausted, so I went straight to bed. When I looked at my bedside clock it read 4:30am. I didn't believe it so I went around my house checking other clocks. All read 4:30. I even checked the car the next day and it was okay too. I don't know what happened. I can't explain it. Maybe I passed out from the pain? I just don't know."

"Very interesting Ryan, very interesting indeed. And you say you started feeling your symptoms the next morning?"

"Yes. I'm certain of it. I thought the owl may have given me rabies or something so I went to my family doctor the following Monday morning to get checked out. Fortunately, everything was good or so I thought anyway."

"Can you describe your symptoms for me?"

"Oh yea, severe stomach cramps! Almost as if I'm starving but if I try and eat anything solid the cramps only get many times worse and I throw-up. I can't keep anything solid down. When I eat, I feel like shit, like someone punched me in the stomach full force. And lately it has really gotten bad. Even liquids are causing me problems now. I know this sounds strange, but it's like mentally I feel like I'm starving to death and often have powerful cravings but when I satisfy them I get sick. I'm starving all the time, but I won't eat because the pain has become so unbearable. I just don't get it Doctor! What the hell is happening to me? I've lost almost 80 pounds in the past six months! I just can't take this anymore!" Ryan said, not so much in a panic but more like he had given up. Ryan's facial expression was one of pure defeat. He looked and sounded like a man who had lost the will to live and the doctor didn't miss the implication.

Settling back in his chair Dr. Wolchek pretended to be analyzing his notes but internally he was conflicted. Investigate and report his finding was supposed to be his mission. But now, seeing Ryan, hearing his remarkable story and most shockingly, his physical similarity to the portrait in his office, the doctor was in a quandary. Ryan's present physical condition did not allow for much time. Truth be told, Dr. Wolchek was amazed he had lived this long. In all his history of investigating these cases he'd never seen anyone in the condition Ryan was in and still have the energy he did. And most importantly, Dr. Wolchek knew Ryan had reached his limits. He caught Ryan's meaning and knew one way or another an end was coming and coming soon. For some reason he did not find Ryan to be a man who bluffèd. He felt Ryan would not hesitate to end his own life if he felt it was his only option. So the question was, what to do?

It didn't take much deliberation. Dr. Wolchek was not one for formal rules and codes. Besides, this young man's life hung in the balance. Maybe Ryan is the one he had been looking for all these years. Maybe the time had finally come. Losing him now because of ridiculous formalities of a corrupt Society that he no longer believed in was not going to detour him. Working himself into a state, Dr. Wolchek looked up at Ryan and said, "Your symptoms are very similar to others I have encountered. I may be able to help you. Would you mind if we try an exercise?"

Cautiously, Ryan agreed.

Dr. Wolchek pulled his chair right in front of Ryan and sat very close, directly facing him.

"Sorry Doc, but I have to ask, what's up with your glasses? They look very dark. Can you even see me?"

"I can see you just fine. You'll have to forgive my glasses. My eyes are very sensitive to light. I wear them all the time these days and I often forget I have them on." the doctor said casually dismissing the question.

"Now Ryan do exactly as I tell you no matter what discomfort you feel. Do you understand?" Dr. Wolchek asked. He took up a position directly facing Ryan.

"Yes." Ryan said, nervously shifting position in his chair. "What are you going to do?"

"A little eye exercise."

Ryan nodded and took a deep breath and then sat up in his chair facing the doctor.

"Now look directly at the lenses of my glasses and focus on them. Your eyes may start to feel a little strange but try not to look away. Keep focused on my glasses and do exactly as I tell you. Shall we begin?"

Ryan nodded and fixed his gaze on the doctor's glasses.

Dr. Wolchek leaned uncomfortably close to Ryan and removed his glasses. When the doctor looked up his stare seemed as if it actually reached out and grabbed Ryan's eyes. Feeling as if his eyes had been forcefully locked into place, panic began to overcome him.

Sensing Ryan's building tension, Dr. Wolchek said, "Relax," without breaking focus.

Hearing his calming voice Ryan felt the tension slowly leave his body. The doctor's close proximity unnerved him, but his attention was focused on the strange sensation coming from his eyes. He briefly felt a slight itching and tingling feeling which quickly passed as he held focus. Almost as quickly, he began to feel a comfortable warmth, like a warm soothing liquid was flowing over them. It was extremely pleasurable. At the same time he felt the pain in his stomach subside for the first time in months. The more he stared into the doctor's eyes, the more relief he felt in his stomach. Almost as if he was finally satisfying the hunger or thirst that he had not been able to quench in months. He kept his focus.

However, Ryan noticed that the doctor was having more and more difficulty maintaining eye contact. He was beginning to perspire and tremble slightly as he strained to keep his gaze fixed on Ryan's eyes. For Ryan, the longer he stayed focused, the easier it became, almost as if he was the one reaching out and into the doctor. Dr. Wolchek, looked like he was experiencing a great deal of physical discomfort. Then abruptly, he shut his eyes and turned away. Ryan felt a sharp pressure in his eyes that quickly subsided. The doctor eased himself back in his chair and held his head with one hand while gently rubbing his eyes with the other.

"Are you okay?" Ryan asked.

"Yes, yes. I'm fine. Just a little tired. How about you? How do you feel, Ryan?"

Thinking about it for a second, Ryan said, "I actually feel good! I can't believe it!" he said as he jumped out of his chair and walked around the room. "For the first time in months I actually feel good. What did you do to me?" Ryan asked, with building excitement.

"Just an eye exercise," the doctor responded notably drained by the experience. Putting his glasses back on and looking up at Ryan Dr. Wolchek continued, "You see Ryan, our eyes play a much greater role in regulating our overall health than most people know. Strain and fatigue can not only affect your vision, but also your entire overall general health. I simply caused you to focus, and in a way, relax your eye muscles."

"So I'm cured? If I exercise my eyes more often I'll be okay?"

"Not so fast. It's not just your eyes Ryan. There is much more to it than that. We still have a long way to go I'm afraid."

"Look, right now I feel better than I've felt in months! I'll do whatever you say just please continue to help me. Please," Ryan pleaded as he spun around on his heals holding his stomach with relief.

Then looking at the doctor Ryan said, "I actually feel hungry. Do you think it's okay if I eat something?"

"Sure, here, have some candy from the mini bar," Dr. Wolchek said, as he tossed Ryan a bag of M&Ms.

As he ate the candy it tasted great. Better than any candy he had eaten before. But before he swallowed he hesitated. When he swallowed he winced and waited for the painful cramp and convulsion that typically followed but it did not come. Instead, it felt good. Satisfying. And he wanted more. He couldn't believe it.

"Christ Doc! I don't know how to thank you. I can't believe it. I can eat again! I feel great! Please Doctor, let me take you to dinner, my treat. Wherever you want to go." Ryan devoured the rest of the candy.

Amused, Dr. Wolchek said, "I'm sorry Ryan, but I'm afraid I'm going to have to decline your offer. I had better stay in tonight. I'm feeling a bit rundown at the moment."

"Are you sure you're alright?" Ryan again asked.

"Oh Yes, my energy level tends to drop from time to time. I'm diabetic."

"Can I get you something at least?"

"No, but thank you all the same. I just need to rest."

Ryan was genuinely concerned about the doctor, but he couldn't help but feel rejuvenated and refreshed. He was raring to go and do something- Anything! He just wanted to move.

Sensing Ryan's eagerness, Dr. Wolchek said, "Do me a favor please will you?"

"Whatever you want just name it!"

"Please come back to see me in two days."

"Aren't you suppose to go back to London soon?"

"No, not anymore. My plans have changed. I have some business here I have to see to first. Two days Ryan. No longer. Okay?"

"Yes. Absolutely. Two days. I'll be back I promise."

Dr. Wolchek then stood and walked Ryan to the door.

"Good night Doctor," Ryan said, as he excitedly shook his hand. "And thanks again. I owe you big." He left the hotel room.

After Ryan left, Dr. Wolchek made his way over to the bed to lay down. As he shut his eyes he said out loud, "Welcome to your new life Mr. Anderson. I hope you can handle it my young friend."

Chapter 5
A New Beginning

On his way home, Ryan stopped at the first fast food restaurant he came to and ordered half the menu. Not waiting to get home he started eating the food right out of the bags as he drove.

Once home and after consuming all the food he bought, he was still way too wired to sleep so he went to his fitness room to work out-something he had not felt like doing in months.

Ryan's house was a large, five bedroom, single-story home located on a wide, deep creek that connected to the St. Johns River. The bedrooms were all very spacious and Ryan had converted one into an office and another into a home gym. Prior to his illness, he often spent hours at a time working between the rooms. Ryan felt he was much more creative when working out so he combined the two. His neighborhood was just minutes from downtown and considered very desirable because of its location and seclusion. The majority of homes were built in the 1960's and well maintained.

Ryan's house was especially unique since its designer was a fan of the Frank Lloyd Wright style of architecture-tall ceilings and a lot of glass. Ryan loved his home and before he became ill, enjoyed using it for entertaining clients and of course, the ladies. The open floor plan and sunken rooms seemed to compliment Ryan's bachelor lifestyle.

The next morning, still feeling energized, Ryan got up early, ate a huge breakfast then did a quick 10-mile bike ride. Feeling the sun and wind on his face and body was refreshing. *Where was all this energy coming from*, he thought as he rode his bike along the familiar route. "Who cares! Thank you Dr. Wolchek," he said out loud. "Thank You Doc!!!" he shouted, pumping his arms in the air. He switched gears and continued his ride.

While getting ready for work, Ryan caught a glimpse of himself in the mirror. He looked different. Still very thin he didn't look the same. Not as sickly. He looked more alive. He even looked different physically-a little more filled out. The changes were subtle, but noticeable.

"Wow!" Ryan said out loud. "Is that really me?"

Feeling energized and more alive than he had felt in months, Ryan decided to drive his Jaguar XK8 to work. He had neglected his prized car in favor of his much larger truck. Getting in and out of his Jaguar in his weakened condition was difficult. But this day, the pain was gone. He wanted the Jag because it drove like he was feeling — powerful!

# # #

Stepping out of the elevator and into the lobby of his firm, Ryan said "Good morning," to a janitor cleaning the floor. He warmly greeted another employee as he made his way through the mostly deserted department to his office. When he arrived at Cindy's desk he was surprised to not find her there. Another employee approached to drop something at Cindy's desk.

"Do you know where all my staff is?" Ryan asked.

Startled, the employee stuttered in her response. "Uh...yes," she said pausing for a moment while inadvertently looking him up and down unable to hide her surprise, "Yes...yes, sir. They're all in a meeting...with Stan in the main conference room."

"Stan? This should be interesting," Ryan said. He nodded and thanked the woman before continuing on to the conference room.

"Wow," the woman said out loud to no one in particular as Ryan walked off. "He looks so much better today. I'd hate to be Stan right now," she added. She smiled and continued going about her morning business.

Stan had been positioning himself for months before making his move on Ryan's staff. Biding his time while quietly manipulating other partners into believing that Ryan would soon be out completely or incapable of continuing in his present position. In order to avoid too much inter-departmental disruption, Stan volunteered to take over Ryan's staff and accounts under the guise of helping to maintain stability within the firm if and when Ryan finally had to step aside. Through numerous back door meetings with senior partners, Stan finally got the permission he had been seeking to begin his takeover. However, the other partners knew the risk involved and told Stan that if Ryan recovered or threatened action, then all bets were off. They knew that they had Ryan to thank for the majority of their success. And sick or not, if Ryan had the desire, he could shut the whole place down. But, Stan was confident Ryan would not do that.

Stan had been watching Ryan carefully-especially the past few weeks-and knew Ryan probably wouldn't like it, but would be too weak physically to do much about it. He knew Ryan was sick. After his last meeting with him, he figured Ryan didn't have much time left. Feeling confident, Stan, with several senior partners at his side, called a meeting shortly after Ryan's staff arrived that morning. He assumed he would be safe since Ryan rarely made it into the office before 11:00am these days.

The meeting had been going on for about twenty minutes when Ryan arrived. Ryan had nine permanent staff members and three other support staff including Cindy. Clearly disturbed by Stan's takeover announcement, reactions among Ryan's staff ranged from visibly upset, to angry and annoyed. Several members openly challenged the validity of Stan's takeover attempt calling it underhanded and accused him of backstabbing Ryan. The partners were getting nervous. Stan, however, would not hear it. He had been planning this for some time and was not about to cave in to his future subordinates choosing instead to be a hard ass. He implied that if people didn't like it, they could go elsewhere. It was no secret to them that Stan was enjoying the meeting. That was due to the fact that many of Ryan's staff viewed Stan in the same light as Ryan, that Stan was basically worthless and only getting ahead through the efforts of others. The partners became even more uneasy. They knew Ryan was only part of the equation. His staff was the other. Driving them off could be just as destructive.

By the time Ryan arrived the mood was sour.

"Good morning everyone," Ryan said, as he walked right into the meeting interrupting Stan in mid speech. "Sorry I'm late. I was not aware we had a meeting scheduled for this morning." Ryan looked directly at Stan with a "fuck you" look.

"Wow. It must be important too since we have such distinguished visitors," Ryan said. He cut the other partners a withering look before taking a seat in an empty chair next to Cindy. "Don't let me interrupt, please continue Stan," Ryan gestured as he leaned back in his chair and crossed his legs.

The mood shifted immediately. Smiles appeared on everyone's lips almost simultaneously. "Oh shit, this ought to be good," a staff member uttered under his breath. Another nodded with noticeable relief while also concealing a big smile.

Completely caught off guard, Stan stuttered in his response.

"Ryan. What are you doing here?"

"I work here Stan. Oh, wait, or do I?" Ryan said. He gestured with his finger from the partners to Stan and back again with a twisted smile. "I think I see what's going on here. Let me guess, good old Stan has kindly volunteered to step in and help me out. Is that it?" Ryan asked, looking directly at Cindy.

Not one to help Stan out of his hole, Cindy decided to throw a little gas on the fire.

"I'm afraid it's worse boss. Good ol' Stan called us together to tell us that he was taking over and that we all work for him now," she said with a devious grin.

"Really? Then, let me ask this." He leaned forward and turned to look at the partners before continuing, "And you guys may want to pay close attention here." Next he looked around the table.

"How many of you want to go work for Stan? Come on now, don't be shy. Raise your hand if you want to go work with Stan," Ryan said in a cocky tone. As expected, no one at the table raised their hand. Some muttered verbal responses that were not flattering to Stan's cause. Smiling, then, looking at the partners Ryan asked, "Now, how many of you want to come work with me," he paused, "at my new firm?" All of Ryan's staff raised their hands. He looked back at the partners.

"So, how does this work guys? I don't have all day," he said. "Do I get some kind of severance package or what?" Ryan had an airtight contract stipulating a buy out and severance package that would practically bankrupt the firm.

Speaking up and trying to make light of the situation while trying to hide his building panic, David Peterson, the General Manager and most senior of the partners said, "Now, now, Ryan, I'm afraid there has been some kind of misunderstanding. We were led to believe that you were gravely ill and incapable of performing your work. Clearly that information was wrong," he said, as he turned and looked at Stan very annoyed.

"But David! Look at him! Come on, you can't be serious!" Stan demanded as he tried desperately to save his rapidly sinking position.

"Enough Stan! Clearly things aren't as bad as we were led to believe. Please Ryan, I would like to apologize to you and your staff. Stan, this meeting is over."

"But sir! Look at him! He'll probably be dead in a week!"

"I am looking at him," David snapped. "Besides maybe needing to gain a few pounds he looks fine to me. What do you say Ryan? Are you and your staff still with us?"

Looking around the table Ryan was clearly moved. All of his staff stood by him.

"That depends entirely on them. Do you guys want me to stay or does anyone doubt my ability to lead?"

"Not at all boss," Cindy said, speaking up and smiling while also putting her hand on his shoulder. "I think I can speak for everyone when I say if you stay we'll stay."

"But, with conditions," Ryan added.

"Conditions?" David nervously asked.

"Yes," Ryan said, just a serious as he would be with any other client, "From this point on, your boy Stan here has nothing to do with me or any of my staff. It's time he pulls his own weight and stops latching on to and mooching off the efforts of other people. Sorry Stan, but it's time to sink or swim, old buddy," Ryan said, in the same condescending tone Stan often used with him. "And this condition is nonnegotiable," Ryan added with a dead pan expression.

"I think we can meet your terms Ryan," David said, as he walked over and extended his hand for Ryan to shake.

Upon hearing David's response, Stan stormed out of the conference room, visibly upset.

Taking his hand and smiling, Ryan said, "Then we have a deal."

Excitedly shaking Ryan's hand, David nervously smiled with relief.

At the same time, Ryan's staff started clapping and congratulated him for getting Stan out of their lives.

Among themselves, the staff commented on how good Ryan looked. Something about him was different, he looked healthier, rested maybe. They couldn't quite place it, but they were just happy to have the old Ryan back.

As David and the other partners left the room David said, "That stupid little shit has gone too far this time. He almost cost us Ryan and his staff! I don't know what's been going on with Ryan's health lately but he sure doesn't look one step away from death to me!"

# # #

Hearing the distant ringing of a far off phone, Dr. Wolchek slowly opened his eyes as he awoke in his hotel room. Still exhausted, he sat up in his bed and looked at the clock. It was 11:30am. Rubbing his eyes he reached for a cigarette, but found only an empty pack. He took a deep breath and with hesitation reached for the phone.

"Dr. Wolchek."

"Alistair? Good morning old friend. Did I wake you?" a voice boomed out over the phone.

"As a matter of fact you did, Henry."

"Sorry about that," Henry paused. "Alistair, they told me you rescheduled your flight. Is anything wrong?"

"No. Nothing is wrong," he responded a little annoyed.

"How is your subject?"

Tapping his fingers on the bedside table, Alistair looked out across the room and said, "I haven't met with him yet. Scheduling difficulties," he quickly added.

"Scheduling difficulties? Really?" Henry said. His tone doubtful."

"It happens from time to time," Alistair answered backing his attempt at deception.

"Alistair, remember who you are. Do not take any action on your own. You are there to evaluate and make a report that is all. Ultimately, the council will decide the fate of your subject. Do I make myself clear?" Henry asked.

"I know why I am here," Alistair barked. "And I'm not the one who needs to be reminded of the rules." Alistair did not attempt to hide his irritation. "If the case proves to be of interest I'll be back with a full report. If it turns out to be nothing, then I may continue on to South America to investigate other possible cases. Either way, you will have something by week's end."

"Good, I look forward to reading your report. Good bye old friend."

Alistair hung up the phone. "A week," he said to himself. "One week is all I have to change a man's life forever, he grumbled as he rolled over to get out of bed.

# # #

For Ryan, the day passed with lightning speed. He took his staff to lunch to celebrate Stan's bitch-slapping, but more importantly, to show his appreciation. After all, these people were more to him than just employees. Their loyalty and devotion went way beyond what was expected and this did not go unnoticed by Ryan. In the first few hours of the morning he'd done a week's worth of work and got his staff going on more new projects than they could handle. Even overburdened, they thrived under the pressure. Working with the old Ryan again was exciting. Cautiously hopeful, they were happy to have their old boss back.

# # #

Still feeling energized, Ryan decided to go to his health club after work. He was still weak in strength and lacked the muscle mass he once exhibited with pride, but was able to plow through his workout with tremendous efficiency. "Where is this energy coming from?" Ryan kept asking himself. Surrounded by mirrors, he was constantly made aware of his physical appearance, but didn't care. His upbeat attitude more than made up for it. Feeling good, he found it easy to flirt with the female members. It was obvious that some were taken back by his appearance and found it difficult to hide but, those who knew Ryan blew it off and flirted back. That added to his self-esteem and boosted his confidence. He felt like a man. He found women interesting again. Even though he knew it might be sometime before he was fortunate enough to have the pleasure of a woman's company, he was content with just being back in the game.

Looking in the mirror he said out loud, "Body, we have a long road ahead of us my friend."

His emaciated image used to disgust him, but now he felt hopeful. Rebuilding his body would be a challenge, but a challenge he looked forward to.

"Today the body. Tomorrow the world!" he joked out loud. He faced his reflection in the mirror and flexed a nonexistent bicep muscle.

# # #

The next day Ryan did not arrive at his office until later in the afternoon. Feeling as upbeat as he did, he decided to use the morning and early afternoon to take care of several out of office appointments. In some cases, it had been months since his clients had seen him so he wanted to reassure them that all was well and that he was still firmly in the picture.

Hearing the elevator bell, Cindy looked up from her computer screen in time to watch Ryan walk in from the lobby. Still very thin, something about him had changed. For the past several days he appeared to be getting better right before her eyes. As strange as it seemed, it was almost as if he was filling out by the hour. She found it difficult to take her eyes off him as he approached. The changes in him were remarkable and she was enjoying the show. He walked with confidence and purpose, like he use to do. Smiling to herself she couldn't help but feel excited. They had a professional working relationship, but they also shared a past. A past that neither regretted, but decided to keep separate.

Cindy was a beautiful young woman of 26. Her shapely body and beautiful long brown hair were nothing compared to her deep green eyes. Eyes that radiated an inviting warmth causing most to become lost in her gaze upon first meeting her. Ryan had long since become immune to her beauty but always enjoyed basking in her radiant glow each morning.

"About time you got here," Cindy said. She cut him a warm, infectious smile.

"Good afternoon," Ryan responded winking and smiling back. "Any messages?"

"Yes, Dr. Wolchek called several times to schedule a follow up appointment. Here's the number," she said handing it to him and lightly brushing his hand with her fingers.

"Thank you," he said. Smiling back and taking the message before continuing into his office.

Grinning sheepishly to herself, Cindy couldn't help but be happy that he was feeling better. It had been months since he had winked at her and even longer since they last slept together...

After settling in, Ryan called Dr. Wolchek.

"Dr. Wolchek, Ryan Anderson, I'm sorry I wasn't able to get back to you sooner but I've been out of the office for most of the day."

"That's quite all right, Mr. Anderson. I just wanted to confirm our follow up appointment this evening."

"Oh yes, about that. Can we do it tomorrow? I mean I really feel great. Whatever you did seemed to have done the trick. I mean I feel cured."

"Yes, Mr. Anderson. I'm sure you do, but trust me when I say that you are not. Your symptoms will return. I can guarantee it."

"Are you sure? I've even begun to gain weight and everything. I haven't had any pain since that night with you."

"I'm positive."

Not really believing him, Ryan reluctantly agreed to meet again at his hotel that evening.

After hanging up, Cindy buzzed in with a question.

"Ryan, are you going to the Long's fundraiser tonight?"

"Oh shit! Is that tonight?"

"Yes. Black tie. Are you in?"

"I'd better be. The Longs have been one of our best accounts!"

He hung up the phone and after thinking about it for a second he buzzed Cindy back.

"Cindy, what are you doing tonight? Feel like going to a fundraiser with an Auschwitz victim?"

"Ryan! You don't look that bad. And sure, I'll be happy to go."

"Great! And wear something extra sexy. Maybe if everyone is focused on how good you look they won't notice how bad I do."

Laughing, Cindy replied, "Can do boss. Pick me up around 7:00?"

"7:00 it is. See you then."

Sitting back in his chair Ryan said out loud to himself, "Sorry Doctor. I'm going to have to cancel tonight."

Chapter 6

The fundraiser was typical. The Longs were one of Ryan's first large commercial accounts. The family owned a grocery store chain. Having met with tremendous success in the Southeastern United States, the company was ready to expand north and west in a big way. Ryan and his team created several successful campaigns which helped catapult the company to the top of the regional market. The Longs were counting on Ryan and his firm to help them continue their success.

After the more formal presentations, Ryan and Cindy pressed the flesh. Cindy did not disappoint. Wearing her little black dress, she was the center of attention. As they worked the room they'd casually eye one another. They lived for these events. Both were made for the public eye. When Ryan was in peek physical condition, the two made a formidable team. Both enjoyed the game, maybe even more so than the victories.

Cindy and Ryan had chemistry. Both understood the other mainly because they were so much alike in their needs. Neither was looking for anything serious and neither wanted to be tied down. However, they did have common interests. They enjoyed life and wanted to live it to the fullest. Both craved attention and enjoyed sampling all life had to offer. Almost from the time they first met they could feel the sexual tension building between them. Given this, they knew a sexual relationship was inevitable. The sexual tension built to such a frenzy that neither was able to function effectively at work. The tension had become all consuming. For several months it simmered, until one evening, unable to restrain themselves any longer, they acted on their wild impulses in Ryan's office. The wait was well worth it. The combination was explosive. Both consumed the other. The raw unrestrained primal experience was wild and exhilarating. The experience more than met their expectations.

After satisfying their sexual curiosity, both were able to settle down and forge a highly productive working relationship. Professionally, they were a good team. Their sexual encounters became somewhat more sporadic, but it was still highly satisfying. Both found it humorous that once they had acted on their urges, they felt a tremendous sense of relief. Neither expected anything from the other; they simply had to get their sexual cravings out of the way. But when they were together, the bedroom chemistry was explosive.

As Ryan skillfully maneuvered through the masses he couldn't take his eyes off Cindy. Breaking away from the crowd, he found a quiet corner across the room where he leaned against the wall with his arms crossed and watched Cindy work her magic. He enjoyed hearing her laugh and seeing her smile. From his vantage point he watched her mingle with various company officials. He couldn't help but notice how perfectly her dress flattered her well-proportioned body. His eyes were drawn to the elegant curve of her neck were he followed it down to the top of her breasts which were exposed just enough. As his eyes continued down her tight stomach, around her shapely thighs, and on to her long sexy legs, Ryan realized that for the first time in months, he was getting aroused. Shifting slightly as he leaned against the wall, he couldn't help but smile.

Noticing Ryan watching her, Cindy smiled and subtlely flipped her hair. Looking past her suitors she gave Ryan a sexy "get me out of here look". He knew the look well and wasted no time responding to her request.

Both wanted the other. Driving back to her place in his Jaguar, they flirted like old times. Cindy teased Ryan by hiking up her dress and gently running her hand along the inside of his leg working him into a highly excited state.

Cindy lived on the 18th floor of a downtown, upscale condominium which overlooked the city and river winding below. After parking in the lower level garage they took the elevator to her floor. On the way up they were all over each other. She threw herself on him with such force that it pushed him up against the elevator wall. Ryan was so turned on. He had to have her. Holding her tightly while passionately kissing her back, he ran his hands over her body. Cindy could feel the energy in his embrace. It was electric. Her body quivered in response welcoming his touch and craving more. She could feel his hands caressing her legs and body then moving up to her breasts where he gently squeezed and kissed them before moving on to her neck and back to her mouth. His hands were warm and inviting. She felt herself getting lost in his touch.

Ryan, too, was highly aroused. He could feel her desire. Her body was electric. Her skin against his was like silk. She pulled off his coat and ripped open his shirt in a wild rage. Running her hands over his shoulders, down his back and then across his chest. Feeling her nails against his skin was invigorating. His senses were so heightened, he was aware of every sensation. Everything was vibrant and alive. All he could think of was her and how much he wanted her. As the elevator ascended, both were lost in their passion.

Finally, the bell rang. Cindy's floor at last. Hardly able to work the door lock, they made their way inside. Once in, they stripped naked. Excited and fully aroused Ryan pressed himself against Cindy with a powerful embrace pushing her against a table in the hallway. Holding each other tight they passionately kissed while frantically running their hands over each other's body trying to satisfy all their physical needs at once. After a deep kiss, Ryan stepped back and looked at Cindy with a devious smile. She smiled back mischievously, then walked away from him. Standing in the hallway wearing nothing but her heals, Cindy's profile was beautifully lit by the dim light coming from a room further down the hall. She tilted her head back toward Ryan and smiled.

"Are you coming?" she asked

Within seconds they were in the bedroom-unstoppable raw energy between them. As Ryan positioned himself over her, he felt her body craving his embrace. His eyes were wild. She could see and feel his primal animal like sexual power. No control, no restraint, just raw sexual energy. As he thrust himself into her he felt a blinding flash of intense pleasure. She felt it, too, and groaned in ecstasy. Repeatedly, Ryan thrust himself deep into her, bringing their pleasure to higher and higher levels. Both were consumed in the act and lost in the experience. He thought to himself that it's never been like this before. Every touch and every sensation was heightened on so many levels. He had never seen or felt Cindy so aroused. She squeezed him between her legs tightly pulling him into her with every thrust. Her nails scratched his back as she clawed him in an uncontrolled response to her intense stimulation. Both were experiencing a noticeably new level of sexual pleasure and savoring every minute of it. He couldn't get enough of her, nor her him. As the pleasure continued to grow to ever greater levels both felt a powerful sense of building anticipation. The climatic relief was getting closer. Both were drenched in sweat as they continued. Ryan felt his body tensing, preparing for the eventual release. Then, in an uncontrolled explosion, he came in repeated deep thrusts. In that moment of perfect mutual sexual pleasure, both simultaneously experienced a powerful explosion of intense orgasmic relief. It was raw sexual pleasure and ecstasy, with both experiencing the same sensations at the same time.

Collapsing on to her Ryan and Cindy lay together, exhausted. Finally Ryan slowly pushed himself off Cindy and laid beside her still out of breath but he managed to say, "Damn! It's never been like that before."

Catching her breath she responded, "No, never. That was incredible."

"And our timing... pretty good I'd say."

"Yeah, pretty damn good."

Rolling over and putting her arm across Ryan's chest both drifted off into a deep sleep.

# # #

Around 2:00am Ryan abruptly awoke. Something was wrong. The pain in his stomach had returned. The exhilaration and energy of the past few days was gone.

"Oh, shit! Not again," he said out loud.

Sitting on the edge of the bed, Ryan felt the pain grow worse. "Fuck!" he thought to himself and clutched his stomach.

Cindy was sound asleep so he stood quietly and walked out of the room. Every step was agony.

"Christ! It's back." Momentarily panicking, Ryan remembered Dr. Wolchek. He gathered up his clothes, dressed and left for the doctor's hotel.

# # #

45 minutes later, he was knocking on the doctor's door. It was now almost 3:00am and Ryan was in excruciating pain.

When Dr. Wolchek answered, Ryan was surprised to find that he had not awakened him.

Hunched over and holding his stomach Ryan looked up and barely managed to say, "Doctor, please help me. The pain is back and worse than ever."

Dr. Wolchek motioned him in.

He stumbled to the closest of the two chairs clutching his stomach. His face was a mask of contorted agony.

Dr. Wolchek sat down and again took up his uncomfortably close position facing Ryan. He then removed his glasses and stared into Ryan's eyes.

"Try to relax Mr. Anderson and focus on my eyes."

Ryan started feeling relief immediately. As the pain subsided, the doctor shut his eyes and sat back in his chair. Ryan was startled by the doctor's abruptness and asked, "Are you okay?"

"Yes Mr. Anderson, I'm fine. How are you?"

"Much better now, thank you. The pain is gone. You really have to teach me how to do these eye exercises. Whatever you're doing seems to work."

Ryan sat back rubbing his stomach with a confused look on his face. "Doctor, what's going on with me?"

Dr. Wolchek stood up and walked away shaking his head. He went to the sink for a glass of water. After taking a sip, he turned back and faced Ryan. "That, I'm afraid is a long story. One I hesitate to tell you."

Immediately defensive, Ryan's aggravation caused him to explode.

"Why? I need to know what's going on with me! Obviously you know something because you seem to know what to do and how to treat it. For God's sake tell me what's happening to me!" he pleaded with a mix of anger and desperation.

"God's sake? Funny you should use that expression. More like God's curse it is," Dr. Wolchek replied.

"What? What curse? What's going on? I'm begging you."

Thinking about it, Dr. Wolchek thought to himself that he could tell Ryan and then kill him if he didn't handle it well. He knew he was more than capable if necessary. He took a deep breath and said, "I'll tell you, but you have to promise to hear me out completely."

"Sure Doctor, whatever. Just level with me."

"No Ryan, I'm serious!" he snapped with an uncharacteristic harshness. For the first time Dr. Wolchek called him Ryan.

Ryan could have sworn he saw something flash in the man's eyes.

"I understand. Please tell me what you know," Ryan said.

Dr. Wolchek walked over to his briefcase and retrieved a very old book.

"Are you familiar with this story Ryan?" he asked handing the book to him.

"Dorian Gray by Oscar Wilde? Sure, I've read it. It's about a guy who stays young and youthful while his picture ages. But what does this have to do with me?"

"That is what I'm about to tell you. Make yourself comfortable. This is going to take some time."

Sitting down in the chair across from Ryan Dr. Wolchek lit a cigarette. After shaking out the match he settled back into a more comfortable position.

"What if Oscar Wilde was inspired to create his fictional character, Dorian Gray, from rumors that persisted about a young nobleman who lived several decades before he wrote the book and was part of a, well... a secret society?"

"A secret society?" Ryan asked with one eyebrow raised expressing his skepticism. "A society of what?"

"Others like him. What if Wilde's character was not alone? What if he was a member of a very old and exclusive society of people?" He paused and added, "People like yourself?"

"Me? I don't think so Doc. I do age and I have no magic portrait hanging in my house bearing all my sins. I think you are very much mistaken here."

"The portrait was not relevant. What if the changes Wilde's character saw on the portrait were only in his head. To anyone else, it looked as it did the day it was painted. You see Ryan, Wilde's character never could accept who he was. Instead, he created a horrible mental image of the monster he believed he was and saw that monster in the portrait. He believed he was cursed by God and continually punished himself for it."

"So the portrait never changed? It was all in his characters head?"

"Exactly."

"Interesting. But what does any of this have to do with me?"

"Well," the doctor said pausing. "Maybe you are afflicted with the same condition as Mr. Wilde's character."

"What? That I'm crazy! I'm only imagining all my pain? I don't think so, Doctor. It's all very real. I can assure you of that!" Ryan was getting irritated.

"That is not what I'm talking about. I'm only saying that you are like him in your needs."

"Needs? What needs? I need to be cured that's what I need!" Ryan barked, losing his patience.

"Regretfully, there is no cure, only treatment Ryan. And like Wilde's character, your willingness to accept your condition will determine if you live or die."

"Accept what condition? Damn it Doctor, stop being so cryptic! What condition? What's wrong with me?" Ryan demanded, losing his patience completely.

Before the last word left Ryan's lips, Dr. Wolchek leapt on him grabbing

Ryan by his neck and pulling him to within inches of his face. The doctor's eyes were glowing a frightening, yet brilliant yellow green. There was no time for Ryan to react. His movements were so sudden Ryan was caught completely by surprise. Staring into those eyes Ryan felt a terrible sensation throughout his body making him helpless to react. His life was rapidly draining from him. It was as if someone was reaching into him and ripping out his heart. Ryan's eyes were locked onto the doctors, his body paralyzed, unable to respond. He could feel his life rapidly slipping away as darkness began to envelope him. Those eyes, those frightening glowing eyes were all Ryan could see as he began drifting into unconsciousness. With no warning, Dr. Wolchek closed his eyes and slowly turned his head away. He released his grip and Ryan fell back into his chair, limp and barely breathing. He heard the faint sound of his heart beating. Helpless, all Ryan could do was look at the doctor as he resumed his position in the chair facing him.

"You are very close to death Ryan. I have drained the life from you . If I leave you as you are, you will surely die. I'm sorry I had to do this to you but I had no choice. I need to prove to you that what I'm saying is true."

Casually cleaning his glasses, Dr. Wolchek continued.

"There is a Society which exists and has existed in some capacity for hundreds of years. It is made up of people like ourselves. The character Mr Gray was possibly based on was indeed one of us, but could not handle his condition and after some time had to be eliminated. He risked exposing us for who and what we are and had to be silenced. There is a council of elders who decides the fate of all newborns such as yourself and determines if they can be trusted with this gift as well as become a useful part of the Society and follow its rules. I came across your case because this is my job. I search medical records across the world looking for signs and symptoms relating to this condition. After responding to your Doctor's request for help with your diagnosis, I determined that you were a possible subject so I came to see you. We do not know why this happens to only a select few in the population, but it does happen. You are one of those few. However, your condition is somewhat unique in that you can trace your onset to a particular event; an animal event at that. That is something that has never been done before. Now, I have much more to tell you but I fear if I do not replenish your life energy soon, you will die."

As before, Dr. Wolchek leaned close to Ryan and placed one hand on his neck. Within seconds of focusing on him, Ryan could feel that warm liquid-like sensation flowing into him through his eyes. It was energy, life energy and it was soothing and refreshing. He could feel his body pulling it in and distributing it throughout. Life force. Raw pure energy. This time he knew what was going on and as if by instinct and sure willpower Ryan forced himself to lock his eyes on to the doctors. With lightning speed Ryan grabbed Dr. Wolchek by his throat. It caught him completely by surprise. Ryan's eyes were ablaze, but unlike the doctors, his eyes were glowing a brilliant blueish white. Dr. Wolchek could feel Ryan's strength-he was extremely powerful. As the doctor struggled, Ryan was able to remain fixed and focused with ease. Desperately, Dr. Wolchek tried to break the connection and quickly realized he could not. He was helpless and unable to break Ryan's hold. Panic set in as he felt his life being drained from his body. All he could do was wait for what he was sure would be his inevitable end.

The look of panic and then complete submission only strengthened Ryan's resolve. It was easy for him now. Almost as if he had awakened some dormant natural ability that his body had long sense forgotten about. Realizing that Dr. Wolchek was the key to his survival, even if he did not know how, Ryan knew he still had much more to tell him. Feeling his strength and energy fully replenished, Ryan felt safe. He knew he had bested the doctor and could do it again if the situation called for it. He did not know how he knew this, he could just feel it in some way. So Ryan closed his eyes and released his grip on the doctor letting him fall back into his chair. Dr. Wolchek was weak, but Ryan knew he was far from helpless.

Feeling strong and somewhat victorious, Ryan said, "Don't ever do that shit to me again!" As he spoke his eyes flashed with a bright intensity. "Now that you have my complete and total attention, I want to know what the fuck just happened!" Ryan settled back into a more comfortable position in his chair guarded and ready if the doctor attempted another attack.

Shocked by Ryan's commanding tone and even more surprised by how quickly he learned to use his new ability, Dr. Wolchek thought how incredible this was. Even in his advanced weakened physical state, Ryan had tremendous willpower. He was truly a unique subject. And those eyes, those blazing blinding white eyes. Never has that been seen before in any subject or society member. "What does that mean," Dr. Wolchek wondered to himself.

Raising his hand in a gesture of submission Dr. Wolchek said, "Okay Mr. Anderson, I'm sure you have many questions. I'll do my best to tell you what I know." He did not have the strength for another encounter and he could tell that Ryan sensed that as well. But more importantly, Dr. Wolchek was desperately trying to conceal his building excitement. Ryan's case was of particular interest to him and now he had the confirmation he had been seeking.

"We do not know when this started, but we know that it has been going on for hundreds of years. Many who go through the change never figure it out and eventually starve to death like you were sure to do prior to our meeting. And then," Dr. Wolchek said, pausing for some time before continuing, "and then there were the others."

Chapter 7

"Others! What others?" Ryan asked.

Hesitating before answering, Dr. Wolchek said, "Unfortunately, our history is not one without incident."

"What do you mean?"

"Well, throughout our history there has been much confusion among our kind as to what or how to feed. Our origins are shrouded in violence, I'm afraid. Early on it was discovered that killing satisfied our cravings most effectively."

"Killing? People?" Ryan asked.

"People, animals, whatever. The vampire legends were actually started by the actions of our kind."

"So, you're saying we're some kind of vampire? You've turned me into a killer!" Ryan shouted. He slammed his hands down on the chair and leaned forward in a threatening gesture.

"Easy, Ryan. You're strong I'll give you that. But, I'm experienced. It is probably best that we do not challenge each other in our weakened states."

Not knowing why, Ryan knew he was bluffing. Still, he decided to go along with it. Smiling he slowly leaned back in the chair.

"Okay Doc, but answer my questions. Am I some kind of vampire and do I have to kill to survive?"

Impressed by Ryan's boldness, Dr. Wolchek smiled.

"No, we are not vampires, not in the literal sense anyway. And no, you do not have to kill to survive. Early on, some of our kind found that killing satisfied their cravings most effectively. Having no idea what it was they were actually satisfying, they believed that the killing and consuming of an individual's blood was the only way to fulfill their needs. The same needs you have but did not know it. Over time, some of us even evolved into very skilled and efficient killers. It wasn't until several centuries ago that we discovered it was life's energy that we were consuming. A person's blood and flesh was only satisfying basic hunger cravings. You see, killing is a violent action. People are basically energy in a shell. When a person is killed, violently, their energy is released. People like us can absorb that energy. As you have experienced for yourself, it can be rejuvenating. For centuries our kind fed on people not knowing that it was their life force we needed not their blood."

"So you're telling me I'm not technically a vampire but I do need to consume a person's life force to survive? And what if I don't feed?" Ryan asked.

"If you don't feed you will revert back to the way you were, starving and wasting away."

"But how can I be starving and still wasting away?"

"Because your body has changed. You are out of balance. You still need to eat real food, but you also need to balance your energy. For whatever reason once we change we are constantly, for lack of a better explanation, leaking energy. Most ordinary people are born with a specific amount of life force that they have throughout the course of their lives. They can create new energy but only in small amounts. They maintain their supply, but never gain any more than what they were born with. We, however, at some point start losing it. For some reason it diminishes. But, unlike ordinary people, we can replenish it."

"For how long?"

"Quite possibly forever. Some of the Society's members are hundreds of years old."

"Do we age?" Ryan asked.

"Not really. The age you are at the point of onset is about as old as you will ever get. The replenishing of energy allows the body to constantly repair and maintain itself. We have even found that we can, to some extent, focus the energy and repair physical damage like cuts, broken bones, and even more serious injuries.

"So we can still be injured?"

"Oh yes. We are still capable of being killed. Physically, we are just as frail as any ordinary person. But unlike ordinary people, we have the unique ability to repair ourselves if in a position to do so. For example, you're in a car accident and badly injured but conscious. If you're able to hold someone's hand, you can possibly take their energy and repair yourself."

"What would happen to the person whose hand I am holding?"

"That depends on how much energy you need."

"Could they die?"

"If you take too much, yes."

"So what about the food? After our last encounter I was starving. I gorged myself for hours before I felt satisfied. Even now I'm very hungry. Why?"

"Because your body is trying to find balance again. As a result of our exchange, you are flushed with energy, life force. Now your body is craving the nutrients it needs to convert that energy into new cells, tissues, etc. You especially need food. Your physical degeneration is so advanced that your body is trying to regenerate now that it has the energy to do so. Before, you were leaking energy so fast that your body could not replenish itself. Food became toxic to you. You still have to satisfy your most basic nutritional needs. Something our early members did not understand. Drinking only blood provided little nourishment. That's why early accounts of vampires always described them as thin with sunken eyes and hollow cheeks. Mostly, they were badly malnourished. Blood is not enough. It is still important to eat a proper diet."

"So theoretically we could live forever if we eat right and satisfy our energy needs?"

"Theoretically."

"What's with the glowing eyes?"

"That occurs when we are feeding and consuming large amounts of energy. A casual touch, handshake, hug, etc. will not cause the reaction. Only a more direct and massive exchange of energy. You feel it in the eyes but you can take and exchange through physical contact too. Something about the absorption of energy creates the effect."

"So what exactly are we?"

"That is a good question Ryan. Some think of us as immortals. Others think we are gods. I, however, like to think we are the next level of human evolution. For centuries we have been trying to understand this condition and have yet to discover why it occurs. We only know that it happens only to a select few in the global population. Finding these people and helping them to understand their condition has been my goal for many years."

"So tell me of this Society? What happens if they don't find me worthy?" Ryan asked.

"Then you will be eliminated. The Society exists to protect us. It is widely believed that the world will not tolerate our existence. We would be wiped out. One thing history has thought us is that man is quick to destroy what he does not understand. Until we have a better idea of what this is, it's vital that we remain hidden in the shadows. Basically, you have to be willing to give up your life and go underground."

Tapping his fingers on the edge of his chair, Ryan looked up at the ceiling and frowned.

"I'm not sure I like the sound of that. You see Doctor, I'm not exactly the joiner type," Ryan joked. His face gave away his obvious concerns.

"I got that impression," Dr. Wolchek responded smiling.

Dr. Wolchek's smile put Ryan at ease. He knew the doctor would not hurt him.

"Will you teach me how this works? I don't want to ever feel the way I felt when I arrived here tonight. I was in excruciating pain."

"I was a bit surprised to see you in such a state so soon. You had lost a considerable amount of energy. May I ask what you were doing earlier?"

"I attended a fundraiser with my assistant. Later, we went back to her place and, well," Ryan paused. Smiled. "We had an incredible round of wild sex. It was quite possibly the best sexual experience I've ever had. A few hours later I woke up with the pain. That's when I rushed over here."

"That explains it. During your sexual encounter you were exchanging energy. Normally, this would not be a problem, but since you are so out of balance you lost a considerable amount of energy to your partner. Ordinary humans can absorb our life force if you let them. You have not learned to cut the flow off from your end yet."

"Did she drain me somehow?"

"Yes. We exchange energy through physical touch and proximity. I imagine there was a lot of close physical contact going on?" he asked.

Ryan did not respond.

"During that time, your energy was flowing into her, charging her up if you will. With normal people it doesn't last for long. It's like a euphoric high that wears off within hours. We, however, can retain the energy for days at a time if we take certain precautions. In time, Ryan, you will learn to take advantage of such encounters to draw energy into you."

"I can feed during sex?" Ryan asked.

"That is one way. There are many others. From this point on you have to understand that it is a constant balancing act. You'll need to continuously strive to balance your energy needs with your nutritional ones. I will help you here."

"But, what about your Society? Don't they have to decide if I'm in or not first?" Ryan reminded him with a cocky tone.

Smiling a devious smile Dr. Wolchek said, "What they don't know won't hurt them. For now I suggest you go home and eat something. Use the energy you got from me to replenish yourself. I will pick you up at 7:00 this evening and we'll begin your training."

"Training?" Ryan asked.

"You can't just go around grabbing people by the neck and draining their life force from them," Dr. Wolchek said, with an uncharacteristic smile. "You have to learn to use your environment. Starting tonight, I'll show you how to exist without giving yourself away."

Rising from his chair Ryan extended his hand but the doctor did not respond in kind. Ryan looked at his hand and retracted it smiling. Nodding to the doctor Ryan said, "Until this evening. Good night, Doc."

After Ryan left, Dr. Wolchek sat back down lost in thought. He was exhausted from the exchange, but excited about the night's developments. Ryan was considerably stronger than he imagined he would be. In the few days since their first encounter he looked so much better physically. His rate of recovery was unprecedented.

If it continues, he could be completely physically recovered in just a matter weeks, if not sooner, Dr. Wolchek thought to himself while shaking his head in amazement. Out loud, he continued, "And once his body is repaired there could be no limit to his abilities."

The exhaustion was setting in. He made his way to the bed and laid down.

"But then again, given his lineage this really shouldn't be a surprise," he said, as he drifted off to sleep.

# # #

As Ryan made his way to his car his mind was racing. Dr. Wolchek had given him much to think about. *Can all this really be true? Is any of this even possible?*

"This is crazy!" he said sitting in his car holding the steering wheel.

"This whole thing is just crazy!" he repeated.

As he sat there thinking, he could not deny his own experience. That feeling of total and complete helplessness was very real. Feeling his life draining from him was real. Unable to move; paralyzed with fear. And those eyes! Those terrifying eyes. They were very real. So was his re-energizing. He didn't understand it, but he knew by the reaction on Dr. Wolchek's face that he had momentarily held the doctor's life in his hands. He knew he had somehow turned the tables on him. And he knew that Dr. Wolchek was both surprised and impressed.

"This evening may prove to be very interesting," he said out loud as he started his car and headed for home.

# # #

When Ryan arrived home, he was met by his cat, Tor, waiting for him by the front door.

Seeing the remains of a half-eaten bird on the steps, Ryan said to him, "You've got the right idea my friend, I'm starving. Let's get something to eat buddy."

Tor had proven to be a master hunter. In the months since he showed up at Ryan's house, he had killed dozens of birds, rats, mice, squirrels, lizards, etc. Ryan felt bad for Tor's victims, but he respected Tor's hunting abilities.

Following Ryan to the kitchen, Tor was meowing and rubbing against Ryan's legs as they walked.

"Okay buddy, I'm getting there. Chill out," Ryan said. He hurried to open the refrigerator.

His eyes were immediately drawn to two steaks on the middle shelf still wrapped. Suddenly he was aware that he was salivating.

"Man, they look good," he said.

Taking the steaks out he noticed a large amount of blood and juice pooling in the package. His hunger was overpowering. Tor jumped up on to the island in the middle of kitchen and continued meowing loudly. Ryan brought the steaks to the island and ripped into the package. Without any hesitation he brought the tray to his mouth and drank the juice spilling some down his chin and neck. *Delicious* he thought. Taking a steak and ripping into it like a wild animal, Ryan chewed the meat savoring the raw flavor. He voraciously consumed the rest, fat and all. Tor, was having at the other steak still in the package. Ryan ripped it to pieces with his hands. He threw some on the counter for Tor and devoured what was left like some kind of starving, wild beast.

Looking up as he licked the juices from his fingers, Ryan caught a glimpse of his reflection in a large picture window across from where he was standing. The image shocked and horrified him. So much so that he actually jumped back when he fully realized what he saw. The image reflected back was that of a monster. The blood running down his chin and stained white shirt, along with his sunken eyes and thin face, revealed a frightening sight. Regaining his composure, Ryan focused on the image and said out loud, "I'll be damned. I'm a fucking vampire!"

PART TWO

Chapter 8

At exactly 7:00pm Ryan watched the rented Lincoln Towncar pull into the driveway from his living room window. He was not surprised by the doctor's promptness. Walking out of his house he couldn't help but feel excited.

Everything was so different now. Drawing energy from the doctor earlier that morning then consuming the raw steak with Tor, made Ryan feel like his body had changed. His senses were heightened. Amplified. He could smell things in the air he'd never smelled before. He watched a moth flying and could here its wings rapidly beating as it danced around the bright light of an illuminated lamppost on the sidewalk outside his house. All day Ryan sat in a chair on his deck watching the wildlife in his backyard fascinated. There was a rhythm to everything. He could feel it. Somehow he knew the trees, plants, animals, insects - even himself, were all connected. It was like he was seeing and feeling everything for the first time. He was completely engrossed and did not miss even the smallest details.

Dr. Wolchek noticed as Ryan walked to the car. He looked so alive. And within only a matter of hours since their last encounter.

"Remarkable," he thought.

"Evening, Doc," Ryan said as he got into the car.

"Good evening Ryan. You look well," Dr. Wolchek said. He circled the big car around the driveway and drove back to the main road.

"I feel great. I can't explain it. I have so much energy."

"Did you eat?" Dr. Wolchek asked.

"Yes and I'm still starving," Ryan replied.

"It will pass. Once your body is back in balance you'll have normal cravings again. That is, unless you over-energize yourself."

"I'm very interested in learning all I can. But I have to admit, I'm still not sure I believe all this. It's just all so incredible."

"Believe it, Ryan. You've already experienced what we can do first hand. Given your physical appearance, you can't deny that you look better than when we first met."

"I can see that my body is recovering and I do feel much better, but I'm having trouble buying the whole thing. You have to admit, it all sounds so Hollywood. Like it's some kind of crazy movie or something."

Dr. Wolchek laughed, "You Americans always refer to the movies to explain your lives. It's like everyone in this country wants to be an actor or a rock star," he said.

"You forget Doc, I am in a band. And hey, we all get to perform in at least one major production. It's called life."

Smiling, the doctor said, "Americans!"

"So where are we going?" Ryan asked. Dr. Wolchek was driving in the direction of downtown.

"The South Winds. Do you know it?" he asked.

"Very nice and it has a beautiful view of the city," Ryan replied.

Within minutes they were pulling up to the restaurant's valet parking. When they got out of the car almost immediately one of the attendants recognized Ryan.

"Evening Mr. Anderson. Good to see you again, sir."

"Good to be seen," Ryan joked, smiling back.

As they walked in, various restaurant staff greeted Ryan with friendly smiles.

"They all seem to know you," Dr. Wolchek said.

"I've entertained many clients here," Ryan said. He tried to be modest.

"Mr. Anderson! We were not expecting you tonight," said a surprised hostess.

"Sorry about that Jane. Is it too late to get my favorite table?" he asked.

"Never too late for you sir," she said with a casual wink and a smile. "This way please gentlemen."

Ryan felt a sense of pride as they made their way to the table. Not so much because people were treating him like someone important, but because they were treating him like a normal person again. He was still a long way from being physically recovered, yet he didn't look like he was one step away from death anymore and he saw that on the faces of the people he interacted with.

"This is very nice," Dr. Wolchek said as he slid into a half curved booth facing a large window revealing a stunning city skyline only made that much more beautiful by the reflections of the tall buildings in the river below the restaurant window.

After being seated and giving their drink orders, Ryan leaned back in the booth.

"So Doc, how does this work? Do we just start grabbing people by the throat and going for it or what? But I have to warn you, we'll probably be asked to leave after the first few," Ryan joked.

Slightly laughing, Dr. Wolchek replied, "No, I don't think we'll need to do anything so dramatic."

"So why the restaurant?"

"Because it's a good place for you to experience using your environment, your surroundings. Being Saturday night, the crowd creates the perfect opportunity for you to practice using your new abilities discretely. And because I wanted to see something of this beautiful city before I leave," he added. He looked toward the window and view beyond.

"To exist you have to learn to blend in and use your surroundings to your advantage. Your chosen profession should afford you many opportunities. Shaking hands, close personal contact, etc., can be very effective methods of casually meeting your needs."

"But I thought the eyes were the key," Ryan said, confused.

"They are the most direct way of channeling energy, but not the only one. Take you for example, given the advanced state of your physical degeneration, I fed you through your eyes because it allowed for the most direct means of delivering a large amount of energy to your starving body."

"And that flow can be made to go both ways," Ryan interrupted.

"Correct, you can take as easily as you can give. Once the person is locked in your gaze, it's difficult for them to get away."

"So you're saying that just by looking at someone I could drain them dry?" Ryan questioned leaning forward with interest.

"Yes and no. Proximity is the key. From across the room, no. You have to be close enough to make a connection. Touching helps."

"Is that why you grabbed my neck?"

"Yes. When I did that it was meant to startle and confuse you. You were thrown off guard. It gave me the advantage to lock on to your energy with little resistance. When a person is scared or injured, it's much easier to dominate them."

"Why is that?" Ryan asked.

"Because they are unable to focus. That split second allows you to move in and take control."

"So to some extent this ability could be used as a weapon?" Ryan questioned.

Dr. Wolchek looked down at the table. "It could and it has."

Noticing that the doctor was holding something back Ryan pressed on, "Is this where the Society comes into play?"

Again hesitating before taking a deep breath, he answered, "The Society has stayed hidden behind the scenes for centuries. We live by a code and part of this code is not to interfere with man's natural evolution. Only occasionally helping mankind when extreme measures called for our help, but otherwise staying out of the way."

"Extreme measures?"

"The black plague of the middle ages is one such example. We quickly realized it was the fleas on rats allowing it to spread as fast as it did. However, convincing others of this took much longer. The time wasted fighting the church, the nobility, and various other superstitions caused many to die and reduced the population of Europe by a third."

"But you helped mankind in the end. Why?"

"The plague was not of man's making. It was not for power or greed. It was an unfortunate event that beset mankind and almost caused his extinction. It killed indiscriminately. Great minds and entire populations were being wiped out. Don't get me wrong Ryan, it was not a decision arrived at unanimously. Many favored doing nothing. After this, there was considerable heated debate over our roles in man's future. For the first time the question arose, is man capable of leading himself or does he need to be led? Europe was weak after the plague. Power hungry groups tried to dominate the continent and wars were common place. Some in the Society believed it was our duty to step in and eliminate these rulers for the greater good. The society was split between those who wanted to passively observe man along his journey and those who wanted to more directly guide him, even rule him.

"So what happened? Ryan asked.

"Several of our more aggressive members left the Society and raised armies in an attempt to carry out their grand ambitions. Most were defeated and eventually killed. Remember, we are not gods. A fact often overlooked given our unique abilities. After that, the Society took a more neutral stance opting to be passive observers instead of active participants."

Ryan sat quietly contemplating what Dr. Wolchek was telling him.

"Why do I get the impression that you're not a happy and content member?" Ryan asked. Leaning toward the doctor he smiled a twisted smile. "A member willing to break the rules and help someone such as myself without getting permission first?"

Dr. Wolchek frowned. "Unfortunately, the last century has caused many in the Society to re-think its role in man's future. Some favor taking a much more proactive role these days," he said.

"Let me guess, the few believe they know what's best for the many?" Ryan said.

"Yes."

"That's not a new concept. Politicians have been doing it forever."

"Yes, but most politicians don't have the ability to eliminate all those who oppose them."

Ryan stared at Dr. Wolchek. "So where do you stand in this debate Doc?"

Chapter 9

"That is difficult for me to answer, Ryan. I do favor some limited involvement. After all, what's the point in living for centuries if you can't use the knowledge you've gained to help benefit your fellow man."

"But?" Ryan asked looking for an explanation.

"Who are we to play God with man's fate? How much help is too much?"

"So what's the problem?"

Clenching his teeth and twiddling his thumbs Dr. Wolchek answered, "The problem is the Society. A few persuasive members are working hard to change our traditionally neutral stance to one of considerably more involvement. Some believe man is incapable of determining his own future because he does not have the benefit of longevity like we do. They believe they are man's only hope if he is to survive."

"You gotta admit the world is a pretty fucked up place these days. It probably wouldn't hurt to remove a few bad apples here and there," Ryan said shrugging his shoulders and smiling.

Dr. Wolchek did not find him amusing. "And where does it stop? One day it's the head of some terrorist group, and the next it's the head of a political party that doesn't think the same way you do. Remember, we can be killed. Controlling people's destinies is not a business we should to be in," Dr. Wolchek said. "I believe, like many in the Society, that man should be left alone to evolve on his own. In his own time."

"I understand what you're saying Doc, really I do. But I don't know if I agree with it 100%. Surely, there are some exceptions. Take Hitler for example. Wouldn't you kill him if given the chance knowing what you know about him now?"

"No Ryan. I would not. And this is what you need to learn. The power you have requires discipline and restraint. You must understand and accept that everything will not always be to your liking. Man has to be allowed to evolve on his own no matter how difficult it is to watch. Once we interfere where does it stop? It is for that reason we created the Council."

"The same Council that is to decide my future?" Ryan said. His tone arrogant. "Yes, tell me more about this Council.

"The Council consists of nine of our more senior members-individuals that have been around for centuries. It is believed that their knowledge and experiences benefit them in making informed decisions. If an exception must be made, it can only be done with their consent."

"Okay. So far it sounds good, so what's the problem then?" Ryan asked.

"The problem is the Council!" Dr. Wolchek said agitated. "It is slowly being taken over by a more aggressive faction within the Society. A group who are not merely content with observing mankind, but instead, what to control and dominate it. They are dangerous, Ryan. And this last century has only served to help strengthen their position."

"It sounds like you guys are on the verge of some type of internal revolution," Ryan said.

"I'm afraid that may soon be the case. Changing our position to one of a more aggressive role will be our undoing. Unfortunately, my voice, like many, is being drowned out by the popular extremist rhetoric of others. Members who appear hell-bent on leading us down a road to ruin. It will be our undoing." Dr. Wolchek said shaking his finger at Ryan. He sat back in his chair to regain his composure.

Noticing that the Doctor was worked up by their conversation, Ryan remained quiet and refrained from asking anything further about the Society. He had many questions and decided they could wait for another time and place. But he couldn't help think to himself what has he gotten into.

The restaurant was filling up. Because of the number of tables, the restaurant patrons were within hearing range of one another. Ryan noticed that the waiter was getting anxious. He had come to the table several times to take their dinner orders but was repeatedly turned away. Deciding that enough people were now seated in the restaurant, Dr. Wolchek waved him over and they placed their orders.

After the waiter left, Ryan leaned forward and nodded to the doctor, "Okay Doc, lets do this."

"First, you have to relax your body, settle back and get comfortable."

Ryan smiled. "So far so good," he said.

"Now focus. Filter out all the extraneous sounds and focus on your needs, your craving. You have to open yourself up and feel the need, then concentrate on satisfying it. It's there you just have to recognize the feeling deep inside."

Ryan was motionless. Focused. Concentrating and tuning out the background noise, he zeroed in on his craving.

"Do you feel it?"

"I feel it!" Ryan said. It was faint, but it was there.

"Good. Now let your mind open, like you're opening a door."

Doing as Dr. Wolchek instructed, Ryan could feel something like a channel opening within him, like a pulling sensation drawing everything to him, energy, sounds, smells, etc. He felt the energy of the room slowly flowing into him. In a strange kind of way it felt natural to him. Something he could do with ease now that he realized he could do it.

"It's everywhere, but very random. It's like I can feel each person in the room in some way."

Dr. Wolchek was unable to hide his surprise. "Really? How so?"

Ryan directed his attention to a woman sitting at a nearby table.

"Take that woman over there. I can feel that she is very worried about telling her husband about a dent she put in his car's bumper earlier this morning. And that man across the way in the corner looks like he's deeply engrossed in the book he's reading, but he's really not. He's more concerned with what other people in the room are thinking about him sitting there by himself. He's alone and embarrassed."

Impressed, Dr. Wolchek asked, "Can you read their minds?"

"No. More like feel their minds. I can't go inside their heads, but I can feel the energy they're giving off."

"Fascinating." Dr. Wolchek said. "I know of no other member in the Society with such an ability. Can you read me?"

Looking at him, Ryan frowned. "No. You're different."

"How?"

"Well," Ryan said and paused. "You're blank. Like a hole in the room. It's strange. I know you're there. I see you, but I almost can't feel you."

"Almost?"

"I can feel... your void."

"Incredible Ryan. Really, it is. This is good though. Do you think you could tell if another one of us was near you?" Dr. Wolchek asked.

"I guess. Maybe."

Surprised by what he was hearing Dr. Wolchek gave Ryan his next instruction.

"Try to feed. Concentrate on pulling energy from the man in the booth directly behind you."

Nodding in agreement, Ryan focused and soon felt the man's energy slowly being drawn into him. It was slow and nowhere near as direct as what he experienced with Dr. Wolchek that morning. But he could feel it.

"Wow Doc! It works. I feel it. It's slow but steady."

Then suddenly Ryan's concentration was broken when a loud masculine voice standing next to him boomed.

"Hey buddy. Long time no see. How's it going?" the booming voice asked. At the same time Ryan felt a hand press down on his shoulder. Immediately, he felt a sharp increase in energy and enjoyed it for a moment before breaking the flow. This was not the case for the man who had placed his hand on Ryan's shoulder. He instantly went limp and stumbled forward off balance. Ryan was able to catch him.

"Randy. You Okay?" Ryan asked. He helped Randy regain his balance.

"Oh man, I feel a little dizzy," Randy said.

"Here. Sit down for a second," Ryan said, as he slid over in the booth.

After a few minutes Randy felt better and said his goodbyes.

"Wow, Doc. I felt a huge surge of energy the second he put his hand on my shoulder. It was like a shock to the system," Ryan said.

"Yes. It's encounters like that, as well as other close brushes, crowded places, and the like, that allow us to feed and exist without causing harm to others."

"I don't know about harm. You saw what happened to Randy. He almost passed out."

"That's because he caught you by surprise," Dr. Wolchek said. Direct physical contact is the most fluid way of getting energy. You were already open and slowly feeding. When he touched you his energy was immediately pulled into you."

"Incredible. It's all just so unbelievable," Ryan said. "Now that I'm actually doing it, it feels so natural. Like I've always known how, but just forgot or something. Is that strange sounding or what?" Ryan asked.

"I've never seen anyone catch on as fast as you. You do seem to be a natural. This is very unusual, but I guess it is possible," Dr. Wolchek responded. "If we do have this ability within us all along but for some reason it's gone dormant, then maybe you've found a faster way of re-awaking it somehow."

"Maybe," Ryan said. He was still surprised by his abilities.

Ryan was quiet, contemplative. "I feel something else too," he said.

Dr. Wolchek raised his eyebrows.

"I don't really know how to describe it," Ryan paused. "It's like there's an undercurrent of energy. Something in the background. It feels huge but just out of reach. I can't quite make out what it is, but I know it's beyond this room. Sound strange, Doc?" he asked.

Intrigued by what Ryan just said, Dr. Wolchek thought to himself, "How remarkable. Can he really feel such an undercurrent? If this is true, he just might prove to be the most powerful of our kind ever discovered." Trying to hide his building excitement Dr. Wolchek suppressed his enthusiasm. "You bring up an interesting point. It is widely believed by many in the Society that there is a greater, unlimited river of energy so to speak, running through the earth."

"Does such a thing exist?" Ryan asked sitting up and leaning in with greater interest.

"We don't know for sure. However, it does seem possible," Dr. Wolchek said. "Think about it. Every living thing has a life force. Trees. Plants. Animals. Everything. The earth is one huge living life form. Therefore, it stands to reason that it, too, gives off energy. Energy that we should be able to theoretically tap into if only we could find a way. Some members have made it their life's work to try and find just such a connection, but they have so far been unsuccessful."

"That's too bad," Ryan said frowning before continuing. "I mean can you imagine it? A huge unlimited amount of energy there for the taking."

"Unfortunately, for now anyway, we have to work with what we know," Dr. Wolchek said. "Lets try another exercise, shall we? This time I want you to take energy from me while shaking my hand."

"Are you sure? Remember poor Randy over there," Ryan said, gesturing in Randy's direction.

"You were already wide open and feeding. This time I want you to control it and focus. Only take a small amount then shut it off," Dr. Wolchek instructed.

Ryan relaxed his body and concentrated on finding and isolating the craving. Within just a matter of seconds he had found it. Now that he knew what the feeling felt like, it was much easier to recall and activate.

"Lets try it," he said. He reached out and shook the doctor's hand.

The jolt was instant, yet smooth and refreshing. It made him smile. He abruptly cut it off. Dr. Wolchek felt the drain but it was over fast.

"Well done. How do you feel?" Dr. Wolchek asked.

"Good. It was a quick burst, but satisfying," Ryan replied.

"Yes. This is one of the best ways to feed discreetly. Any physical contact works as long as you don't get to carried away. I personally like massage," Dr. Wolchek suggested.

"What about the people we take the energy from? Does it hurt them?" Ryan asked.

"Not as long as we don't take too much. Small amounts can be regenerated but large amounts will seriously affect a normal person's ability to function. They can't regenerate energy to the extent that we can. Taking too much will permanently damage them and possibly even kill them in time."

"But ordinary people can also drain us right? I mean, according to you, my encounter with my assistant last night drained a lot of energy from me. How do I prevent it from being pulled into someone during such encounters? Please don't tell me I have to give up sex Doc. That would be a major deal breaker," Ryan said. He was smiling but his tone was serious.

"No, you don't have to give up sex. But you do have to learn how to control the flow of your own energy," Dr. Wolcheck said smiling and shaking his head.

"How?" Ryan asked.

"The same way you just did shaking my hand. Focus on the energy, the craving, and block it. Concentrate on holding it back. It's like shutting the front door on your house. You do this to keep the air conditioning inside so it won't escape into the hot July outdoors. Same thing applies to your energy. When I'm not feeding and I shake someone's hand, I close myself off and prevent any energy from escaping. I think of a wall. It can be done. You just need to practice. Might I suggest looking into various meditation and concentration exercises."

"I feel like a kid on his first day of school," Ryan replied.

"Over time your ability will be as natural as breathing. It just takes practice."

A few minutes later the waiter arrived with their food.

"About time. I'm starving. Lets eat," Ryan said picking up his knife and fork.

Chapter 10
Tor

From his favorite lounge chair on Ryan's deck, Tor looked out over the backyard with sleepy cat eyes. The summer sun had set and night was falling. This was Tor's domain and hunting ground. The creek and the wilder more natural sections of the yard provided the perfect environment for an abundance of wildlife.

Standing up in the chair and stretching like cats do, Tor faced into the warm breeze blowing off the river and creek. Catching a faint sent of something on the wind, he jumped off the chair and walked to the edge of the deck. The moon had not yet risen and the yard was shrouded in darkness. Tor's eyes were big as they scanned the creek bank in the direction the smell was coming from. Motionless, he stared out frozen in place. Seeing movement by the stairs leading to the dock, Tor crouched down. His eyes were locked on a shape moving along the top of the creek bank. It was a large rat.

The Rat moved quickly. Not far from the dock was a bird feeder hanging off a limb over a small clearing. The birds scattered bird seed on to the ground when they visited. To Ryan it seemed the birds wasted far more than they ate but he still made it a point to keep the feeder filled. The ground below the feeder was well known to the rat and he visited it nightly when scavenging for food.

Tor excitedly watched the rat with the intensity of a seasoned predator as it moved along the creek bank. His instincts were heightened eyes locked on his prey. After losing sight of the rat when it disappeared behind a small shrub, Tor ran down the deck stairs and disappeared into the darkness. He could smell the rats sent in the air. Crouching down, he stealthily made his way along the edge of the yard toward the feeder using plants and shadows for cover. Making no sound, Tor slowly and methodically approached. Careful not to give himself away.

The rat also moved cautiously. Predators were a constant threat but this was a large old rat. His instincts had served him well throughout his life. Occasionally he would stop and smell the air for any sign of danger before continuing. Unfortunately, the breeze was blowing off the river this night.

Chapter 11

After dinner, Ryan and Dr. Wolchek went outside to take in the view as well as allow the doctor to indulge in his after dinner cigarette. The restaurant was elevated two stories above the south bank of the St. Johns River. The view from the balcony was beautiful.

"I see life energy isn't your only craving," Ryan said with a smile. He nodded toward the cigarette the doctor was holding.

"We all have our vices Mr. Anderson," Dr. Wolchek grinned.

Ryan was thoughtful for a moment.

"If this is all about balance, then what happened? I mean how did I get out of balance?" he asked.

"Good question Ryan. I'm not really sure. But I'm convinced it had something to do with that owl," Dr. Wolchek replied pointing his cigarette at him.

"The owl?"

"I think the owl drained some of your life force that night to repair its damage and in a way left the door open so to speak when it flew away. As a result of the encounter, you have been leaking energy ever since."

Shaking his head and looking down Ryan asked, "Is that even possible?"

"We are not the only species with this ability. There are others and owls are one of them."

"Fascinating. It's all so unbelievable. And now that I've been opened, I have to keep feeding in order to survive?"

"Yes. But remember, your aging process has halted and theoretically, barring unforeseen accidents, you can possibly live forever."

"Like vampires?"

"Something like that," Dr. Wolchek said. Amused by his comment Dr. Wolchek patted Ryan's shoulder as they strolled around the balcony.

"So then to recap, casual interaction, close physical contact, drawing from public events, and eating well is how we are to survive?" Ryan asked.

"Yes. We blend in and use our environment. Remember, for now anyway, secrecy is our best defense. I don't believe the world at large is ready for us. Not yet anyway."

"No. Probably not yet. Still, I owe you my life. Thank you. I know you didn't have to do this."

"No thanks necessary Ryan."

Pausing before continuing, Ryan put his hands on the balcony railing and looked up at the brightly lit skyline. Reflecting on the recent events he was humbled but also grateful. He knew if Dr. Wolchek had not chosen to help him he would probably be dead by now. Suicide was not something Ryan gave much thought to in his healthier days but as his condition worsened it was becoming more of a daily consideration. The quality of his life had degraded drastically over the past six months. With each passing day ending his suffering was becoming a very real possibility. Taking a deep breath Ryan exhaled a sigh of relief. The doctor had saved him. Grateful but curious Ryan turned to Dr. Walchek and asked, "Why did you decide to help me?"

Dr. Wolchek's face was emotionless. It was obvious to Ryan he was lost in thought. For a long time he said nothing as if he was replaying past events over in his head. Looking down and walking away Dr. Wolchek took a long drag on his cigarette then exhaled the smoke into the night air. Turning back to face Ryan he said, "Because you remind me of someone I use to know a long time ago."

"The night we met you seemed surprised when you first saw me. You said I reminded you of someone. Is it the same person?"

Hesitating then turning away and looking out over the open river, Dr. Wolchek answered with a solemn, "Yes."

Not one to miss the obvious change of mood, Ryan continued. "What happened?" he asked.

"A long story I'm afraid Ryan. One I'll have to tell you some day but lets leave that tale for another time shall we?" he said as he forced a smile and dropped his cigarette to the ground before patting it out with his shoe.

Getting the message, Ryan decided not to pursue the matter. But he could tell this was a sensitive subject for the doctor. "I understand. For another time then." Shifting to a more up-beat tone Ryan asked, "So what's next on the training schedule? Are we going to meet tomorrow?"

"I'm afraid I can't. I must be going," Dr. Wolchek replied.

"Already?" Ryan was surprised. "What about the training?"

"You know what you need to know to survive."

Dumbstruck Ryan's face showed his surprise.

"Really? I just figured it would take a lot longer to learn. I mean, I thought it would be a much more complicated process."

"Normally it is. But you seem to have developed the ability rather quickly Ryan. Usually it takes months of intense training for new converts to fully grasp the concept of feeding. But not you. I've never seen anyone transition as fast as you have. You are different that is for certain."

"It seems, well, kind of easy, actually almost natural in a way. I don't mean to brag, but it just doesn't seem that difficult of a concept to grasp," Ryan said shrugging his shoulders and looking at the doctor a little confused.

"Most need a considerable amount of time and help. They need to be fed like I did you until they develop the ability. But you...well...your another story altogether," Dr. Wolchek said. He lowered his head and paused. Then he looked at Ryan with a humbled expression.

"I've never been bested before. Not in all my many years. When you reversed the flow and then drained my life force, I was quite surprised to say the least," Dr. Wolchek said. "Not even knowing what you were doing you took to the ability naturally, as if by instinct. You are a remarkable subject, Ryan."

"Remarkable?" Ryan said rolling his eyes. "I was dying. I'd have tried anything to stop that pain. But, thanks for your vote of confidence. And speaking of votes, what are you going to tell your Society? I haven't forgotten what you said. A council will decide if I'm worthy or not? That I'll have to give up my life and go underground? Basically join this Society or be eliminated? You didn't paint a pretty picture Doc. And like I told you, I'm not really the joiner type." Ryan said crossing his arms and leaning back against the deck railing. "So what are you going to tell them about me?"

Dr. Wolchek chuckled. "Oh, I don't know. Maybe I'll tell them it wasn't what I thought. I'll be creative. Perhaps you've made a full recovery," he said chuckling again. The thought of deceiving the Society amused him.

"Is it really going to be that easy?" Ryan asked with genuine concern.

"Sometimes. I don't want to give you a way to the Society either. I believe you are different. The full extent of your abilities are yet unknown. Once your body is fully recovered, who knows what you might be capable of doing," he said. Dr. Wolchek began pacing. "No, Ryan. I need to give you the time you need to recover physically."

"Will I see you again?" Ryan asked.

"Of that I am certain."

"So where are you going?"

"I'll travel for a few months. That should give you plenty of time to heal and practice feeding. I'll go investigate other cases in this country then head to South America for a spell. The sooner I leave the better."

"Why is that?"

"It will aid in convincing the Society that you are not of interest. You see, by the rules, I should have gotten the council's permission to drain and feed you which I did not. Then, you would have to be brought to our compound in London for training and conditioning. But mostly, they would never believe that I would leave someone newly changed so soon. It's just not done. Remember, most don't take to this ability as quickly. By moving on and investigating other cases, it shouldn't arouse suspicion," Dr. Wolchek replied.

"So, you're going to abandon me," Ryan said. He tried to make it sound like a joke and express his gratitude. It was one thing to accept all the doctor was telling him but another to be abducted from his life and then forced to join some Society he'd only learned of a few days ago. He appreciated that Dr. Wolchek was willing to conceal his existence. He needed more time to take all this in.

Dr. Wolchek shrugged his shoulders.

"Only for a few months." he said. "Just long enough to direct attention away from you. Then I'll be back and your real training can begin."

"Real training?" Ryan asked.

"We've only scratched the surface my boy," Dr. Wolchek said. He patted Ryan's shoulder before leading him back inside the restaurant.

Chapter 12

Reaching the edge of the clearing, the rat paused for a long time trying to sense if the area was safe. Driven by hunger he cautiously entered the small clearing under the bird feeder. Half way to the center he paused again and sniffed the air before reaching the birdseed littered ground. In a frenzy the rat started eating. Completely exposed, he gorged himself.

Tor was crouched down by the base of a tree on the opposite side of the clearing hidden by plants. His muscles tense-eyes locked on his prey, ready to spring.

Lost in the moment and dangerously exposed, the rat had no idea Tor was watching from the shadows. The abundance of food overwhelmed the rat causing him to let down his guard as he scavenged the ground in a frenzy.

Tor watched with the patience of a skilled predator waiting for his opportunity. If he miscalculated his attack there was a chance the rat could escape into the dense underbrush. But his predatory cat instincts served him well. He remained as still as a statue.

Completely engrossed in scavenging, the rat was unaware of what was lurking on the edge of the clearing. In a fateful move, he turned his back to the darkness. Tor sprang from the shadows and pounced on the rat. In one deadly move he had the rat's neck in his mouth and clamped down. The rat squealed and kicked violently but there was no escape. Tor's eyes glowed as he drew in the rat's life force. When he drew in the last of the energy his eyes returned to normal and he spit the rat out. Energized, Tor playfully swatted the rat's lifeless body into the air and chased after it. He played with his kill for a few minutes before carrying it to the front door. Ryan was use to coming home and finding the remains of his victims. Tor had proven himself to be a master hunter in the months since moving in. After placing the rat on the front porch doormat, Tor proudly waited by his kill for Ryan to return.

Chapter 13

For Ryan, the evening passed with lighting speed. At Dr. Wolchek's direction, he continued practicing feeding off and on throughout the evening. Finally, it was time to leave. Having taken up the table for the entire dinner sitting, Ryan felt bad for their server. Ryan knew they had denied him at least two rounds of tips for the evening so he apologized and gave the young man a substantial gratuity.

While waiting for the valet to bring the car around, Dr. Wolchek noticed the couple they observed having dinner earlier in the evening also waiting for their car. They had apparently spent the remainder of the night in the lounge. The husband was very intoxicated. His wife was just barely able to keep him on his feet. When their car arrived, Dr Wolchek noticed the rear bumper. Just as Ryan had said, there was a large dent in the molding. Dr. Wolchek nudged Ryan in the side and nodded toward the bumper. Ryan noticed it and chuckled.

"What is it?" The doctor asked.

"Shaking his head, Ryan replied, "Now she's thinking she's going to tell her husband he did it on the way home. He's so drunk, she'll probably get away with it."

After returning to Ryan's house, Dr. Wolchek put the car in park but did not turn off the engine.

"Would you like to come in for an after dinner drink?" Ryan asked.

"Maybe another time. I have an early flight."

Ryan groans. "I still have so many questions."

"I'm sure you do," Dr. Wolchek responded. "There will be plenty of time for that. Right now I must leave in order not to arouse any suspicion. Business as usual I think is the term."

"Thank you again Doctor. I know you didn't have to do any of this," Ryan said humbly.

Dr. Wolchek paused for a moment. When he spoke, his tone was serious.
"I need you to promise me something Ryan."

"Anything."

"Promise to keep a low profile. Do not abuse what you have."

"Of course not."

"No Ryan, I'm serious."

Ryan could tell that something else was troubling him. "What's the matter, Doc?"

For a second Dr. Wolchek wondered if Ryan could read his energy. "I'm afraid the Society may send someone to verify my findings."

"Why? You don't think they'll believe you?" Ryan asked.

Frowning, the doctor answered, "I don't know anymore. Maybe. Maybe not. The Society and I are becoming more and more estranged these days. The trust is not like it once was."

"Then maybe it is you who should be careful, Doc. After all, didn't you say your Society tends to eliminate all those who oppose its rules?"

Shaking his head and fumbling with the steering wheel, Dr. Wolchek answered, "I did say that didn't I?"

"Then don't go back. Stay here," Ryan said. He sat up in his seat, folded his arms across his chest and gave Dr. Wolchek a defiant look.

"I can't do that. I must continue on. It's safer this way. Promise to be careful, Ryan. I'll try and warn you if I can. Just don't give yourself away."

"Now you're starting to worry me," Ryan said. He shifted uncomfortably in his seat.

"I don't mean to. Just be discrete. Continue practicing feeding and try not to give yourself away to anyone. Even those you love and trust the most. No one can know what you are. Do you understand? No one can ever know."

"I won't. I'm still not sure I understand all this myself."

Smiling and breaking the more serious atmosphere, Dr. Wolchek shook his shoulder. It will all make sense someday. Just give it time my young friend," he said.

Shaking his head and also smiling, Ryan opened the car door. "Just be sure to come back. We still have a lot to discuss," he said.

Ryan got out of the car and noticed Tor walking toward him. "Hey buddy. Where have you been all day?" Ryan asked. He bent down to acknowledge the cat.

"You have a cat?" Dr. Wolchek asked abruptly in more of a statement than a question.

Surprised by the doctor's tone, Ryan answered, "Yes. His name is Tor. He showed up the night I hit the owl."

Ryan picked Tor up and faced Dr. Wolchek as he held him. Frightened, the doctor abruptly pushed himself back against the car door. At the same time, Tor hissed and bolted out of Ryan's hands startling him.

"Strange, usually he's very friendly. I wonder what's gotten into him," Ryan asked.

"You said he showed up the night you encountered the owl?" Dr. Wolchek asked.

"Yes," Ryan answered. He was puzzled by the doctor's reaction to Tor. "He reminded me of a cat I use to see downtown at a warehouse the band and I used to rehearse. That night, after the owl flew off, he came up to me and let me pet him. It looked like it was about to start raining so I let him in the house, fed him, and he's been around ever since. Other than being a vicious hunter, I have no complaints. He's the perfect roommate," Ryan joked. "Why were you so surprised by him?"

Regaining his composure Dr. Wolchek answered, "It's just unusual for people like us to associate with cats. Cats, owls, and various other lifeforms are, to some extent, considered enemies of the Society."

Scrunching his face, Ryan could not believe what he was hearing. *How can a cat be an enemy,* he thought.

"Why? What can a cat possibly do?"

"More than you know. Believe me they are dangerous. Haven't you heard any of the stories about cats stealing souls or taking peoples' breath when they're sleeping?"

"Of course I have. But those are just old wives' tales. Surely you don't believe that nonsense?" Ryan asked.

"There is much truth to those old stories. Cats in particular have the ability to channel energy both ways. He could drain you dry if he wanted too," Dr. Wolchek claimed.

"Please, get real Doc. My cat wouldn't hurt me. The whole time I was sick, being with him was really the only thing that kept me going. Just being around him made me feel better in a strange kind of way."

"Very interesting. Then somehow he must have been feeding you," Dr. Wolchek said thinking out loud.

"What? No way. Is that even possible?" Ryan asked.

"Yes it is. He was feeding you. Not much, but enough. Enough to help you. Somehow he was able to sense your condition. The owl changed you and the cat felt it," Dr. Wolchek responded. "How extraordinary."

"But why, Doc? Why would he want to help me?"

"I don't know, Ryan. Be grateful that he did. He probably kept you alive much longer than you would have lived without him. Actually, I was surprised to see you functioning as well as you were when we first met. I've never encountered anyone in as good mental condition as you were."

"So somehow he knew I was sick?" Ryan asked.

"Yes, but he was too small to help you like I did," Dr. Wolchek said. "But he was trying. You said he was a vicious hunter. Why did you say that?"

"Because he kills everything. Birds, rats, mice, squirrels, moles, everything. Why?" Ryan asked.

"He's consuming their energy probably in an attempt to give it to you. He's been charging up by the most basic of methods - killing. Still, it wasn't enough to do anything more than give you temporary relief."

"If this is true, then I owe him big. So if cats can help, why does the Society fear them?" Ryan asked. He looked at Tor who was now siting by the front door bathing himself while waiting for Ryan to let him inside.

"Because they are wild animals and cannot be controlled. Remember, they can also take. Tell me, since meeting me, does he still give you comfort?" Dr. Wolchek asked.

"Yes. Actually, after returning from your hotel, he was all over me."

"Be careful Ryan. He can take your energy if he wants. He could easily drain you dry."

Ryan rolled his eyes and shook his head in disbelief. "He would never do that to me! I can't explain why I feel that way but I know he would never do anything to intentionally hurt me. Besides, if I do really owe him my life, then maybe letting him drain a little energy from time to time is the least I can do."

"The Society sees it differently. They see these animals as uncontrollable and threats to their very existence."

"Come on, Doc, a cat?"

"Yes. And owls."

"Why owls?" Ryan asked.

"Because they can also take energy. Have you ever heard any of the legends about owls?"

"I know there's some Native American beliefs about owls knowing when people are going to die or something. Some believe they show up when something bad is about to happen, like a bad omen," Ryan said.

"Exactly. It's believed they somehow know when people are close to passing and then they show up and collect their life energy, or soul if you wish, as it ebbs away."

"That's ridiculous."

"Ridiculous? Dr. Wolchek asked. Remember, humans are relatively new to this-at least new in respect to understanding and being aware of this ability. But other life forms have possibly been doing it for thousands of years if not longer. We know owls are capable of taking and even completely draining human energy. This is what happened to you."

"But, it didn't kill me. Why didn't it kill me? It only took what it needed to fix itself," Ryan said.

"Yes, and that is very interesting," Dr. Wolchek replied.

"Interesting how?"

"It somehow knew only to take what it needed. It could have easily killed you if it wanted. We've done experiments where owls and cats feed until we stopped them. They seem unwilling or unable to stop feeding on their own," Dr. Wolchek said.

"You've done experiments?"

"Yes. We have been researching this phenomena for a long time. These animals can be very dangerous to our kind." Tor was sitting as still as an Egyptian statue looking in their direction.

"If this is true, then why didn't my owl kill me that night? And why did Tor choose that particular night to befriend me?" Ryan asked.

"I don't know. Somehow he sensed that you were hurt and for whatever reason decided he wanted to help you," Dr. Wolchek said. He looked at Tor. "Tell me Ryan, can you read his energy like the people in the restaurant?"

"I don't know, lets see." Ryan said. He turned from the car and looked at Tor. It took a second, but he quickly found his rhythm. Tor's energy was more wild and free flowing. Much more open than a human's. Still, it was familiar. Ryan smiled and turned back to Dr. Wolchek. "He's hungry."

"Extraordinary!" Dr. Wolchek whispered under his breath. He was unable to contain his excitement. Shaking his head in amazement, the doctor continued, "Like I said, Ryan, you are a very interesting case. Your abilities are unprecedented. There is no telling what you will be capable of once your body has regenerated."

"That is, if your Society doesn't present me with an offer I can't refuse," Ryan said.

"Don't worry about the Society. Leave them to me," Dr. Wolchek said. "In the meantime, practice feeding and be discreet about it. Wait for me to return. And I promise I will return."

"Okay Doc. I look forward to our next encounter." He extended his hand to Dr. Wolchek. Ryan wondered if he would take it. He did. Neither tried to exchange any energy. Smiling, Ryan said, "Thanks again. I've got a lot to think about."

"I look forward to our next meeting Ryan."

"As do I Doc. Good night and have a safe trip." Ryan shut the door and patted the cars roof indicating it was clear to pull out.

# # #

As Dr. Wolchek drove back to his hotel, his mind was racing. "An owl and a cat! This is indeed an extraordinary young man!" he said out loud. He couldn't help but feel a strong sense of relief. Seeing that Ryan could feed on his own as well as feeling secure in knowing that he appeared to have a firm understanding of his ability, Dr. Wolchek felt much better about leaving. He knew the faster he got away from Ryan, the better he believed his chances were of convincing the Society that Ryan was of no interest to them.

# # #

Over the next several weeks, Dr. Wolchek visited other possible subjects throughout the United States and Canada before continuing on to South America. He submitted a preliminary report on Ryan basically concluding that he was not a person of interest to the Society. Dr. Wolchek attributed his deteriorating health to other medical conditions. Though he knew he would eventually have to present a more detailed report to the Society's review board, for now his goal was to buy Ryan as much time as possible. Ryan was strong, but Dr. Wolchek knew he would have to be much stronger if he was to face what lay ahead.

PART THREE

Chapter 14

Since the doctor's departure, Ryan found everyday held new surprises. Eager to learn how to better use his new abilities, he sought out different situations in which he could practice feeding discretely. Dr. Wolchek was right about his profession providing opportunities to draw energy. Shaking hands proved to be very effective. As his health continued to improve, he soon found that his health club also offered many interesting possibilities as well.

It wasn't long before Ryan was settling back into his normal workout routine. Before the onset of his mysterious illness he would sometimes visit his health club in the morning prior to work and then, energy permitting, again on the way home. He enjoyed working out and pushing his body to its physical limits. He usually worked out on his own but every now and then he partnered up with other regulars. Competitive by nature, working with others motivated Ryan to excel beyond his normal routine; something his home gym could not provide.

As the weeks passed, Ryan noticed that peoples' energy signatures were very different. He often compared these signatures to flavors and fingerprints; each was unique in its own special way. For instance, he found that healthy people radiated much stronger energy signatures. Their level of health seemed to parallel the strength of their energy field. Diseased or sickly people tended to radiate weaker and more erratic energy signatures. Smokers, addicts, and other substance abusers, gave off distorted energy fields. It was possible to feed from any of these sources but Ryan found the healthier people to be the most satisfying. To himself, he referred to the health club as an unending buffèt. And for this reason most of all he looked forward to going. Each day presented him with new and interesting flavors to choose from.

One evening after work, Ryan was working out alone. His attention was drawn to three loud and annoying extremely over-developed young men throwing weights around and attracting a lot of attention with a constant barrage of harsh language. He could sense that they were on something. Their energy signatures were artificially wild and erratic. The closer he got the easier it was for him to focus on their energy. It was like static electricity in the air. They were bench pressing large amounts of weight and throwing the bar back onto the rack with unnecessary force. Casually taking up a position on the bench next to the group Ryan loaded the bar with his normal 225 pounds and prepared to lift the weight. At the same time he was open and casually drawing energy from the men. When he lifted the bar off the rack he noticed that it was very light. Wondering why, Ryan stopped feeding and tried it again. This time it was the weight he expected. "Strange," he thought. Somehow he was able to convert their energy into strength. "I gotta try that again," he muttered to himself. After adding more weight, he got back into position under the bar. Opening up and drawing their energy in, he focused and lifted the additional weight with minimal effort. Smiling, Ryan couldn't resist the opportunity to show off a little himself. Without all the noise and obvious attempts at getting attention, Ryan casually stacked more weight on his bar equaling what the guys next to him were lifting, 315 pounds. Noticing Ryan, one of the guys motioned to another. Laughing, neither believed he would be able to move it.

"Hey buddy, you need a spot?" one asked with a cocky tone.

"No thanks," Ryan responded. "I'm just warming up." Then as effortlessly as ever, Ryan lifted the weight and pressed ten full reps. Amazed, the guys huddled and then stacked more weight on their bar. The biggest and strongest of the three men took up his position on the bench and lifted the bar off the rack. Immediately his face turned red. The blood vessels swelled and his arms strained and noticeably shook, as he slowly lowered it to his chest and then pressed it up. He did this six more times before returning the bar to the rack. Exploding with excitement, he jumped up from the bench.

"Six reps baby! 350 pounds! Beat that bitch!" he yelled.

Ryan smiled. "Impressive. Let me give it a try."

"It's your funeral man," the big guy laughed. He motioned to the bench. "Be my guest."

As Ryan took his position under the bar, the guys laughed between themselves. Ryan was 170 pounds and probably a good hundred pounds lighter than the smallest of the group. None of them believed he would even be capable of lifting the bar from the rack.

"Okay, here goes. One. Two. Three."

To everyone's surprise, Ryan lifted the weight off the rack with ease and did another ten reps as effortlessly as before. Casually placing the bar back on the rack, Ryan sat up and said, "Not bad. That was ten wasn't it?" he asked. His nonchalant attitude was pissing them off.

"No way, man! There's no way you can lift that much weight! Put on another fifty!" demanded the big guy. As instructed, his buddies loaded the bar. Again taking up his position, the big guy was barely able to lift the bar clear of the rack. After pausing, he slowly lowered it to his chest and with great effort forced it up. To Ryan's surprise, he managed two more reps before his buddies assisted him with returning it to the rack. He then stood up and howled excitedly while beating his chest like some kind of hyped up Neanderthal.

"Impressive. What is that, 400 pounds? Let me give it a try." Ryan said. He took up his position and with little effort lifted the bar from the rack and did another ten reps. Silence fell over the group. The big guy's jaw dropped.

"You know guys, I'm just not feeling it. Put another fifty pounds on will you?" Ryan asked. He laid back down under the bar. Looking at each other, the guys added two forty-five pound plates instead of the two twenty-five ones he asked for. Ryan knew what they did. He could feel it. But it would make no difference. Ryan had been steadily drawing on their energy to assist him in lifting the weight.

"Okay, you're ready," one of the guys said. He smiled a cocky smile at Ryan.

"Alright. Let's do it. One. Two. Three." Ryan lifted the weight with little effort but this time he only did five reps. At this point, even he felt ten was showing off. "Wow! Only five. I must be off my game today. Oh well, I guess we all have a bad day every now and then." He smiled as he stood up.

"No fuckin' way, man! No way you could lift that much weight," the big guy shouted. His buddies were just as stunned.

"Yea. I'm surprised too. Usually I can get at least ten reps with 500 pounds." Ryan shrugged his shoulders. "Well, it's been fun gentlemen, but I have cardio to do. Later." He headed off to the indoor track. Stunned, none of the group said a word. They watched in silence as Ryan walked off toward the track area.

Halfway around the track, Ryan heard someone yell-out his name.

"Anderson!"

Stopping, he turned and saw one of his former band mates chasing after him.

"James! What's up buddy?"

"Man, you look great! You look fuckin' great! What happened? Are you cured? What did you have? I have to tell you, we thought you were one step away from death. What happened?"

Laughing from the bombardment of questions, Ryan motioned for him to relax.

"Slow down, man. One at a time. Yes, I am cured. I had something wrong with my eyes. A doctor from overseas diagnosed my problem and was able to help me," he said.

"Thank God! I'm serious. We all thought you were a goner," James said. He was relieved and happy to see his friend healthy.

"Not yet. So what's up? How's the band?" Ryan asked. "You guys working on anything new?"

James frowned. "Ryan, that new guy just isn't working. He won't listen to a damn thing we tell him. He's so hard-headed it's unreal. Brad's going to fire him this Friday after our show. I wish he would do it now and just cancel the gig. That jackass changes everything in mid-performance. We can't keep up. I'd rather cancel and pay for it than let him fuck up the music again." All of a sudden a big grin appeared on James' face.

"Any chance you might want your old job back, pal?" he asked.

Ryan pretended to think for a second. "Sure. What the hell. I always liked playing weekend rock star."

"Hot Fuckin' damn!" James yelled and jumped up into the air. "Yes! I'll call Brad right now and give him the good news!"

"You do that buddy. Just let me know when you guys want to practice. I gotta get back to my run. Later man. Great seeing you again," he said and took off down the track.

Smiling from ear to ear, James waved him off as he reached for his cell phone.

# # #

Ryan stumbled into the lead singer position with the band after James and some of the other band members heard him singing with friends one night at a bar. Ryan was drunk at the time, but his voice got their attention. He always liked to sing, but mostly he just played around and performed in front of friends or when he had too much to drink. The band was local and struggling. They were a good mix of modern alternative rock with a techno element mixed in. It was a good sound and prior to losing their lead singer, they were developing quite a local following. Their previous lead singer developed a major problem with crystal meth. Having tried repeatedly to help him, the band finally had to cut him loose. The timing could not have been worse. After months of performing and saving money, they were on the verge of cutting a demo CD. The session was booked and paid for, but with no lead singer, it looked like they would have to cancel the session and lose the money. This was particularly unfortunate since all the songs were written by the remaining members. Even if they couldn't perform shows anymore, they still wanted to have some of the songs recorded so they would have something to market.

After hearing Ryan, they approached him about singing for the demo session. They promised to pay him for his time if he could help out. Ryan was shocked by the offer. He didn't think of himself as a singer, but after trying out with the band and liking their sound he discovered he had real talent. Refusing the money, Ryan told them he would be honored to do it for free. Within a week he had most of the songs down and what he didn't, he used notes and cue-cards to get him through the recording session.

When the recording session was over, they asked Ryan if he would like to join their band. He was flattered but told them he was serious about his advertising career and that, for the time being, had to be his priority. Still, he was willing to help on the side as long as he could. The band was agreeable and appreciative. They were mostly looking to write and sell material. Performing was a bonus since they all enjoyed the stage element. With an audience, they got to play rock star. None of the band members outwardly expressed the desire to go big, but they all secretly dreamed of the day.

Meeting Ryan also had other advantages for the band. Having access to money, Ryan was able to get better equipment as well as help out by paying for recording sessions. He even footed the bill to have several hundred additional CD's made so they could have something to sell at local venues. And he refused taking any profits from the sales. He just enjoyed performing. The stage and audience invigorate him. The energy from the crowd was intoxicating and Ryan soon found he really liked the lifestyle that came with playing weekend rock star. The band and Ryan had a bond. Maybe this was because of his lack of family life. He thought of them all as brothers and always enjoyed working with them. They were like a family.

But with the onset of his mysterious illness he had to take time off. Ryan had not sung with the band in months and this really bothered him. He felt like he was letting his band-mates down. They said they understood and wanted him to concentrate on getting better. But he knew they were struggling with the replacement singer.

As Ryan did his laps he couldn't help but smile to himself. He missed his fellow band members and looked forward to singing with them again. But he also wondered what new and interesting feeding opportunities performing to an audience would present.

Chapter 15

London, six months later

Standing in the office doorway observing the beautiful young woman working at her desk and consumed by her research, Lord Henry Malcolm said nothing. He stood silently taking in her radiant beauty in only the way an older man can. Feeling a presence, Christine Wolchek turned toward the doorway.

"Lord Malcolm. I did not know you were there," she said.

"Sorry to startle you, Christine. Interesting reading?" He undressed her with his eyes.

Oh, not really," she answered. She tried to hide the repulsive feeling building inside her.

"I guess your father is off on another one of his wild adventures again. I don't suppose you have any idea when he plans to return?"

"He did not inform me of his itinerary," she responded. She tried to be inconspicuous as she slid a picture of a young man under a pile of papers on the desk.

"Are you sure?" Lord Malcolm asked. His tone was one of doubt as he walked into the room.

"Yes," Christine replied. She was blunt. No pretend pleasantries.

Lord Malcolm walked around the room casually inspecting Dr. Wolchek's many trinkets collected from around the world before returning to take up an uncomfortably close position in front of Christine's desk. Leaning over, he slid the picture out from under the pile of papers. For a split second his expression registered shock and surprise. As if by instinct he looked toward the portrait hanging in the office. To Christine, he looked as if he had seen a ghost. However, Lord Malcolm was not a man who startled easily. He quickly regained his composure and smiled a sinister smile.

"That's unfortunate. Well, it has been a pleasure young lady. If you do talk to your father anytime soon please give him my regards and tell him we eagerly await his findings. Good day."

"Good day Lord Malcolm."

As he left the room, Christine felt a cold chill run down her spine. Lord Malcolm always left her with an uneasy feeling and today was worse. She'd been caught hiding the photograph. "Oh father, I hope you know what you are doing," Christine said out loud. She exhaled a long sigh and looked toward the portrait hanging on the office wall.

Truth be known, Christine knew where her father was and why. She was very much involved in his work. They had been secretly investigating possible cases together for decades. Like her father, she was a member of the Society and was not happy with the direction it appeared to be heading.

Christine looked like a young woman in her mid to late twenties, but she was actually over a century older. Like her father, she too had the "gift" and with his guidance, learned how to live with it long ago. Unfortunately, her mother and three sisters did not. She and her father had long outlived the rest of their family. That was always the sad, but unfortunate reality of their situation. Relationships were difficult. Watching those one loves grow old and die while always staying untouched by time slowly hardens one to the truths of life and death. Christine and her father were lucky in that they had each other.

Christine slammed her fist down on the desk.

"Dammit! How could I be so careless," she said. She held her head in both hands looking at the picture still sitting where Lord Malcolm had left it. It was a picture from a medical file of a man in his late twenties. A few minutes later the silence of the room was broken by the chiming of a small clock on the fireplace mantel. Breaking her concentration, Christine looked at the clock and sighed. "Time sure flies when you're having fun," she said with obvious sarcasm.

She pushed herself back from the large desk and stretched. Standing up, Christine walked around the room lost in thought before returning to the desk and packing the file's contents. She picked up the picture of the young man again and looked at it. "Are you really the one we've been looking for all these years, Ryan Anderson? Is it possible that we've finally found you?" She put the picture in the file and locked it in the office safe. Concerned about Lord Malcolm, she decided it was time to call her father.

# # #

Christine went for a walk along a small river shaded by beautiful centuries-old trees. Like many members of the Society, Christine and her father had offices and kept a residence at Kingsley Hall, the Society's headquarters located twenty miles outside of London. Situated on 3700 acres, Kingsley Hall was a large 16th century manor house. The property had been used by the society for nearly 400 hundred years. Having been rebuilt and expanded over the centuries, surviving multiple wars and various internal uprisings, it now consisted of the main house, and six large out buildings converted for commercial and residential use. Here members met and conducted business as well as debated their roles in the Society.

Through a wide variety of methods, the Society and its members controlled a significant amount of the world's wealth. Their financial influence could be exerted across the globe at will if necessary. By controlling various markets, owning multiple large mega banks, insurance companies, and investment firms, as well as being the largest "unofficial" owner of international real estate, the Society and its members could influence world economies with ease.

In addition to business, many in the Society also actively debated the future of the human race. With more members growing tired of the Society's policy of non-involvement, exploring the possibilities of a more proactive role was often a popular topic of conversation. Since WWII, the Society had been faced with a steadily expanding internal rift that was now threatening to tear it apart. Tired of existing behind the scenes, a loud group of members advocated change. They wanted more involvement and control over mankind. They believed if the human race was to survive, then they would have to be the ones to lead it. However, that went against all that the Society was originally created for. At first, the internal unrest went unacknowledged. But, after the horrors of WWII, the small minority began gaining supporters. By the turn of the 21st century, the number of members leaning toward more involvement was almost equal to those supporting the more traditional role. However, a steadily increasing number of members favored some amount of limited intervention; many believed man was unable or unwilling to lead himself successfully. Daily stories emerged in the world's media that only served to further strengthen the opposition's position. It often disturbed Christine and Dr. Wolchek to hear their fellow Society members discussing the future of humanity as if it were some kind of game. The arrogance and disrespect displayed toward the human race astounded them.

As the twentieth century drew to a close, Lord Malcolm and other charismatic members took the lead in organizing the opposition into a formidable force within the Society. Although his charms were lost on Christine and Dr. Wolchek, Lord Malcolm's ability to manipulate others was unsurpassed. Even Hitler paled in comparison to his ability to speak and influence an audience. As the leader of the opposition, he was dangerously popular in the Society. Dr. Wolchek and a slight majority were all that prevented Lord Malcolm and his followers from dominating the council. It was rumored that Lord Malcolm, with the help of his trusted aid Roger, had been secretly recruiting and training new members to be part of an elite hit squad. Loyal members willing to follow his orders without question. Lord Malcolm denied such rumors, but Dr. Wolchek and other members of the council had their doubts. Unfortunately, they had no proof of any wrong doing yet. For this reason most of all, Dr. Wolchek took the lead in evaluating and indoctrinating new members.

Over the years Dr. Wolchek and Christine noticed a disturbing pattern. New and old members opposed to Lord Malcolm's policies were finding themselves the victims of strange and bizarre accidents. Usually fatal. Lord Malcolm's opposition was little by little being eliminated. Dr. Wolchek could not prove that Lord Malcolm or his hit squads were directly linked to any wrong doing, but he and Christine had their suspicions. Knowing Lord Malcolm was determined to dominate the Society at any cost in order to gain control of its vast financial resources, Dr. Wolchek, Christine, and other council members were doing all they could to hold him at bay. However, it was becoming painfully obvious that they were fighting a losing battle and time was on Lord Malcolm's side. Dr. Wolchek was often successful in finding and converting new members, but he played by the rules. Lord Malcolm, on the other hand, did not. Christine and Dr. Wolchek knew time was running out. In order to defeat Lord Malcolm, Dr. Wolchek would have to resort to extreme measures himself. And Ryan Anderson possessed the key to their survival.

Knowing the office phones were bugged, Christine left the compound when calling her father. As she strolled along the bank of a small river that ran next to the manor house, she disappeared further into the trees out of sight from prying eyes that may be watching her. When she felt safe, she pulled a small satellite phone from her jacket pocket and called her father.

He answered on the second ring. "Christine? Are you okay?"

"Yes Father, I am fine. But, I'm afraid I have some bad news," she said. "It's Lord Malcolm. I'm sure he suspects something. He saw the picture of Mr. Anderson. I should have been more careful. He snuck up on me while I was reviewing the file."

The phone was silent. Christine felt her heart skip a beat. She could feel her father's concern.

"I'm sorry, Father," she whispered. Her voice was trembling.

"It's been six months since I turned Ryan. He should be well in to his recovery by now I would think."

"But, how can that be? He's only six months old. That's impossible!"

"He's different. He's strong, Christine. I've never seen another like him. Almost immediately he learned how to feed. I suspect it was more from instinct. Still, it didn't take him long to learn how to use his abilities. It's like there was something in him that just needed to be awakened. When he was draining me..."

"What? What do you mean draining you? How did he drain you?" Christine asked. She cut him off with noticeable concern in her voice.

"It was extraordinary. After I drained his life force to get his attention and began to re-energize him, he suddenly took over and turned the tables on me," he replied.

"That's not possible Father. Not from someone who just turned!"

"I know, but it happened. He had me as helpless as any ordinary human. He could have killed me if he wanted, but he did not. He was able to control himself and released me but only after weakening me to where I was no longer a threat," he said. "I don't think he really understood how he was doing what he did. It was like some kind of self-defense survival instinct kicked in. Even in a weakened state, I was doing all I could to hide my excitement."

"This is just not possible," Christine repeated.

"But, it is I assure you. Later that evening I took him out to begin his training and by the end of the night he was able to draw energy as if he'd been doing it for years. And that's not all. He seems to have the ability to read people's energy; their thoughts and feelings."

"Are you saying that he can read minds?"

"No. Well, yes. Kind of. He can read their energy. He said he can't go into their minds, but he can tell what they are thinking by the energy they give off."

"Fascinating. Do you believe him?"

"Yes. A situation presented itself that offered proof. However, he could not read me. He said I was like a hole in the room a void that he could somehow feel."

"A void?" she asked.

"Yes. I told him this might be a good way for him to sense if others like us are around. A way for him to have a kind of warning."

"How much did you tell him about us and our kind?"

"I told him enough. No need to overload the man at this point. I think he has plenty to deal with for now," Dr. Wolchek said. "There is something else too, something I just do not understand."

Christine waited until her father put his thought together.

"He seems to have a connection with animals. Owls and cats to be exact," he said.

"But how can that be? They are dangerous to our kind!"

"I know. And that's the most amazing part. They don't drain him. His pet cat had been feeding him for months probably the only thing that kept him alive. I have to tell you Christine, I think he's the one! He's strong, strong I tell you. With enough time, there is no telling what he may be capable of once his body if fully regenerated."

"That's just it, Father. Enough time. You know Lord Malcolm will send someone to evaluate your findings. After seeing the picture this afternoon I'm sure he's already figured out that you lied about Mr Anderson in the report you sent to the council."

"Yes, you're probably right. If that's the case, then there is no reason for me to continue this attempt at deception. I'm coming home. Time to put our plan into action."

"Thank God. It's about time we abandon this sinking ship! And the sooner the better too," Christine said.

"Make the necessary arrangements and we will leave for good shortly after I return. We'll pick up Mr. Anderson along the way then go into hiding. Sound good?" her father asked.

"My bags are already packed."

"I thought they might be," he replied. "I'll see you in a few days. I love you Christine."

"Love you too, Father. Good bye."

# # #

"She's taking her walk again," said a large intimidating man. He watched Christine from a corner window of the manor house as she disappeared under the canape of trees lining the river.

"Calling her father I suspect," said Lord Malcolm. He did not look up from his desk as he finished writing a letter.

"Should I have the surveillance team monitor her conversations?"

"No. Let Christine and her father have their little intrigue for now. It may even prove useful to us later," Lord Malcolm answered. He casually folded the letter closed.

"How much longer do we have to wait your Lordship? Now is the time to strike!"

"Patience my dear friend," Lord Malcolm said. "Patience. It has taken a long time to get this far. We cannot act hastily now that we are so close."

Lord Malcolm's sneer agitated his associate.

"But, sir, this is the perfect time to strike. When they least expect it. If the council won't yield to your leadership we must force them too!"

"He gave the man a withering look that quickly faded into a grotesque smile.

"Don't worry," Lord Malcolm said. "Our time is coming. There is no reason for us to do what the good doctor and his lovely daughter are going to do for us. Let them play their little game. It won't make any difference in the end."

Changing the subject Lord Malcolm stood from behind his desk and handed the folded letter to the man. "Now be a good man and take this letter to Roger for me."

"Yes your Lordship. Good day," he said. With a slight bow he turned on his heal and exited Lord Malcolm's office closing the door behind him.

Nodding at the man as he left the room, Lord Malcolm walked over to the window and looked out just as Christine emerged from the trees.

"Do you really think you can stop me Alistair?" he asked out loud to no one.

# # #

A short time later, there was a knock on Lord Malcolm's office door.

"Yes," Lord Malcolm said. He sat back in his chair at his large desk as if he had been expecting someone.

"You sent for me, sir," said a large, hard looking man. He walked into the office carrying the letter.

"Have a seat. I'll make this brief," Lord Malcolm said. He held up a copy of Dr. Wolchek's report on Ryan Anderson. "It appears our good doctor is up to his old tricks again."

"Another bastard," the man asked. He looked at Lord Malcolm through cold black eyes, eyes that have seen and caused countless numbers of deaths over the centuries.

"I'm afraid so."

"Do you have a name?"

"Ryan Anderson. He lives in the U.S. Jacksonville, Florida to be exact."

"I'll take care of it," he said. No emotion.

"Not so fast my friend. I only want you to check him out for now. Alistair has gone to great lengths to hide Mr. Anderson from us. I want to know why first. If this Mr. Anderson is what I think he is, he may even prove to be of use to us."

"What? You want a bastard to join our ranks?" The man snapped.

Looking at the man with an equally cold and emotionless expression, Lord Malcolm responded in his superior aristocratic tone. "I want you to find out what's so special about this particular subject and report back to me. If he proves to be of interest then maybe you will return and present him with the same choice we give to all those we deem worthy." His eyes narrowed and he smiled a sinister, twisted smile at the killer sitting across from him.

"And what about Wolchek and his daughter?" the man asked returning the twisted smile.

"Leave them to me. I'll take care of that little problem when the time is right, Roger."

Chapter 16
Roger

It had been six months since Ryan and Dr. Wolchek's eye opening dinner at the restaurant. And since that time, Ryan actively explored the extent of his new power. With his body completely recovered, he found the more he practiced, the easier he was able to absorb and manipulate the energy. It seemed so natural to him now. He not only mastered drawing energy from crowded places and casual contact but he had also learned how to cut himself off so ordinary humans could not draw on his energy. Dr. Wolchek was right. In a matter of days Ryan learned how to prevent himself from being drained through every day and even more intimate encounters. Cindy, was unknowingly participating in numerous nighttime experiments. Remembering what the doctor said about using such encounters to his advantage, Ryan was eager to give it a try. Not only could he drain energy from Cindy during sex, he could exchange large amounts with her as well. By energizing her to some extent he was able to heighten their sexual experience. It was as if he could feel her pleasure through her energy along with his own and by exchanging his energy with her she could feel his. The stimulation was so intense, they often found themselves consumed by the passion. It was as if they were experiencing twice the pleasure simultaneously.

As he learned how to feed and replenish his energy he discovered that there were many other benefits. Working out at the gym, showed him he could convert power into strength. The restaurant revealed that he had the ability to read a person's thoughts through their energy a handy technique he used to entice new clients to the firm. He did not understand how he could do these things, but he knew he could do them.

He also felt that there was so much more to be discovered. Since his encounter with Dr. Wolchek, Ryan felt like his body had been reborn.

Everyday held new surprises. New situations and surroundings offered untold opportunities to feed and learn more about his capabilities.

The band was a blessing in disguise for Ryan. He always enjoyed playing weekend rock star and since running into his former bandmate at the gym, they had already played several small local venues. When discovered that Ryan was back on lead vocals, news spread quickly and soon the crowds were swelling. Ryan enjoyed the feeling he got when performing in front of a large audience. Something about it energized him and he used these encounters to his advantage. During a show he would often get drunk on the power he consumed. However, feeding on such large quantities caused his eyes to glow. He tried to control it, but found it necessary to wear dark glasses when performing. Being performers, this didn't arouse much curiosity. But, if anyone asked, he told them he wore the classes because the stage lights bothered his eyes.

With Ryan's health fully restored and his new abilities, he burned the candle at both ends. On the weekends, he played local rock star. He enjoyed the pseudo celebrity lifestyle and discovered many new ways to play the role. But during the week he led his team at work often staying late into the evenings to put the finishing touches on various projects. On the eve of a potentially lucrative project, Ryan worked late into the night finalizing a presentation he was presenting the next morning. The meeting was scheduled for 11:00am. If successful, he would bring the firm its largest client to date. It was a huge, multinational corporation desperately in need of a regional image facelift after a very public and nasty clash with the state and several environmental groups. Ryan was privately pleased that the company had taken such a public and humiliating beating in the media. He felt he and his team were more than up for the task of helping them rebuild their public image and looked forward to the opportunity.

Deciding to call it a night, Ryan rose from his desk and stretched. Feeling good, he packed his briefcase and headed to the elevator.

"Coming over tonight?" Cindy asked.

"Sorry, not tonight. You know, superstition," he said. He was smiling and lowered his head sheepishly.

"The night before the big game?" she teased. She winked and smiled back at him.

"Exactly!" he said. "But can I walk you to your car?"

"No thanks. I'm waiting on a fax. Unfortunately, it looks like I may be here for awhile."

"Have you been here all night?" Ryan asked.

"No. I went home earlier and then came back. They said they were sending it around 8:00, but that was 45 minutes ago."

"I'm going to have to talk to your boss. You should get a raise for going above and beyond," Ryan said.

"Yes. You do that. I think I often go above and beyond."

Smiling back, "I'll see you tomorrow. And don't stay too long," he said. He lightly touched her hand as he walked by her.

"Night, Boss. And good luck tomorrow."

As Ryan stepped into the elevator he thought maybe he should go to her place. But then he thought better. The night before the "big game" might jinx the deal. Even though he knew this was a stupid superstition, he decided not to chance it. Besides, tomorrow night's victory celebration would be so much better.

# # #

The presentation went well. Ryan and his team were professionals and it showed. The multinational corporation agreed with all of their ideas and suggestions. Eager to get started as soon as possible on the new campaign, the company representatives surprised everyone when they decided to forgo the usual evaluation period and instead opted to hire Ryan's firm on the spot. Needless to say, Ryan and his team were ecstatic. To celebrate, Ryan announced that he was taking everyone out for a victory lunch.

On his way back to his office to get his car keys, Cindy let him know that someone was waiting to see him.

"Who is it?" Ryan asked.

"He says his name is Roger Franklin. He's from England and knows Dr. Wolchek."

"Really?" Ryan said with noticeable skepticism. "Show him in."

As Ryan positioned himself behind his desk, he questioned the man's credibility. Remembering Dr. Wolchek's warning, Ryan felt pretty confident the doctor wouldn't be sending anyone without informing him first. "This should be interesting," he thought out loud.

A moment later Cindy walked the man in and made the introductions.

Ryan stood and extended his hand. "Nice to meet you Mr. Franklin." He smiled a friendly smile to hide his skepticism.

"The pleasure is mine," Roger said. He had a puzzled expression and spoke slowly. "The pleasure is mine." he repeated. His amazement showed as he studied Ryan's face.

Noticing Roger's sudden partial paralysis, Ryan shook his hand and asked him if he was okay.

"Yes, yes. Oh forgive me. You look like someone I have not seen in years," Roger answered.

"I hope it was someone you liked. Because for a second there you looked as if you had seen a ghost," Ryan said. He tried to chuckle lightly and shrug off a sinking feeling.

Forcing a smile, Roger laughed. "For a second there I thought I had."

"Please, make yourself comfortable," Ryan said. He gestured to a chair behind Roger. "That will be all, Cindy."

Cindy nodded as she walked out of the office shutting the door behind her.

"So, how can I help you, Mr. Franklin?"

"Please, call me Roger," he said. "I'm an associate of Dr. Wolchek's. You see Mr. Anderson, my job is to follow up on all of his patients. You know, checking to make sure your case was handled professionally and what not. Our Foundation is very specific about such matters. In order for us to receive funding, we have to do loads of paperwork and document every case thoroughly."

Ryan knew what Roger was. He felt the void surrounding him from the second he walked into his office. Remembering Dr. Wolchek's warning, Ryan remained guarded. He could not read Roger's energy like an ordinary human, but he knew something wasn't right.

Listening carefully as he studied the man, Ryan figured Roger to be in his mid 40's. But like Dr. Wolchek, he could be far older. Unlike Dr. Wolchek however, he lacked the refined upper-class qualities of a gentleman. Even well-dressed, there was a hardness about him; a coldness that made Ryan feel uneasy. And he could tell Roger felt out of place playing a professional role. Still, Ryan was curious and played along.

"I do understand. The paperwork never ends. You should try the advertising business sometime," Ryan joked. "So Roger, tell me how can I help you?"

"Well Mr. Anderson, I must admit you don't look as close to death as I was led to believe."

Laughing, Ryan said, "No, not anymore. Thanks to Dr. Wolchek that is."

"Really? How fascinating. May I ask what your diagnosis was?"

"Ryan quickly recalled the story he and Dr. Wolchek agreed on. "It was really a combination of things, but mostly I was having intense side effects to some of the medications I was taking. The more I took, the worse things got. Dr. Wolchek immediately took me off of everything. My primary doctor disagreed, but I was better in days." He paused before continuing. "But surely you know this? Wasn't all this information in Dr. Wolchek's report?"

"Oh yes, but I must follow the rules of the Foundation. I'm required to do a personal follow up. You know, procedures and such," he replied.

"You mean bureaucracy and bullshit." Ryan joked.

"Yes. Bullshit," Roger repeated half smiling. "But tell me, how did you recover so fast? The report recorded your weight around 120 pounds, emaciated and so fourth. I must say, you look to be in remarkable shape now," Roger said. It was clear he was skeptical of Ryan's explanation.

Ignoring his tone, Ryan continued with the cover story. "Once the pain was gone I began eating like a horse. And since I was use to working out and staying fit, I guess I was able to recover fast. Just lucky I suppose." Ryan knew Roger wasn't buying it.

"Yes, you were fortunate the good doctor came along when he did."

"Yes. I owe him my life." Ryan was trying to get a reaction out of him.

"Well then, I won't keep you," Roger said.

As Ryan stood, Roger looked around before standing almost as if he was checking to see if anyone could see them. Ryan sensed Roger was up to something and prepared himself. His office was in a corner section of the building. With the exception of the windows facing the city skyline, there was no other view into it.

Roger stood and extended his hand. "It has been a pleasure meeting you Mr. Anderson."

"Likewise," Ryan said.

As he shook Roger's hand, it was as if he'd been struck by lightning. Roger smiled a grotesque smile and his eyes flashed a brilliant yellow green. Momentarily caught by surprise, Ryan cringed in pain. Then, in an almost convulsive spasm, Ryan was able to stop Roger draining him and turned it back on him. Roger's face registered his surprise. Within a fraction of a second Ryan had the upper hand and was reversing the flow.

"I don't think so my friend," Ryan said with a tone of arrogance. However, unlike Dr. Wolchek, Roger fought back with tremendous force.

There was an unexpected knock on the office door followed by excited voices telling him he owed them a free lunch. The interruption broke them up. The door opened and in walked several excited members of Ryan's staff.

"Sorry, Boss. We didn't know you were with someone."

"My guest was just leaving," Ryan said. He quickly regained his composure and offered Roger a chance to go.

"I'm sorry Mr. Franklin, I'm afraid we're going to have to continue this conversation another time."

Not as recovered, but trying to appear so, Roger said, "Yes, I look forward to it."

"As do I." Ryan said. He gestured toward the door with a cocky smile.

Roger cut Ryan a withering look before nodding and walking out of the office.

His team members had noticed the tension. "We're really sorry, Boss. We didn't know you were in a meeting," one of his staff said.

"That's okay Billy," Ryan said. He playfully slapped him on his shoulder. "You guys might have just saved my life." He motioned toward the door. "Lets go to lunch. I'm starving."

# # #

After exiting Ryan's building, Roger climbed into his waiting car.

"Take me to the plane," he hissed.

"Yes, sir," the driver answered.

"Lord Malcolm must know of this. Wolchek has gone too far this time. Too far!" He stared out the window at the passing scenery on his way back to the airport.

Seven hours later, Roger was relaying his story to Lord Malcolm.

"So, Alistair has found another bastard," Lord Malcolm said shaking his head disgusted.

"Yes your Lordship. But this one is different. Besides the striking physical resemblance, he seems to have a rather advanced understanding of his power."

"So you say," Lord Malcolm said. He stared through Roger lost in thought.

Roger lost his patience, "He must be eliminated as soon as possible. Unlike the doctor's other bastards, I feel this one could be trouble," he demanded.

"Now, now. Not so fast my friend. If he is indeed as strong as the good doctor hopes, then maybe he can be of use to us."

"What? Join the Society? That is completely unacceptable!" Roger snapped. He could not hide his contempt for Ryan.

Lord Malcolm did not respond but instead fixed Roger with a stern superior aristocratic look reminding Roger of his position in life. Roger had outlived countless generations of nobility, but he still had the misfortune of being born into the lower classes. Something he was powerless to change.

"All in good time my friend," Lord Malcolm said once Roger was reminded of his status. Tapping his fingers on his desk and contemplating something, he said, "I think I want to meet this Ryan Anderson."

"Yes, your Lordship. As you wish," Roger replied. But he knew he would never let that happen. Even if it meant defying Lord Malcolm; something he had never done in all his years of service. Roger knew there was no way he would allow Ryan into the Society.

"But first we have business here. Is it true the doctor's plane is due to arrive tomorrow night?"

"Christine will be picking him up at the airport."

"Good. When he arrives, have your men inform him that he is to address the council immediately. I think it is time that we confront him and the council about this matter." Lord Malcolm paused. "It's time my friend. Alistair has finally given us what we need to make our move. Have your men standing by tomorrow night. The Society will be reborn in our image."

"Yes, your Lordship. Our time has finally come," Roger said.

"And with all the Society's resources at our disposal nothing will stand in our way," Lord Malcolm said. They exchanged sinister smiles.

Chapter 17

After lunch, Ryan went home to rest. His earlier encounter with Roger was still heavy on his mind. He managed to put on a good show during lunch so he wouldn't damper the celebratory mood, but still needed some time to himself before meeting Cindy later in the evening.

Having taken Dr. Wolchek's advice, Ryan found meditation to be very relaxing. His back yard was perfect for these exercises. Because of the way his house was angled on the lot, it was totally secluded. One side was bordered by a deep creek which led out to the St. Johns River. The creek had been dredged by the neighborhood so people who lived along it could have a wide variety of boats and other watercraft. Some were quite impressive. Ryan had a dock where he kept a 24-foot Monterey speed boat. The remainder of the lot was bordered by large trees and dense over growth he let grow wild along the borders for complete privacy. Within this sanctuary of solitude was a large swimming pool to one side of the yard. Outside his bedroom windows was a pond and cascading rock waterfall. He built an artificial rocky, stream from the pond that wound through the yard to a lower pond closer to the woods on the other side of the lot. There were two bridges that elegantly spanned the steam at specific points to connect stone paths. The landscaped portion of the yard resembled a manicured Japanese garden. Ryan found it easy to lose himself in the tranquil beauty of his surroundings.

Since his "change", Ryan's senses were constantly on overdrive. Learning to accept and control these new sensations was difficult, but he found it easier to do as his mind became stronger. Meditation helped him concentrate and learn to control and make sense of this flood of information. The natural energy of the yard, along with an abundance of wildlife provided for a more soothing environment. Something about being surrounded by such an array of naturally occurring stimuli helped Ryan focus and calm his mind.

The yard also provided something else. Since that night at the restaurant with Dr. Wolchek, Ryan was aware of another sensation; something in the background. A constant presence. It was subtle background noise like the soft hum of a florescent light. It wasn't disturbing, but Ryan was curious about its source. When engaged in a state of deep meditation, he felt like he was being pulled toward it, sometimes even feeling like he was actually closing in on the strange sensation but it always felt just out of reach.

Having settled into a comfortable position at his favorite location next to the pond under a large shady tree, Ryan found it easy to lose himself in the peaceful tranquility of his surroundings. His thoughts of Roger were replaced by the calming sensations of the many natural stimuli in the yard. He let his mind focus on that mysterious background presence and before long found his mind drifting peacefully in its direction. This was a common experience. He felt like his body was floating on a gentle river of energy leisurely pulling him in the direction of the mysterious sensation. He felt as if he was being drawn to it, but knew he could never get there. Still, the ride itself was always a pleasant experience.

Relaxed, Ryan suddenly became aware of another presence. It was Tor. He was approaching from behind him. Ryan could feel his energy as he drew closer. Tor did not disturb Ryan but instead took a position next to him. Sitting as still as an Egyptian statue, Ryan could feel Tor's energy signature. It was wild and free flowing, but it had a pattern. In his deep state of concentration Ryan could feel their energy signatures crossing. Together, he felt their strength. Their power. It was almost as if he could channel his energy and Tor's.

With Tor he felt a whole new level of strength. It was very strong. He wasn't draining Tor, just focusing his energy, taming some of his wild pattern. For the heck of it he decided to try and reach that strange background sensation hoping that their combined strength may give him the extra boost he needed to get there. Focusing and channeling both their energies, Ryan soon found himself rapidly gaining on the mysterious background presence.

For the first time he felt like he may actually be able to tap it. Focusing harder, he drew on more of Tor's energy. Tor seemed to have no problem with Ryan borrowing his energy. He remained open allowing Ryan to channel what he needed at will.

Ryan felt as if he was in a speeding car rapidly gaining on another. The experience was exhilarating. "Am I finally going to be able to reach it?" he thought. He did not know, but the excitement was building with each passing second. Then, in a flash of warm intensity, he made a sudden connection to something very powerful causing a jolt of energy to spike through his body. It was pure and refreshing. Not like what he got from casual feeding this was much stronger and far more intense. Within seconds, he felt refreshed and fully charged. The sensation was so overpowering, he felt himself knocked to the ground when his body was fully gorged with energy causing him to lose focus and abruptly sever the connection. Ryan laid there laughing as he felt the energy coursing through his body. He looked over at Tor who was also in an excited state.

"Wow, buddy! That was cool. Was it as good for you as it was for me?" he asked. He extended his hand in Tor's direction. Tor excitedly rubbed against Ryan's hand purring loudly. "Yes buddy, me too. I'm starving. Lets go in and see what we have to eat." Crying in agreement, Tor followed Ryan into the house.

To Ryan and Tor's disappointment, there wasn't much to be found. After finishing off some leftovers from the refrigerator, both of them were still famished. "Well, I guess we gotta go to the store, bud," Ryan said. Meowing in agreement, Tor followed Ryan as he grabbed his car keys off the counter and headed to the garage. Once they reached the car, Ryan opened the door and Tor jumped in. Ryan was not concerned. He could read Tor's energy and knew Tor was just as driven by his hunger as he was.

There was a large supermarket just a few blocks away. Ryan parked, got out and Tor followed. Showing no fear, Tor walked beside Ryan as they approached the store entrance. Without hesitation both walked in as the automatic sliding doors opened. People were looking and pointing. Tor was walking right next to Ryan, they were on a mission.

"Steaks buddy. We need steaks," Ryan said. He led the way to the meat counter.

Noticing them enter the store, the assistant manager said, "Excuse me sir, you can't bring that cat in here."

"He's my seeing eye cat man. Sorry," he said brushing him off and not even slowing down. Ryan smiled mischievously, shrugged his shoulders and kept on walking. After getting several pounds and a wide variety of meats and other food, they made their way to an empty checkout line. As Ryan began removing the meat from his basket, Tor jumped on to the conveyer and began meowing. "Okay buddy here," he said. He ripped open the plastic wrapping on a steak tray so Tor could lick the meat and juice. As the conveyer moved Tor was undaunted and continued licking the open package. People in other lines were staring and pointing. Many laughed and whispered among themselves. The assistant manager was not happy as he looked on with a stern, disapproving look.

"Seeing eye cat? Really?" the checkout lady commented.

"If you think that's something, you should see him drive. Good day," Ryan said as he took the meat and walked out with Tor crying and following close behind. When they got home both gorged themselves until they could eat no more. A few hours later they fell into a deep sleep. Bloated and exhausted, they slept for hours.

PART FOUR

Chapter 18
Coming home

Christine sat in her Bentley Continental GT anxiously tapping her fingers on the steering wheel as she looked out the rain soaked window. She and her father owned many cars, but this one was their favorite. Not only was it quick and agile, but also very comfortable. Just what she thought her father would appreciate after such a long flight. Usually driving the car made her feel good, but that was not the case this night. Glancing down at the clock again for what seemed like the millionth time, 8:30pm shined back in pale blue numbers. She often picked her father up from the airport after his trips, but this time was different. The anticipation had been steadily building for months. Since her father's first meeting with Ryan Anderson, Christine's curiosity had piqued. But after their most recent conversation, Christine could hardly conceal her excitement and growing concern. Lord Malcolm was on to them and she knew it. She knew her father might have to explain Ryan to the council exposing him and possibly making Ryan a target of Lord Malcolm's hit squads. But, for now she just wanted him home. There was much to discuss, but at the moment she just missed him in only the way a daughter can miss her father.

Christine and her father were unique and fortunate in that they had each other. Many immortals only have themselves their families and loved-ones died years ago. Hearing the light rain falling on the roof of her car, Christine looked out the rain-speckled windshield in the direction of the runway and sighed.

Drover Airfield was built for bombers during WWII and used by allied forces to launch nighttime air strikes on Germany. After the war, the field was kept open and used by private aircraft. Because of its relatively close location to London and the fact that it was much less crowded than the larger commercial airports, many corporations kept their planes there. The

Society had many private planes in airports like Drover around the world. Private planes and small airfields made traveling much easier for Society members. As countries grew and traveling and immigration restraints and documentation became stricter, it was necessary to find alternate ways of beating the ever-changing international travel requirements. Christine and her father had a fleet of planes available for use at a moment's notice. Privately, they also kept their own planes unknown to the Society. These planes were for their personal use and when they needed to travel under the Society's radar. Through numerous forged identities, they also kept residences, planes, vehicles, and bank accounts around the world just in case they needed to make a sudden and unexpected departure from the manor house or even the Society itself.

Going "underground" in an effort to defect from the Society had always been a possibility. And now, with the rise of Lord Malcolm and his growing following, Christine and her father began making contingency plans in the event such an escape proved necessary. But, this night was business as usual. Christine openly waited for her father by the hanger the Society owned and housed its five Gulf Stream business class jets in. Since Dr. Wolchek had been traveling on official business, there was no reason to hide.

"Come on, Father. Where are you? You should have been here thirty minutes ago," Christine said out loud as she strained to see down the runway. The rain was becoming worse and visibility had dropped off considerably. Then, far out in the night sky she could just barely make out the lights of an approaching air craft.

"Finally," Christine said. She breathed a sigh of relief as she got out of her car and walked into the shelter of the hanger.

The large hanger doors had been opened in anticipation of the returning plane. From inside she watched as her father's plane touched down then taxied in her direction. A few minutes later, the plane entered the hanger and throttled down. When the sound of the engines faded, Christine made her way to the plane's door just as it was opening.

"Father!"

"Christine. What are you doing here in this god-awful London weather?"

"Picking you up of, course. You know I wouldn't leave such an important task to Lord Malcolm's goons."

"Thank you. It's so good to see you," he said. He reached out to embrace her in a smothering hug.

"I can't wait to hear all about Mr. Anderson." Christine whispered. Dr. Wolchek held her tightly.

He saw the plane's crew loading his luggage into the trunk of Christine's car. "I'll tell you all about him on the drive back to the compound," he whispered.

She held him at arm's length and looked him squarely in his eyes. "Do we have to go back? Let's just get back on the plane and go. Just go," she said.

Hugging her again, Dr. Wolchek said, "Not just yet. Now more than ever we need to act normal. He's the one we've been looking for!" Dr. Wolchek said trying to keep his voice down. "For now we act normal. Business as usual," he said as he patted her back and led her to the car.

"If you insist. But I still think it would be better to just get back on that plane, pick up Mr. Anderson and disappear."

"All in good time, Christine." Dr. Wolchek said chuckling.

Christine's comment about not trusting her father's safety to the care of other Society staff was not a joke. Recently, through an unfortunate sequence of events, several high-level Society members had either mysteriously gone missing or had been the victims of strange accidents. Christine and her father knew Lord Malcolm was involved, but could not prove anything. Knowing her father was Lord Malcolm's chief critic and main detractor, Christine made it a point to see to his safety and security herself. She may have had the look of a young woman in her mid-twenties, but the reality was far different.

Christine took it upon herself to become proficient in a wide variety of self-defense techniques. She was well schooled in multiple forms of hand to hand combat and also knew how to use weaponry from across the world. And if this wasn't enough, Christine was a skilled driver constantly training to keep up-to-date with the latest defensive driving techniques. When her father was in London, she insisted on driving him wherever he needed to go. Sometimes this annoyed her father, but he knew he couldn't be in safer hands. Knowing the security details patrolling the estate could no longer be trusted, Christine figured the best way to protect her father was to do it herself.

On the drive back to the compound Christine was bursting with excitement.

"It's so good to have you home, Father. I've missed you."

"And I've missed you. I should not have been away so long," he said. He reached over and patted her arm affectionately.

Becoming serious, Christine focused on her driving. "Lord Malcolm has been acting very strange. I'm sure he suspects something. After sneaking up on me in your office and seeing the picture, he's been acting even more suspicious. Do you really think your extended trip doing evaluations will fool him?"

"I hope so. I hope I didn't spend all that time in those god-forsaken countries for nothing," he replied.

"For both our sakes as well as Mr. Anderson's I hope you are right. I really do. Still, I feel we need to be careful. I don't trust Lord Malcolm or his evil henchman, Roger!"

Dr. Wolchek shook his head and looked out the window at the passing rain soaked London scenery.

"We must be careful now more than ever. Our every move will be watched. We must play our parts perfectly so we don't cast any suspicion on Ryan," he said.

"Tell me about him. I have to admit, what you've told me so far was fascinating, but I'm having trouble believing it," Christine said.

"Believe it!" Dr. Wolchek boomed. His voice was loud and excited.

"We've finally found him!"

"Tell me everything!" Christine demanded. Her father's excitement was infectious.

"It's fascinating," Dr. Wolchek said. He leaned back in the comfortable seat to stretch his legs. "He was turned by an owl of all things!"

"How is that even possible? Owls are deadly to our kind," she asked.

"Yes, but not to him. He was driving home late one night when he struck the bird with his car. He saw it tumble off to the side of the road so he went back to try and help it. When he picked it up, it clamped down on his finger and would not release. He said it was very painful but he did not panic and took it home to care for it. He thinks at some point he must have passed out in his driveway because he recalled a discrepancy in the time. Several hours passed before he awoke. When he did, the owl released its grip on his finger and flew away. Unfortunately for Ryan, or fortunately for us, that was the point of transition. The owl somehow opened the door and began his transformation."

"If this is true, this is the first documented transition to happen by way of an animal-an owl no less! Incredible," Christine said pondering the information.

"There's more. Guess what had been keeping him alive for months following the transition?"

Not responding but clearly interested, Christine motioned to her father to continue as she watched the road.

"A cat!"

"You mentioned he had a pet cat in our last conversation. You're telling me he was turned by an owl and then kept alive by a cat. How can that be possible? Cats and owls are deadly to our kind."

"They are deadly to us but not to him. I was there and saw it firsthand. The cat not only lives with him, but to some extent protects him as well," he said.

"Unbelievable," Christine said. She was not sure of what to make of all her father was telling her.

"So how did you explain this to him? How did he handle it? You know new converts are often difficult. They tend to be in a state of denial. What did he say? How did you explain his condition to him?" she asked, rambling on excitedly.

Dr. Wolchek was amused by his daughter's barrage of questions. Christine rarely let her emotions overcome her. "That, too, was something of an experience," he said. Shaking his head, he chuckled as he remembered the encounter.

"What happened?"

"After I fed him the first time he felt so much better, but he ignored my warnings and went about life as normal. His body was so emaciated. The cat had been keeping him alive with its energy but Ryan was still wasting away. He did not know how to feed or about the physical side of our condition. Two days later he crashed and crashed hard. When he came back to see me he was almost completely depleted so I did the usual number on him," Dr. Wolchek said.

"Oh Father, you didn't. The poor man..."

"Poor man hell! He almost killed me!" Dr. Wolchek interrupted.

"How was that possible if he was so weak?" Christine asked.

"He was very weak. I even did the drain him to the point of death routine to make sure I got his attention," he replied.

"Father. Really? So dramatic."

"Yes. But you have to admit, it does get their attention."

"What happened next?" Christine asked. She was having a hard time focusing on the wet road and listening to what her father was telling her.

"I went to recharge him after my you will surely die speech and he recovered fast, so fast that he caught me off guard and got a lock on me! I've never experienced anything like it before," Dr. Wolchek said. Christine saw him smile slightly out of the corner of her eye.

"How is that possible? You are one of the strongest of our kind," she asked.

Still smiling, Dr. Wolchek said, "Because he's the one! He's the one I tell you!" He slapped his knee leaning forward in his seat laughing.

"Father please! You could have been killed," Christine said.

"I know but it was worth the risk."

They continued in silence for several minutes as Christine exited off the busy highway and on to a smaller road leading to the countryside.

"So? Go on." Christine said, now expressing more concern than curiosity.

"Well, like I said, he turned on me so fast that before I knew it I was the one being drained. Me. He put me in a weak state. Can you believe it?" He asked. More to himself than Christine. "Even as I felt my life slipping away, I was impressed. Only just transitioned and he was already able to best me." Dr. Wolchek said thoughtfully.

"Do you know how dangerous that was? She asked. Her voice rose as she spoke. "You know new converts can't control themselves. They need training and discipline. He could have drained you dry!"

"But that's just it. He didn't. He stopped when he felt he was safe and I was no longer a threat to him," Dr. Wolchek said. "He stopped on his own totally in control."

"Unbelievable!" Christine uttered under her breath.

It was 20 miles from the airport to the manor and the time was passing quickly. The rain had let up as well as the traffic. Deep in the country side she turned on to another small road that was completely deserted. This was the last long stretch and by her estimate she figured they had about 15 minutes before reaching the manor. As absorbed as she was in her father's experience with Mr. Anderson, she could not shake the nervous feeling building inside her.

"And then what happened," she asked.

"He sat back and demanded I tell him everything," Dr. Wolchek responded.

"The nerve!" Christine said looking at her father with a furrowed brow.

"I'd say. But he did have me at a disadvantage."

"What did you do?"

"I told him."

"Everything?"

"Not everything. I said nothing about his bloodline. But I have to say, he's a dead ringer for his ancestor. Having met him in person, I was surprised by the similarities. Even as decimated as he was I could still see the physical resemblance."

"Remarkable," Christine whispered.

"Yes, remarkable. He should be completely restored by now. Maybe even someone you might take a fancy to," Dr. Wolchek said. He nudged her in the ribs teasing her.

"Oh please! Stop trying to set me up," she said.

"He's someone you might like that's all," Dr. Wolcheck said.

Christine brought the conversation back to a more serious tone to hide her embarrassment. "I know Lord Malcolm suspects something. What are you going to tell the council? If they find out about Mr. Anderson, you know Lord Malcolm will send his assassins," she said.

"I'll tell them it was a medical condition then I'll ramble on about the dozens of other cases I investigated throughout the Americas," he replied.

"Do you think they will believe you?"

"I don't know. The most important thing for now is to try and buy Ryan as much time as possible to recover," he said. He paused for a moment. "We will make our escape and go underground with him. Soon we'll be on the run and hunted like animals. Are you ready for that life?" Dr. Wolchek asked?

"The sooner the better," she responded. They drove on in silence both thinking about what lay ahead for them all.

The quiet was soon broken by the clicking of the car's turn signal as Christine exited off the dark country road and on to the long gravel driveway leading to Kingsley Hall.

A few minutes later the compound emerged out of the darkness. At one time, the sight was soothing. For over a hundred years Christine and her father called it home. It used to fill them with warm feelings of comfort and tranquility. Here they could live with others of their kind in the security of familiar surroundings safe from the outside world. But, now it was different. With the rise of Lord Malcolm, peace and tranquility had been replaced with an atmosphere of tension, treachery, and deception. Two distinct groups had formed within the Society. The stage was being set for an eminent showdown between the factions. It was only a matter of time. Christine and her father knew Lord Malcolm wanted the resources the Society and its members controlled all to himself. He needed them to carry out his master plan of eventually dominating the human race.

As the main gates approached, Christine looked at her father.

"Welcome home, father. Home sweet home," she said. She waved to a security guard as he motioned them through the gate. Moments later, Christine drove down a ramp leading to the large garage under the South wing of the main house.

After pulling into her parking space in the garage she noticed several security guards approaching. As she and her father exited the car one of the guards approached Dr. Wolchek.

"Welcome back, Doctor. Lord Malcolm and the rest of the council request your immediate presence in the Grand Council chambers."

"Can I at least freshen up first?" Dr. Wolchek asked. His irritation showed in his tone.

"I'm afraid not, Sir. I have orders to escort you to the Council Chambers immediately."

"And me?" Christine asked. She stood tall, jaw locked as she asked the question.

"No ma' am. I was told only to bring your father."

"Well I'll be damned if he's going anywhere without me," she replied.

"It's okay, Christine. I'll be alright," said Dr. Wolchek.

"I should come with you," she pleaded.

"Go on up to the apartment and see to our travel arrangements. Hopefully, this will not take too long."

Catching his meaning, Christine knew exactly what to do. "Travel arrangements" was code for their emergency escape. Using all her strength to remain calm and in control of her emotions, Christine humbly replied, "Yes, Father."

Smiling then slightly nodding his head to her, Dr. Wolchek addressed the guard. "Shall we go?" he asked.

As they turned to walk away Christine could no longer hide her feelings.

"Father!" she shouted.

When he turned back to face her she threw herself into his arms. "Please be careful," she whispered. She pushed herself back to face him with tears in her eyes.

"I will dear daughter. Now hurry along and see to those travel arrangements. We have much work to do, the two of us."

Choking back her tears she looked down and nodded.

As Dr. Wolchek and the guards walked away Christine sat back down in her car and buried her head in her hands. Unable to stop the tears, she let her emotions flow unchecked. After taking a few minutes to regain her composure, she exited her car and headed to the elevator. Looking normal and in complete control, Christine was focused on the mission at hand. Still, she had a horrible feeling that she may never see her father again.

Chapter 19
The Council

The Grand Council chamber was a large, impressive room located three stories under the main manor house. It had been built at the beginning of World War II as a bomb shelter to protect the Society's members during German bombing missions. In the decades following the war it had been repurposed several times to better meet the needs of the council. In its present configuration it was a large, opulent, two story deep, nine sided room with each side devoted to a single permanent member and his or her staff. The ground floor was where the council met. Above this were recessed galleries where other members could view all public council activities. These members were part of the Society but did not participate directly in council decisions. The Society's members created and debated Society policies then presented final versions to the permanent counsel to be discussed and ruled on. Mostly this centered on how to use the Society's resources to better mankind without directly interfering in its future. Once voted into their position, council members were permanent and could not be replaced. They served a life term. However, they could step down at any time. This had unofficially become the normal operating procedure. Most members usually served a decade or two then stepped down in order to allow others to serve.

When it was time to choose a replacement, candidates would often campaign in much the same way modern politicians do. A candidate would try to rally as much support as possible from the Society's members before the election. Lord Malcolm's campaign was one of the most heated and divisive the Society had ever experienced. It created so much debate that it actually polarized the Society and threatened to become as destructive as what happened centuries earlier when the Society split with many members leaving to try and dominate mankind. Lord Malcolm preferred to abandon the Society's main directive of not interfering in man's social evolution. His campaign proved to be popular with many members. He was a master of playing on their ignorance and arrogance. He was elected to his seat by a slim majority. There had been rumors Lord Malcolm's supporters bullied and intimidated some of the Society's members in order to get them to vote for him. Unfortunately, this could never be proven and the results of his election were allowed to stand. Unlike other Society council members however, he did not step aside after a decade. He and Dr. Wolchek were two of the longest serving members. Neither was willing to step down while the other served.

The rooms ornate decor never failed to impress those privileged enough to experience its grandeur first hand. The eighteen massive marble coated columns supporting a huge golden domed ceiling were a sight to behold. It was as if one had entered a sacred Greek temple. Behind each permanent council member's section, was a set of double doors recessed under the galleries above. Here council members could exit the chamber and retire to their private quarters to debate council business.

Most council meetings were open to all Society members, but not today. As Dr. Wolchek was led to the floor of the main chamber, he quickly realized this was a closed meeting. Only the permanent members were present and from the looks on their faces he could tell some were quite apprehensive.

Banging his gavel to bring the council to order, Lord Malcolm stood.

"I'm sorry to have summoned all of you here tonight with such short notice but I have recently learned of some very disturbing news and felt it was important to share it with the entire council immediately."

Tired and irritated, Dr. Wolchek was not in the mood to listen or debate Lord Malcolm in a public forum. Assuming this had something to do with his extended trip, Dr. Wolchek stood up from his center seat and cut Lord Malcolm off practically in mid-sentence.

"Is this really necessary to do now? I've just returned from a long trip and would like some time to freshen up and prepare my reports," Dr. Wolchek said.

Undaunted by the doctor's complete lack of respect for him, Lord Malcolm smiled.

"It's good you brought up your trip old friend, because that is exactly why we are here tonight."

"Really?" Dr. Wolchek asked. "Give me a few days to put my reports together, Henry, and you can analyze my findings to your hearts content." Dr. Wolchek never addressed Lord Malcolm by his title. He insisted on calling him by his first name, Henry, believing nobility had no place within the Society.

Low snickering could be heard coming from several council members and their aids.

"I don't think that will be necessary Alistair. I'm sure you can tell us all what we need to know right here tonight," Lord Malcolm replied.

It was obvious to Dr. Wolchek that Lord Malcolm knew something at this point. Why else would he go to such an extent unless he had something he could use against him publicly? Despite Lord Malcolm's growing popularity, Dr. Wolchek still had the respect of the council; something Lord Malcolm did not. He figured Lord Malcolm was going to use something against him in order to tarnish his reputation. After talking with Christine and then being summoned to this meeting as abruptly as he was, he was sure Lord Malcolm knew about Ryan. Depending on what would be presented to the council, Dr. Wolchek figured his best bet would be to stall for time. Enough time for him and Christine to escape. "Let the games begin," he thought to himself.

"Well Henry, if it's such a matter of urgent importance, I'll do my best to provide whatever information the council seeks," Dr. Wolchek said. He smiled and nodded to Lord Malcolm in a condescending way.

Leaning forward in his chair, Lord Malcolm wasted no time getting to the point.

"Tell us of your findings, Alistair. More specifically, tell the council about Ryan Anderson," Lord Malcolm said.

"There it is," Dr. Wolchek thought. Lord Malcolm knew about Ryan. He remained calm and pretended to try and recall from memory.

"Oh yes, Mr. Anderson. My first subject. Forgive me council members, but I've been traveling for almost six months now," he said. "Yes, Mr. Anderson. Not much to tell really. He had been suffering from a severe gastrointestinal infection. Prior to my arrival, his doctor had already diagnosed the problem and begun an aggressive antibiotic treatment program. By the time I performed my evaluation, he was already on his way to recovery. The problem, however, was that he had been over medicated and was having side effects from the medications he was on. After taking him off of some of the medications, he began to feel better almost immediately."

"So Alistair, you're telling the council that Mr. Anderson is not one of us and is of no further interest to the Society?" Lord Malcolm asked. He leaned back in his chair with a confident, cocky grin.

"Yes Henry. That is exactly what I am telling this council."

"And that is your official position?"

Knowing Lord Malcolm had something and was just waiting to spring his trap, Dr. Wolchek took an irritated stand with him.

"Yes, that is my official position. What's going on here Henry? Why such interest in this particular subject? If you wait a few days I'll present you with reports on all the subjects I encountered. Now I'm tired and want to retire for the evening," Dr. Wolchek said. He stood up to leave.

"I'm afraid that won't do Alistair," Lord Malcolm said. Standing and addressing the full council with a confident, devious grin, he continued. "I have proof that our good doctor here is lying to this council in an attempt to mislead us about Mr. Anderson's true nature." Looking directly at Dr. Wolchek, Lord Malcolm said, "Why the deception Alistair? What are you trying to hide?"

Clearly irritated, because he knew Lord Malcolm was right, Dr. Wolchek continued his attempt at concealing Ryan's true nature.

"Henry, what are you saying? What is the meaning of this? I protest this whole line of questions!" Dr. Wolchek said. He slammed his fist down on the table. "I am a loyal and devoted senior member of this council and I will not sit here and listen to these ridiculous accusations. If you have proof to the contrary then present it," he demanded. "As far as I'm concerned, Mr. Anderson is of no interest to this Society."

"Are you sure about that Alistair? Roger, has information to the contrary," Lord Malcolm responded.

Fearing Ryan had been found and killed by Roger, Dr Wolchek hissed between clenched teeth. "You mean your lead assassin for that murdering gang he runs for you?" Dr. Wolchek shot back.

The council members were growing uneasy with the direction these proceedings were taking.

"I resent that as I'm sure Roger does," Lord Malcolm replied. Roger stared at Dr. Wolchek with cold, empty eyes.

Lord Malcolm was undaunted. "My fellow council members. Roger paid Mr. Anderson a visit last week. A visit that was, at the very least, interesting." He turned and addressed his assassin. "Roger, you have the floor. Tell the council about your discovery," he commanded.

As Roger stood and made his way to the railing to address the council, Dr. Wolchek felt an overwhelming sensation of dread and loss. He was sure Roger was going to report that he had discovered what Ryan was and killed him.

"Thank you, Lord Malcolm," Roger said. Yes, it is true. I did visit Mr. Anderson after getting some additional information about Dr. Wolchek's patient. I presented myself as an associate there to do a typical follow up evaluation. When we shook hands at the end of our meeting, I attempted to drain a little energy from him to see if I could provoke a reaction."

"And what happened then?" Lord Malcolm asked. He could barely contain his excitement.

"Well, he somehow cut me off and reversed the flow, pulling his energy and some of mine back to him! It happened so fast that I was caught off guard."

Dr. Wolchek had to lean forward to conceal a smile remembering how Ryan had done the same thing to him. He knew this was not a smart move by Ryan to reveal himself and was sure Roger had killed him. "No point in pretending anymore," he thought. With Ryan dead, his best and only hope now was to try and save himself and Christine by turning the tables on Lord Malcolm and his assassins. Quickly devising a defense, he decided he would admit his attempt to deceive the council in an effort to protect Ryan from Lord Malcolm's goons.

"Then you would agree that not only was Ryan Anderson one of us, but he was also unusually strong?" Lord Malcolm asked.

"I have to admit that he was strong, but still very green. Like I said, he caught me off guard," Roger repeated attempting to protect his ego.

"He bested you?" Lord Malcolm asked. He smiled which irritated Roger.

"No, your Lordship," Roger said. "He just caught me off guard. It won't happen next time."

And there it was. Dr. Wolchek caught it immediately. Ryan was not dead. Feeling temporary relief, Dr. Wolchek felt a renewed surge of strength.

"So Alistair, in light of this new information, what have you to say?" Lord Malcolm asked.

Hesitating, Dr. Wolchek rose to his feet. In a show of respect he looked at each council member before speaking.

"It is true. Ryan Anderson is what he is. I apologize to the council for my deception but I did it for Mr. Anderson's own protection."

"Then you freely admit to willfully deceiving this council?" Lord Malcolm interrupted.

"Yes, I did it to protect him from you and your thugs Henry," Dr. Wolchek answered.

"What are you talking about, Alistair?" Lord Malcolm asked. He pretended to fain ignorance.

"You know damn well what I'm talking about Henry! You and that group of killers Roger leads have been going behind my back and the Council's killing anyone opposed to you and your policies. The sheer number of unexplained 'accidents' has increased drastically over the past fifty years. All of the new converts that I and others have identified were never allowed to live long enough to be trained and become members. As soon as you get the impression any new convert does not share your views, they suddenly have an accident or simply go missing. I may not have proof that you and Roger have had a direct hand in these murders, and yes I am calling them murders, but you as well as many in this room know it to be true," Dr. Wolchek said. He stayed composed as he finished. "So yes, I freely admit to lying about Mr. Anderson. I did it to protect him from you!"

"There it is out in the open," Dr. Wolchek thought. He knew many suspected Lord Malcolm of manipulating Society members. He hoped that by diverting the council's attention to Lord Malcolm, he'd be able to buy enough time to get Christine and escape. All that mattered now was getting to Ryan and seeing to his safety.

"These are serious accusations you make Dr. Wolchek," one council member said. "Even though you cannot offer proof, I agree there are many suspicious incidents that deserve further investigating."

"I agree," said another member. "Given the circumstances, I believe further investigation is necessary to determine if Dr. Wolchek's concerns are valid."

"Lord Malcolm, how do you respond to such accusations? Is it true that you have been using your teams to carry out unsanctioned assassinations? You know full well that any intervention in our ranks or the human race requires the permission of the full council," said yet another member.

Emboldened by the unity within the council, other members began questioning Lord Malcolm about his alleged activities.

Feeling more comfortable, Dr. Wolchek settled back in his chair and enjoyed watching the tables turning on Lord Malcolm. Hearing the council's questions and seeing Lord Malcolm's growing frustration warmed his heart. Unfortunately, this would be short lived.

During the meeting, Roger's men had been quietly infiltrating the council chamber and taking up positions in the shadows behind the council members. When the last one was in place Lord Malcolm rose to his feet and slammed his fist on the table in front of him. "Enough!" he said.

The chamber went silent. Lord Malcolm spoke with a tone of absolute authority.

"Yes, it is true. I have been thinning the ranks so to speak. But only to help grow the Society."

"Grow it in ways that favor you and your views. You eliminate anyone opposed to your agenda. Not any more Henry," Dr. Wolchek interrupted as he sprang to his feet and stood defiantly pointing his finger at Lord Malcolm. "I'm calling you out for what you are. A monster. Assassin of innocents! You are consumed by your quest for power. You want to take over the Society and use its resources to dominate the human race. Well that's not going to happen! You've been exposed for who and what you are before this very council!"

Unusually calm, Lord Malcolm smiled a dark smile. "You think so Alistair? Do you really think you and this pathetic excuse for a council can stop me? Think again." He looked out into the room. "Gentlemen. Come forth." As if they were ghosts, Roger's men appeared from the shadows pointing guns at the council members' heads.

"What is the meaning of this?" a council member demanded. Lord Malcolm simply nodded in that direction and the gunman behind that member discharged his weapon into the council member's head causing it to explode across the chamber. Twitching in uncontrollable spasms, the body fell to the floor where it went lifeless in seconds.

The room fell silent. "Now that I have everyone's attention, I'm taking over. The fact that I have not killed all of you shows that I'm willing to be civilized about this. After all, I could use everyone's cooperation." He made his way to the lifeless body. "However, it is not completely necessary. Anyone who disagrees will meet with a similar end," he added kicking the lifeless bloody body.

Unable to contain his mounting anger, Dr. Wolchek's eyes flashed and he lunged for Lord Malcolm. But Roger had his gun aimed at Dr. Wolchek since the coup and with one shot, Roger hit him in the shoulder knocking him to the floor. Lord Malcolm reached down and grabbed Dr. Wolchek by the neck. His eyes ignited. "Oh Alistair. Do you really think you can stop me?" he asked. "I'll tell you what I'm going to do. First, I'm going to drain the life from your body. Then I'm going to find that beautiful daughter of yours and drain her too, but not before having my way with her."

Dr. Wolchek was strong, but being wounded, he couldn't maintain focus. Holding Lord Malcolm off for much longer would be impossible. Loss of blood was making it difficult to remain conscious.

Lord Malcolm could feel the doctor's resistance weakening. "You can't fight me, Alistair. You are weak and getting weaker. I can feel your life slowly slipping away," he said.

Dr. Wolchek knew it was just a matter of time. No way to prevent the inevitable. Mustering what strength he could, he managed to say in a weak voice, "You'll get yours, Henry. Your time is coming..." He fell into unconsciousness.

"I doubt that Alistair," Lord Malcolm said. He drew in the doctor's life force with ease.

Dropping Dr. Wolchek's lifeless body to the ground, Lord Malcolm looked at the remaining council members. "I, and only I, am the head of the Society now. I will decide the future direction and our role in the world. It's time for change ladies and gentlemen. A new direction. A new order!" Feeling the doctor's energy coursing through his body Lord Malcolm felt energized. "We are better than man. We have more experience. Man has proven time and time again that he is not capable of deciding his own future so we will do it for him!" Roger and his men erupted in cheers and applause.

"To the new order," Roger cheered.

"To the new order!" his men cheered back. The council members buried their heads in their hands and wept.

# # #

Watching from a small side office connected to Dr. Wolchek's chamber seat, Danny Overstreet, a trusted and loyal aid, witnessed everything. Fortunately, Since Dr. Wolchek had been brought to the center table on the ground floor of the council chambers, Roger did not order his men to secure Dr. Wolchek's council seat or office. Danny was able to witness the entire meeting unnoticed. Now, with the doctor dead he knew Christine would be next. He had to get to her before Lord Malcolm.

Chapter 20

As Christine sat in her office thumbing through her father's real file on Ryan Anderson, she found herself captivated by every line. He was a fascinating subject. She couldn't help flipping back to the first page of the report where her father had attached a more recent picture of him. As she read, she'd occasionally look to the picture, often losing herself in thought before looking at the portrait on the wall.

"Remarkable," she thought out loud. "The similarities are incredible."

The office doors burst open. Out of breath and in a panic, Danny Overstreet ran in and shut and locked the doors behind him. He spun around.

"You have to leave. Now!"

She quickly jumped to her feet. "What's happened?" she asked.

"It's your father," Danny managed to get out between breaths. "He's... he's dead"

"What?" Christine asked. She sank back into her chair. Shock and horror showed on her face.

"How?"

"Lord Malcolm and Roger killed him right in front of the council. Then Roger's men stormed the room. In the confusion I escaped. Christine, you must get out of here! He'll be coming for you! He knows about Ryan Anderson! He knows everything!"

As if a switch flipped, Christine's mind went in to autopilot. She and her father had rehearsed a number of escape strategies. Knowing time was critical, she immediately went to the wall safe and extracted her emergency passports and other alternate forms of identification as well as 100,000 U.S. dollars in cash. She walked to a corner bookcase and pulled it out from the wall. To Danny's surprise, it revealed a hidden passage way.

"Are you coming?" she asked Danny as she stepped through the opening.

Shaking off his surprise, "Let's go," he said.

Following her through the passage, they disappeared into a dark tunnel.

"Where does this lead?" Danny asked.

"To the parking garage under the manor."

"Did you and your father build it?" he asked. His tone was uneasy as he felt the dust and cobwebs brushing against his skin and face.

"No. It was here before us."

"Does Lord Malcolm know about it?"

"I don't think so, but just in case let's step it up."

After reaching the garage, they were relieved to find it empty of security staff. Quietly and quickly, they made their way to Christine's car.

"So far so good," she said. She drove up the ramp to exit the garage. Just as she emerged into the courtyard, an armed security team began approaching from the opposite side. "Brace yourself," Christine said giving Danny a serious look. She pulled out a small box not much bigger than a keyless remote entry device from her coat pocket. It had one red button. She looked at Danny. "I hope this works," she said. She pressed the button. An explosion erupted from the corner of the manor house completely engulfing her and her father's office suites in a massive ball of fire. Within seconds, pieces of building were raining down all around causing the security team to run for cover.

"Hang on!" Christine said. She slammed the accelerator down and aimed the car in the direction of the closing courtyard gates. What was left of the security detail scrambled to get out of her way as she burst through the gates and rocketed down the gravel driveway.

Her escape was far from over. Within seconds of escaping the compound, the car was hit with a barrage of gunfire.

Looking in the rearview mirror, Christine saw a security truck in hot pursuit. She could see a man firing an automatic rifle from the passenger side window. Bullets were tearing into the car as Christine zigzagged to keep from giving him a clear shot. The rear window exploded causing

Danny to scream as he dove to the floor to escape the hail of glass and bullets. Christine's car had a turbo engine, but the security truck was also well equipped. Within seconds, the truck was on her bumper ramming into her -trying to force her into a spin. Christine's years of defensive driving training kicked in and she countered. Her car was heavy, an advantage she knew she had. She slowed allowing the truck to come alongside the car. With a sudden swerve, Christine slammed the car into the truck. The car's lower profile and weight forced the truck off the road at just the right time to send it crashing into a large, old oak tree. The impact was loud and violent. They heard pieces of the truck fall onto the car.

"You can come up now," Christine said. She nodded as Danny pulled himself off the floor of the passenger seat.

Danny had been with Dr. Wolchek and Christine for many years and learned to expect the unexpected, but in all his years he had never experienced anything like this. Trying to regain his composure, he climbed back onto his seat.

"Nothing like a spirited drive in the country," he said.

Reaching into her coat pocket, Christine produced a satellite phone and called a small private airfield where she and her father kept a plane for such an occasion. Under one of her emergency ID's, she ordered the plane made ready for immediate departure. The plan was to get to the European continent, then make their way to the US. Once they were sure they were safe, Christine knew she needed to get to Ryan before Lord Malcolm. She hoped she wouldn't be too late.

PART FIVE

Chapter 21

The Excalibur

Within weeks of meeting Dr. Wolchek, Ryan was well on his way to a full recovery. Feeding on both energy and food, Ryan's mind and body were growing stronger by the day. Not only was he excelling at work, but also socially. Having rejoined the band several months ago he and his fellow band members were regaining their rightful place within the hierarchy of local bands. With renewed energy, it wasn't long before Ryan helped propel them to the top of the local music scene but this time they were performing on a whole new level. Everyone, especially his band mates, were enjoying themselves and most importantly, having a good time.

Ryan's energy was contagious. There was something about playing in front of a live crowd that energized the members and helped drive them to perform at their best. Ryan was especially attuned to this. He found feeding in large crowds to be easy. The energy created by a mass of people felt much like the energy field he tapped into when meditating. But this was all human energy, young, healthy, wild, and pure. Since the energy was everywhere, all he had to do was allow himself to take it in. The only drawback was that feeding on such a large scale caused his eyes to glow. He found a solution to this problem. Sunglasses. Having already told everyone that his previous health problems had to do with his eyes, it was an easy sell. Besides, sunglasses and musicians are a natural fit.

As the weeks and months passed, Ryan and the band's performances only got better. Word spread that Ryan was back on lead vocals and it wasn't long before they began selling out local venues. With renewed confidence and enthusiasm, Ryan also helped with the recording of new material. To everyone's surprise, they began to make money. More than they were spending, anyway. The new music, combined with the energetic live performances, drew new fans every night. This got the attention of local venues throughout the area and the band became one of the top billing acts in all of northeast Florida. But this was not the primary motivator for Ryan. Singing and preforming were a release for him. After playing the professional all week, their performances allowed him to let loose and be a weekend rock star; something he enjoyed more and more now that he was developing his newly discovered powers. The upcoming performance at the downtown club, Excalibur, further validated the band's success.

The Excalibur was an old five-story building located in downtown Jacksonville, Florida. In an attempt to attract night life to that area, the building was converted to a multi-use club. The first two floors were gutted giving it 30,000 square feet of prime entertainment area converted into several performance venues. From the time it opened, it was the popular hot spot. Local bands competed to perform there on the weekends. It was also one of Jacksonville's premier dance clubs. Each weekend had a different theme. And Saturday night was reserved for the top acts. Only the best bands were invited to perform. Not only had Ryan and the band been invited to perform, they were billed as the featured act-an honor they were excited to receive. To be billed as the featured act at the Excalibur was considered making it to the "big time" in the local music scene. Ryan and his bandmates joked that playing the Excalibur on a Saturday night would probably be the closest they would ever come to feeling like real rock stars.

# # #

It was late Saturday afternoon when Christine's plane touched down at a small private airfield just outside Jacksonville. It had been two days since Christine and Danny escaped the Society's compound. Both were exhausted but knew they had much to do. Not knowing how long it would take to convince Ryan to go with her, Christine sent Danny to the next rondevu point with specific instructions. The airfield had a small airport offering commuter flights to other regional cities. Under an assumed identity, Danny booked a flight and headed west to await her arrival. Christine knew they needed to keep as low a profile as possible. Private planes and small airfields gave them an advantage and more escape options. She was an experienced pilot after all. Between Christine and her father, they had amassed a small air force stashed around the world. Having her own planes and flying herself eliminated the need for additional people to be involved. No ticket agents. No tickets being booked. No trail to follow. The fewer people involved, the better. The plan was to land in Jacksonville pick up Ryan and get out as soon as possible. The sooner they were on the move the faster they could escape into hiding.

It was nearly 8:15 in the evening when Christine arrived at Ryan's house in her rental car. She parked in the driveway and noticed that the house was dark. She decided to knock on the front door anyway. After waiting a few minutes no one answered so she convinced herself it could wait. She knew time was against them, but couldn't dismiss the fact that she was both mentally and physically exhausted. She decided she would get a hotel and some much needed rest then catch up with Ryan in the morning.

A neighbor noticed her as she was walking to her car.

"Are you looking for Ryan?" asked a sickly looking woman standing in a bathrobe holding her dog's leash.

Mustering up the strength to be polite, Christine responded, "Yes, I am. Do you know where I might be able to find him?"

"He's playing at the Excalibur tonight," the neighbor said.

"Playing? Playing what?"

"His band. They're performing at the Excalibur."

Christine was confused. She did not know Ryan was a musician.

The neighbor saw Christine's expression. "The Excalibur is a night club downtown. I wish I could go but I got side tracked by a rotten summer cold. They're the worst!" she said as she wiped her runny nose with a tissue.

"Where is this club?" Christine asked the chatty neighbor.

"Off Bay Street. You can't miss it. It's the glitzy building all lit up with neon and the works. Should be a good crowd tonight," the woman replied.

"Really?" Christine asked. She was intrigued at the thought of Ryan playing in a band in a popular night club.

"Now that Ryan is back with the band again they're better than ever."

"Was he away?" Christine asked.

"Well, with his illness and all he had to take some time off. He just couldn't do it the poor guy. Thank goodness he's better now. To be completely honest, we," the woman said gesturing toward the neighborhood, "We all thought he was a goner. Nothing but skin and bones."

"He looked that bad?" Christine asked.

"Honey, he looked like death warmed up! Fortunately they were able to figure out what was wrong with him."

"So he's better now?"

"Oh yeah, and then some..." the woman said with an obvious lustful expression that Christine noticed.

"Well, thank goodness for that then," Christine said smiling.

"And how do you know Ryan?" the woman asked. She did not do a good job hiding her deeper interest.

"Ryan and my father are colleagues. They occasionally work together. I was in town and thought I would drop by and say hello. Strictly business I assure you." Christine said with a wink and a smile.

"Forgive me honey," the woman said. She looked around before continuing. "But there isn't a single or married woman for that matter on this block that doesn't secretly lust after that man. And now! Well, I gotta say, he has made a full recovery and then some," the woman said. She had a dreamy, longing look in her eyes.

"Sounds like he's quite a specimen," Christine said. She was growing more amused with the conversation.

"Oh honey!" the woman said. She paused as if she just realized something. "Wait, you haven't actually met Ryan?"

"I'm afraid not. He and my father work together, but I have not yet had the pleasure. Well, thanks again for the information," Christine said still pretending to be pleasant.

"Sure. Good luck," the woman said. She turned to walk back up her own driveway. Her initial pleasant curiosity was replaced by a more jealous demeanor.

# # #

As Christine approached the Excalibur she noticed a huge crowd and was taken back by the enormity of the event. She really knew nothing about Ryan Anderson except what she had learned from her father. Ryan's public life could make his extraction more complicated, but she was determined to do what she had to do to keep him safe.

She approached a doorman who smiled a big toothy smile.

"Well, what have we here? I'm afraid you're just too fine to come in, Baby!" he joked. He loved flirting with beautiful women. "You might start a riot in this place!"

She smiled and tossed her hair flirting back at him.

"No need to worry about me. I plan on being a good girl tonight," she said in her sexy British accent.

"Now that's just too bad baby. I'm only letting the bad girls in tonight."

Tiring of this little game and still inwardly exhausted, Christine faked a mischievous smile and placed her hand on his bulky forearm. "I like a guy with muscles," she said. She ran her hand up his arm to his shoulder and neck, then with the force of a sledge hammer she pulled a large amount of energy from him. It was so sudden that the guy passed out falling to the floor in a crumpled mass. Pretending to be concerned, she called for help and another doorman arrived. When he was distracted, Christine slipped into the crowd and entered the club. Not really sure what Ryan looked like now, Christine staked out a position about half way to the stage and waited for the show to begin.

At 10:00pm, the opening acts were finished and it was time for the main event.

The lights went out and the crowd erupted in excited applause. A loud voice boomed over the sound system, "Ladies and gentlemen. Please join me in welcoming to the Excalibur for the first time, The Immortals!" The lights came on in a blinding flash and the music started with a powerful beat. The music was fast. The flow was fluid. Christine could feel it pouring over her. The crowd burst into cheers and applause when Ryan's voice suddenly exploded over the sound system.

Ryan was a natural. He worked the stage and crowd like a true rock star. He enjoyed what he was doing and the rest of the band was also having a good time. As they played, they worked the crowd into a frenzy. Each song surpassed the previous in entertaining the crowd. It was obvious to Christine that each band member put everything he had into his performance.

From her position, she could see the stage and more importantly, Ryan. He was indeed handsome and had a good physical frame. It was hard to believe that six months ago he was as bad off as her father reported. He looked completely recovered. Nothing like the sickly thin picture that had been attached to his file.

As Christine continued to watch she noticed how Ryan's energy seemed contagious, almost as if it was somehow energizing the band and crowd. Christine usually didn't like this kind of music, but more than once she found herself caught up in its beat and energy. She also noticed that Ryan was the only one wearing sunglasses. Not really all that unusual. After all the stage lights were bright. But something about the glasses puzzled her.

Like everyone else, Christine watched with a hypnotic fascination as the band performed. It did not hurt that all the members were somewhat attractive, but she couldn't take her eyes off Ryan. He intrigued her. His physical appearance was so different from what she expected. His movements, too, captivated her.

After performing all their familiar favorites and a few new surprises, the band wrapped. They were called back for encores twice before finally concluding the show. After thanking the crowd for a final time all five of the members hugged each other then exited the stage. Christine tried to follow as best she could, but was stopped by another security guard before entering the backstage area.

"Sorry miss. I can't let anyone back here without a pass. Only band members and guest," he said.

"But I am a guest of Ryan Anderson," she said faking it.

"Then where is your pass?"

"Pass?" Christine asked playing innocent.

"All guest have passes. I can't let you in without one," the security guard replied.

"Oh, I see" Christine said disappointed.

As she was turning to walk away, she pretended to slip. Being the chivalrous guy the security guard was, he managed to catch her in order to prevent her from falling.

"Thank you," Christine said looking up at him holding his arm. As with the doorman, Christine pulled a large amount of energy from him causing him to collapse.

# # #

The back stage party was in full force and it took some time for Christine to locate Ryan. After asking several people where he could be found, she was eventually directed to the showers. Behind the stage in one of the auxiliary dressing rooms was a bank of showers for band members to use. More often than not, the showers usually turned into an orgy. As Christine made her way through the shower room she finally located Ryan. He was standing completely naked in a shower stall with his arms raised holding the shower head as it sprayed down over his face and body. Shocked by what she saw, it took a second for the sight to sink in. Not one, but two naked women were on their knees taking turns giving Ryan oral sex. Still, something was different. She could tell he was enjoying the experience. She could also tell that he was feeding.

Sensing a presence, he tilted his head out from under the shower spray. He kept his eyes closed until he was facing it straight on, then he opened his eyes. Locked in his gaze, Christine did not turn away and continued looking directly at him. Almost as if he was throwing down a gauntlet, he smiled slightly and flashed his eyes. By doing this, he actually pushed energy at Christine causing her to stumble backwards. Still staring, he kept his gaze firmly locked on her but did not make another challenge. Momentarily caught off guard by the force of the exchange, Christine caught her balance. She did not return the gesture. She looked down at the girls, smiled and walked out of the shower area. Ryan did not sense she was dangerous, but he knew she was one of his kind. Closing his eyes, he tilted his head back under the warm spray and let himself get lost in the experience.

Chapter 22

After the show and subsequent "clean up" activities, Ryan and the band members loaded into the limo he had rented for the evening and headed to after parties around the city. As expected, he got his money's worth out of that limo. Always combining work and play, Ryan used the show at the Excalibur to do some advertising work. Entertaining both clients and fans at the after parties, Ryan found himself doing what he did best; socializing and entertaining all those around him. Even with the success of the evening, he was aware of a presence. He knew the woman from the shower was following him. Occasionally, they caught each other's eye, but each time he attempted to approach her, she disappeared into the crowds. This heightened Ryan's curiosity even more. He felt a game of sorts was at hand. After his encounter with Roger the other day, he felt confident, but aware. Was she another Society member sent to check on him? Was she dangerous? He did not know. For some reason he didn't feel she was a threat. At least not yet anyway.

Christine followed Ryan throughout the night and kept a casual eye on him from afar. Occasionally catching each other's eye at a distance, Christine always managed to disappear into the crowd before Ryan was able to spot her again. At 3:30am, she followed the limo back to his house. She parked her rental car down the street. From her vantage point, she observed Ryan and a female companion emerge from the car. After thanking the driver and tipping him, she could hear Ryan and the woman laughing as he put his arm around her and led her into his house. She noticed the lights come on and decided to try and get some rest. She figured she would catch him as soon as possible in the morning and, hopefully, be on the move shortly after that. Settling back in the car seat Christine drifted off into an uneasy sleep. Thoughts of her father, the Society and the chase haunted her dreams causing what little sleep she could get to be fitful.

Around 7:00am, Christine was awaken by the sound of a car horn. When she opened her eyes she noticed a taxi in Ryan's driveway.

"How nice of him. He called her a taxi," she thought. She attempted to fix her hair and remove the traces of yesterday from her face. After feeling she was as presentable as she could be, she looked at herself in the rearview mirror. "Well, I guess there's no time like the present," she said out loud. She opened the car door and headed toward the house.

About the time Christine reached the front porch the door opened and a beautiful blond woman hurried out. Startled, the woman stepped back.

"Excuse me, I didn't see you. Can I help you?" the blond said.

"Is Ryan home?" Christine asked. She smiled at the woman.

"You're in luck, he's in the kitchen. Go on in. He's all yours." The woman hurried down the sidewalk to the taxi.

Not one to just walk in, Christine knocked on the front door.

"Mr. Anderson?"

"In here," Ryan replied directing her to the kitchen.

Christine followed his voice and found herself in a large open concept kitchen/dining room area. Leaning against a counter still wet from his morning shower with a towel around his waist, Ryan sipped coffee. As she rounded the corner he lowered the coffee mug.

"The mysterious woman from the club. And what brings you to my home so early in the morning?" he asked. He held her in his line of sight. Knowing what she was, he wasn't taking any chances.

"The mysterious woman has a name. It's Christine," she replied.

"So Christine, what can I do for you?" he asked. He sipped from his mug never breaking eye contact.

Christine put her purse on the counter, pulled a stool out and sat down.

"You are in serious danger, Mr. Anderson. I need to get you out of here as soon as possible," she said. Staying calm and keeping the level of intensity to a minimum was her plan.

"Really?" he responded. "From who? You? Or that other goon you people sent to see me last week?"

Christine was confused. "What other goon are you referring to?" she asked.

"Come on, Christine. You know the guy. The scary looking English fellow with the black empty eyes. That guy is a piece of work. A cold blooded killer if I ever saw one."

"Roger..." Christine uttered under her breath.

"Yeah, that was his name. Roger."

"You met Roger?" Christine asked. She was surprised. She knew that Roger knew about Ryan, but she did not know all the details of their encounter.

"Surely you knew he was coming to visit me?" Ryan asked.

"No I didn't," she replied. "I'm surprised to find you still alive. Usually anyone who encounters Roger does not live to tell about it."

"He tried to kill me alright. He made no attempt to hide his intentions as he tried to drain the life from me in my office at work."

"And you survived?" Christine asked doubting his story.

Ryan looked at her.

"Roger is a trained assassin the best at what he does. He must have intentionally let you live," she said.

"I doubt that. His expression did not look like one of mercy."

"Impossible...," Christine uttered under her breath. "There is no way you could have bested him."

"Maybe he was having a bad day," Ryan snapped. "Look lady, who are you and what do you want? And make it quick. I'm losing my patience," he said. He flashed his eyes and locked on to her with an intense stare.

"I'm Christine Wolchek. Dr. Wolchek is my father."

Ryan was completely caught off guard.

"Dr. Wolchek's daughter?" he asked. His eyes returned to normal.

"Yes." Christine replied. She lowered her head and looked down at the floor.

"Where is he? I need to talk to him," Ryan said.

"I'm afraid that's impossible. He's dead."

"Dead? How?"

Christine fought her emotions. "He was killed in a coup."

"A coup? Within the Society? I told him not to go back!" Ryan said. He fought both anger and sadness at hearing the news.

"The Society has been taken over by one of the more radical members. A despicable, power hungry, dangerous man named Lord Henry Malcolm. I'm afraid his first order of business will be your elimination."

"Why me?"

"Because of who you are."

"And what the hell does that mean?"

"I'm afraid it's a very long story, Ryan. And I promise I'll tell it to you but first we need to get you out of here as soon as possible. They'll be coming. I can assure you of that," Christine pleaded.

"Get out of here? Go into hiding? Live on the run? I don't think so. I have a life here. People depend on me. This is my town. My city. I can't just go running off into the blue with a complete stranger! Forget it lady!" Ryan said. He slammed his coffee down on the counter.

"You don't have a choice Ryan. Roger and his thugs will be coming. I have risked everything to come here and take you to safety. They are after me, too. I can't go back. Our only chance is to get to a safe location."

"I'm not running Christine. I'm sorry you came all this way for nothing, but I can take care of myself. If you want to run, be my guest. I'm not going anywhere." He turned to leave. "Excuse me I need to get dressed."

As Ryan left the kitchen, Christine stood up to follow him but lost her footing and slipped on the tile floor.

Hearing the commotion, Ryan returned.

"Are you okay?" he asked. He bent down to help her to her feet. He noticed how tired she looked. Exhausted.

"I think so. Thank you," she responded softly before bursting into tears.

Kneeling down next to her Ryan tried to comfort her. Her exhaustion was obvious.

"It's okay, Christine. Everything will be okay."

Christine was inconsolable. "I miss my father so much. It was not supposed to happen like this. He should be here with us too. He told me to get to you and keep you safe. Ryan, please listen to me, you're in great danger. We must get you out of here!"

Mostly in an effort to calm her he agreed.

"When was the last time you had any sleep?"

"I don't know," Christine said. "A few days ago?"

"That settles it. I'm putting you in the guest room so you can get some rest for a little while at least."

"No, Ryan. There isn't time for that. We need to get going now."

"This is not negotiable. Either you get some sleep or the deal is off."

She relented.

"Only for a little while. Then we must leave."

As Ryan helped her to her feet he pulled her up and in the direction of a nearby counter so she could use it for support. At the same time Tor jumped onto the counter next to her. He immediately arched his back into a defensive mode and hissed at Christine. His eyes flashed a brilliant yellow as he locked her in his deadly stare.

Christine jumped back and froze against a wall. She was petrified with fear. Tor had her in his sites and looked as if he was about to attack. Ryan was intrigued by the interaction between the two. Tor had no fear and Christine looked as if she was about to be killed. Finally, Ryan ordered Tor to stop.

"Tor! Enough! She's my guest!"

Begrudgingly, Tor complied. His eyes returned to normal, but he would not leave. He sat on the counter watching Christine occasionally making a low pitched growl.

Ignoring Tor, Ryan went to her.

"Come with me. He won't hurt you," he said. He led her down the hall to the nearest guest bedroom.

"That's your cat?" She asked. She emphasized "your."

"I can't really call him mine. Let's just say he's my roommate."

"Incredible..." Christine mumbled. "You live with a cat. Truly incredible...." Christine again repeated as he helped her into the bed.

"Your father was also surprised by that," Ryan said, but he doubted she heard him. She had already drifted off into a deep sleep.

After helping her to bed, Ryan turned off the light and stood at the door. "Sleep well, Christine. I have many questions for you later." He shut the door. Tor had followed them down the hall and was waiting outside the room. "And you, Buddy. What am I going to do with you?" Ryan bent down to rub his head. "What do you think about our guest? Is she dangerous? Is she here to hurt me? Fortunately I have you to protect me," Ryan joked. He continued to rub Tor's ears. "Okay. Let's go get some chow. I don't think we need to worry about her for a while." He led Tor back to the kitchen for some breakfast.

Chapter 23
The Truth

It was Sunday and usually the day following any "big show" is a mellow one. Ryan typically uses the day to relax and do things around the house. Not having any major plans meant Ryan could stay home and see to his guest.

Off and on through the morning and early afternoon Ryan checked on Christine. Learning of her father's assassination deeply troubled him. Ryan had only known Dr. Wolchek for a short time, but he still felt a profound sense of loss. After all, it was Dr. Wolchek who saved his life and introduced him to his new world. Ryan knew that Dr. Wolchek was aware of the risks he was taking by helping him, but never believed things could become this serious. For months, Ryan looked forward to his and the doctor's eventual reunion so he could finally get answers to his ever growing list of questions. Often his emotions shifted from angry to hopeful, always wondering if he had been forgotten or if he was being ignored on purpose. "How could the doctor do this to me?" Ryan asked himself. Change him into this and then just disappear? With every new discovery Ryan made about himself and his abilities his anger gradually turned into curiosity and wonder. He needed information; someone to explain to him what was going on. With the exception of his encounter with Roger, most of his experiences had been positive and innocent. But news of the doctor's death brought a sudden and tragic end to this period of ignorant bliss. Dr. Wolchek's death showed him that there was a darker side to his condition. There was a "Society" and politics involved that were far greater than himself. Christine's warnings and desperate pleas to leave and go into hiding did little more than anger Ryan. He did not ask for this! Their agenda was not his own. He couldn't care less about some ancient organization or their stupid politics. All he wanted was to be left alone so he could live his life as he saw fit. Still, he had so many unanswered questions. With all of his confusion and curiosity, he clung to the hope of eventually seeing Dr Wolchek again so he could continue his training and get answers. With him gone, Ryan felt empty. Christine was Dr. Wolchek's daughter and had risked her own safety to travel halfway around the world to warn him. Ryan hoped she would be able to provide the information he sought and somehow help him make sense of everything.

# # #

Christine finally woke up mid-afternoon. She found Ryan swimming laps in his pool. The moment she stepped out on to the pool deck, he felt her presence. On his return lap he angled himself in her direction. When he reached the wall in front of her, he pulled himself up and climbed out of the pool. The speedo swimsuit he was wearing flattered his swimmer's frame. Still half asleep, Christine could not stop from staring at his well-proportioned body. Catching her obvious full body scan Ryan smiled back at her as he walked over to a table for a towel and dried off.

"Sleep well?" he asked.

"Yes, thank you. I guess I really needed that."

"Would you like something to eat?"

"That would be wonderful," she replied.

"Sit here in the shade while I round up some sandwiches and something to drink."

Christine felt relaxed for the first time in days. The long nap was just what she needed. Lost in thought as she looked around at the beautifully manicured yard, her concentration was broken when Ryan returned carrying a tray with drinks and a couple of sandwiches.

"I hope you like ham and cheese and cold sweet tea."

"Right now I could eat just about anything. Thank you," Christine said. She eyed the sandwiches and felt real hunger for the first time in two days.

Ryan served the tea and sandwiches.

"I'm really sorry to hear about your father. I owe him my life," he said. He was leaning forward in his chair. He was humble and sincere.

"Thank you," Christine said. She fought the tears welling in her eyes.

Ryan took her hand and gently squeezed it. He sat back in his chair and shook his head.

"He warned me that my life might be in danger, but did not say that his was. I don't understand Christine. Why would anyone want to kill him?"

"It's a long story. I'm really not sure where to begin. My father and I have been at odds with Society policy for some time now. I just never believed it would ever come to this."

"Was he killed because of me?"

Christine hesitated before answering. "Yes and no. If you had not been discovered I'm afraid the outcome would have been the same sooner or later. Your discovery just accelerated things." She tried and failed to make light of her last comment.

"But why me? Why would a Society half a world away give a shit about me? Who am I to them?" Ryan asked.

"It's complicated," she said. She shook her head as she looked far off into the distance.

"Please tell me what you know. I deserve to know why people are out to kill me," Ryan said. His mounting confusion added to his irritation. "Your father said I was like Oscar Wilde's character, Dorian Gray. He also said that story might have been based on a real person and that he, too, was hunted and killed by the Society! Why? Who was this guy and why did the Society want him dead? What's the connection to me?" Ryan was pissed at this point. "Dammit Christine! I didn't ask for any of this. And I sure as hell didn't ask to get involved with some fucked up ancient secret society of ex-vampires!" Ryan snapped.

Christine remained motionless gathering her thoughts before responding. "You deserve answers. I had no idea my father told you as much as he did. I guess the best thing to do is start at the beginning. Make yourself comfortable Ryan, this is going to take some time" she said. She sat back and sighed. "It is believed by many that Wilde's story might have been inspired by rumors involving a young nobel, Robert Wellington, who lived about 50 years prior to his fictional creation. He was the only son of Lord Wellington and Lady Sara Cornwall. Lord Wellington and his wife were very much in love. They traveled the British Empire and the rest of the world determined to learn all the secrets life had to offer. Ancient cultures were of particular interest. Unfortunately, their love was not meant to last. Lady Wellington died from complications giving birth to Robert. Lord Wellington was devastated. He blamed his son for killing his wife and could never allow himself to accept the child. Shortly after Robert was born, Lord Wellington committed suicide unable to live without his beloved. Robert was sent to live with his grandfather. Robert's grandfather was not an affectionate man. He made sure Robert had the best care and education one could have in those days. He was sent to the best schools and universities. Like yourself, he excelled in his academic requirements and also found comfort in sporting activities and competitions," Christine paused for a moment before continuing. "Robert grew to be an accomplished student and by all accounts a striking young man. He and his grandfather were never close, but when his grandfather died, Robert inherited a huge fortune and title."

Ryan could relate to Roberts childhood. Having been orphaned himself at such an early age.

"Young Lord Wellington was only in his late teens or maybe early twenties when he came into his fortune so he was considered quite the catch by the women in society. For three years, he enjoyed his playboy role and was often involved in scandals. It was believed his good looks and charm were irresistible to women and even men throughout London," Christine said giving Ryan a sly smile.

He blushed and motioned for her to continue.

"Near his 22nd birthday, Robert was badly injured in a carriage accident. Most believed he would die, but it was not to be. He somehow pulled through. For weeks he was thin and malnourished. He was reported to be mad and just barely clinging to life. Then something happened. Nobody knew how, but a chambermaid was found dead beside his bed one morning. Shortly after that, he began to recover. Within weeks he had regained his strength and appeared to have been restored to perfect health. But to those closest to him something was different. He still was as attractive as before, yet something about his personality had changed and he was not the same person he was before the accident. He would disappear into the forest on his estate and be gone for days at a time. Nobody knew what he was doing out there. Some believed he was practicing black magic; others thought he was worshiping the devil. Many in society shunned him. Others tried to maintain a formal relationship, but rumors and gossip continued. Before long it was dangerous to be associated with Robert for fear of damaging one's own reputation."

"But why? What had so drastically changed that caused such a public back lash?" Ryan asked.

"He changed. The places he openly frequented; opium dens, brothels, etc., and the company he kept. Death also seemed to surround him. Many years after his accident he did not appear to be aging which generated even more gossip. People even said he had sold his soul to the devil to always stay young."

Ryan rolled his eyes. "How ridiculous," he said.

"Be that as it may, you have to remember times were different then. The Society existed in those days, but was still weak after many years of infighting. Members were just beginning to organize and understand their common condition. It was my father who first figured out what Young Lord Wellington was."

"How?" Ryan asked. He was captivated by her story.

"Father believed the carriage accident was the trigger that began his transition into our kind.

However, the real proof came one night when my father was helping the London authorities try and solve the mystery of who was behind a string of horrific murders practically paralyzing the city every evening," she said shaking her head remembering the events.

"The murders were extremely violent. Some believed a wild beast was on the loose because of the condition of the bodies. Father investigated the killings and with other Society members helped patrol London's streets. One foggy night, he came across a ghastly scene. A man was stooped over a woman in a dark alley. The fog was glowing bright yellow. He thought it was a Society member feeding. But when Father approached, he found Robert covered in blood and drunk on life energy while crazily hacking up the body of his victim with a large knife. He tried to stop him, but Robert was too strong."

"What did your father do?" Ryan asked shifting in his seat.

"Going to the local authorities risked exposing all our kind so he reported his findings to the council. Because Robert was one of us, it was decided that we had to be the ones to stop him. Not only was he creating considerable panic and unrest in the population, but if he was captured and it was revealed what he really was the risks would be too great for the Society to take. Father convinced the council that they needed to help him so several efforts were made to try and capture Robert but it did not go well. All efforts to capture Robert ended badly."

Ryan paused a moment as he took in everything Christine told him.

"But why? Why couldn't they catch him? Clearly he was out numbered," Ryan asked.

"Yes, but my father said there was something different about him. He was stronger than any other member he had ever encountered. Father later hypothesized that his strength might have developed because he feed mostly on other people. Literally."

"People?"

"Yes. A person has considerable life energy and when killed, it is released. If one of our kind is present, we can consume it. It has even been found that the more violently a person is killed, the greater the energy discharge. Something about the fear felt by the victim enhances the energy. My father believed Robert probably figured this out by accident and once he had a taste for it, he became addicted. The murders had been mostly sporadic and seemed only to occur every few months. But, by the time my father discovered Robert, they were occurring every few nights. He and the Society decided it was time to get involved. Panic and public unrest had reached a critical point. Citizens had lost confidence in the ability of the police to protect them. Riots and a complete social breakdown was not far off."

"So his accident started his change and then feeding on people made him strong?" Ryan asked. "Does the triggering event contribute to how strong a person may become once transformed?"

"Father thought it did. We have found that people develop their abilities differently. It seems to depend on what it was that set the change in motion. Someone who is badly injured in an accident and recovers tends to be stronger than say someone who survived a near death experience from a disease or sickness. It's like there is a trigger in all of us but how it is pulled has different consequences to the individual. Honestly Ryan, we do not know why some transition and others do not. To some extent, we believe it may be an evolutionary process and can even be hereditary. I transitioned after I contracted yellow fever when I was in my mid-twenties. My mother and two other sisters did not. They lived normal lives. My father had transitioned many years before. He was almost killed on a battlefield."

Ryan was mesmerized.

"This is all so unbelievable. So what became of Robert?"

"The situation really deteriorated. People claimed they saw glowing fog then a body would be discovered. Rumors and gossip were out of control. The city was on the brink of mass panic and my father and his people could not capture Robert. On a few occasions they came close, but he was so strong and crazed they were no match for him. Finally, it was decided he had to be eliminated. Not only was he creating mass panic, but his capture risked exposing us all. After bribing one of Robert's house servants, my father and two other members gained access to his house one night and waited for him to return. When he did they killed him."

"According to Wilde's story, he killed himself by stabbing his own portrait."

"It's true there was a portrait. The original hung in my father's office until recently. Father believed it was the purity and innocence reflected in the image that eventually drove Robert mad. It was reported that he kept the portrait locked in a private room. His servants said he would often lock himself in the room and talk to it. They heard him yelling, crying, even laughing. It's a sad story. The poor guy never knew what he was. We believe he thought he was cursed and eventually drove himself mad with guilt and fear."

"So how did they finally stop him?" Ryan asked.

"Father, Roger, and Lord Malcolm waited for him in his house one night. As I said earlier, a servant tipped them off to his nightly habits and gave them a key to his private room where they waited. When Robert arrived home, he was extremely out of sorts. He burst into the room and began wailing at the portrait. They attacked catching him by surprise. Father said Robert put up quite a fight and almost killed Lord Malcolm. I wish he had now," Christine said. The bitterness in her voice was not missed by Ryan. "Father felt terrible about the entire incident and was never able to put it out of his mind."

"So how do I figure into the story?" Ryan asked.

She gave him a mischievous smile. "Robert did not always kill people. Like you, he learned to feed through a variety of means. Feeding by killing is the most direct injection of energy, but it is not necessary. Robert also used sex and other forms of contact. He is believed to have sired hundreds of offspring during his 50 years," Christine said. She paused for a moment before continuing. "You are a direct descendent of his. Father followed your bloodline for generations to see if the trait ever developed. Remember, we suspect to some extent that it can be passed down from generation to generation."

Ryan was shocked by the information. "Wow, I was not expecting that. So I'm a descendent of a crazed killer? Nice," Ryan said. He was not sure how to take all of this new information.

"Yes. Father followed many possible descendants but only a few ever developed the condition."

"What do you mean?" Ryan asked.

"After Robert was assassinated, the council ordered that all of his offspring be destroyed. His mental illness and strength scared the council. The Society worried that his decedents would be just as dangerous. Father objected and wanted to study future generations but was voted down. So he manipulated documents and records in order to protect some of the bloodline.

"Why was your father so interested?" Ryan asked suspicious of the motive. "Why would he care?"

"Because he believed that this condition was just the beginning. He did not think it was fair or even natural to try and stop it from its evolutionary path. Unfortunately, others did not see it this way, Lord Malcolm for one. He feared others like Robert Wellington, mostly because of his strength. Lord Malcolm saw him as a threat and wanted him eliminated. He and Roger along with my father carried out the first sanctioned assassination in Society history. After that night the dye was cast. Father refused to participate in any more assassinations but Lord Malcolm and Roger relished the opportunities. They became the Society's hit men and took care of whomever they perceived as troublemakers or anyone who could threaten the Society's existence. Unfortunately, being an assassin was not enough for Lord Malcolm. After WWII, Lord Malcolm wanted more power and control over the Society and its resources which, by the way, are considerable. He wanted the Society to take more of a proactive role in determining man's future, something the Society has always tried to stay out of. Their belief has always been that man should be left alone and allowed to make his own future," she said.

Pausing, Christine looked out past the pool as if she was attempting to fight building emotions. "So, now he has what he wanted. Total control. The Society I knew is gone." She looked directly at Ryan. "And he knows about you. He knows you are a descendent of Lord Wellington and fears your existence. He will use all the resources of the Society to see that you are eliminated. He will be coming for you Ryan. This is why we need to leave now and get you some place safe. My father thought you were special; thought you may have power that the rest of us do not have. He wanted to make it possible for you to develop into whatever it is you can. His wish was for us to help you get to safety."

Ryan did not know what to make of everything Christine was telling him. It all sounded so incredible, yet he knew it was true. He stood up from his chair and turned away from her for a moment.

"I need some time to think about this. I wanted answers and you've given them to me," he said. He turned back to face her. "It's just a lot to take in all at once."

"I know, but we really need to get out of here now for your safety," Christine insisted. "For our safety."

"I just can't up and run," he replied. "My life is here. There's things I have to see to."

"We're running out of time!" She said. "Roger will be coming soon. Of that I'm certain."

Ryan forcefully pushed a chair out of his way and walked to the edge of the pool.

Christine knew this was a lot for Ryan to absorb so she decided to stop pushing and give him some time to let it sink in.

"I'm sorry, Ryan. This was never our intention. My father and I hoped that this would not be necessary, but given the circumstances within the

Society, it left us with no choice. You are who you are and your case is very unique. Never have we encountered anyone where the transition was brought about by an animal exchange. And you're stronger than the average member. For these reasons most of all I want to get you some place safe so you can continue to develop your power in safety."

"I just can't up and run. I have things I need to do first," Ryan said again but this time more humbled and subdued.

Christine tried to put herself in Ryan's position. Hearing all this must be overwhelming. Yet, all things considered, he did appear to be handling what she had told him well. She wondered to herself how she would have reacted had the situation been reversed. After trying to see things from his point of view she took a deep breath and smiled.

"I know this is a lot to take in. Forgive me. I'm almost two hundred years old and you just transitioned six months ago. I sometimes forget how incredible it all is," she said. "But, please understand, time is against us."

"I know," he said. He was quiet and thoughtful.

By now it was late in the evening and both were tired. Ryan had much to think about. After treating Christine to a light dinner he decided to turn in for the evening. His mind was turning over and over with everything Christine had told him. He looked at himself in the large bedroom mirror. "Well, you wanted answers. Now you have them."

As he drifted off to sleep he felt a thud on the bed then heavy feet. Opening one eye he found Tor standing on the bed next to him. "So what do you think, buddy? Are you up for a vacation?" Tor climbed on Ryan's chest, curled up and began purring as he settled into a more comfortable position. "Okay, a vacation it is. Good night, Bud," Ryan said.

Christine decided to sit by the pool a little while longer before going to bed. Lost in thought, she sat there thinking about her father and considering possible future courses of action. But, more importantly, Christine was standing guard. She was still concerned that Lord Malcolm would be sending someone at any time and wanted to be ready just in case.

Chapter 24

Christine could not sleep. As she lay in her bed staring at the ceiling she began to cry. This was the first time in days she had time to reflect on all that had happened. Ever since learning of her father's death, she had been on the run. Sneaking out of the compound, blowing up their quarters, and then escaping England had taken its toll on her. Fortunately, she and her father had planned for just such an emergency escape many times. They had created new identities and alternate passports in the event they were needed. Realizing the significance of Lord Malcolm's growing popularity as well as their own precarious position within the Society, they knew it was not a matter of if, but when they would need to go on the run. All the precautions had been taken and escape strategies were rehearsed constantly. They had multiple avenues taking them to a variety of preplanned safe house destinations. Dr. Wolchek had even taken extra precautions by opening off shore accounts in different countries accessible only to him and Christine. Nothing was ever written down or recorded. All account information and safe house locations were committed to memory. They took no chances. The Society's reach would be considerable and they knew it would be difficult to stay off the radar for long.

Christine and her father long dreaded the inevitable day they would have to put their plan into action. Still, both held to the hope that maybe something would happen and they would be able to keep some form of balance within the Society. But, as Lord Malcolm's popularity grew, they found themselves rehearsing their emergency escape strategies more frequently.

"I made it father, just like we planned," she said out loud as she wiped the tears from her eyes.

# # #

Christine tossed and turned for hours. "Was coming to Ryan really the right thing to do?" she asked herself. "Will he be safer going on the run with me?" No matter how she thought about it, she always answered the same. Yes. She had to warn him that his life was in danger. Lord Malcolm knew of his existence and would be sending someone. Her father did not have the chance to tell her much about Ryan. But he believed that Ryan was special or could become something special if he only had the chance to develop his abilities. Dr. Wolchek wanted to be the one to train him, but that would never be. Her father was gone and there was nothing to stop Lord Malcolm now. She had to convince Ryan that his life was in grave danger and he needed to leave with her as soon as possible. So much to do she thought to herself.

Hungry, she went to the kitchen for something to eat. Ryan's house was impressive. She liked the openness, the glass walls and open floor plan. As she walked down the hall she noticed Ryan's bedroom door was slightly open. Looking in as she passed she froze in place and her mouth fell open in shock. It was easy to see in the room since almost one entire wall was a huge picture window allowing a clear view of a small pond and the pool. The pool light was on causing a warm, aquatic glow in his room. Christine saw Ryan on his back with only a sheet covering his lower body; Tor slept on his bare chest. "Incredible," she thought. She heard Tor purring from outside the door. Then suddenly the purring stopped and Tor's eyes opened. Christine did not move. Tor's wide open eyes glowed a bright yellow green as he stared right at her. Panic consumed her. She couldn't move. Tor watched her with great interest. To Christine, he appeared to be guarding Ryan and was ready to attack at any moment.

She saw Ryan's right hand raise up and gently stroke Tor's head and back.

"It's okay, she's not here to hurt us," he said.

"Does Ryan know I'm standing here?" Christine wondered. She remained still.

Tor put his head back down on Ryan's chest and shut his eyes, but not all the way. From the door, Christine saw a slight glint of yellow-green coming from his mostly closed eyes. He began to purr. It was not as loud as before, but it was constant and peaceful. Hearing this, Christine silently backed away and continued down the hall to the kitchen.

The belief that cats stole people's breath while they were sleeping actually originated within the Society. Early in the Society's existence, it was discovered that cats could take the life energy from someone who had transitioned. It wasn't clear if it was something they could control or more of an involuntary response to the presence of a person with this special ability. But, it was clear that cats could take far more energy than they gave back. They never seemed to fill up. The Society labeled cats dangerous and viewed them as threats to its members. If it was ever discovered that cats were dangerous to the Society, the fear was that they might somehow be used against them. They themselves used cats for executions. By placing a cat in the same room as the sentenced victim, the cat would drain his energy until he was dead. Nobody could explain why it happened. They just knew it did. Owls, too, possessed this ability. For these reasons, the Society waged a silent campaign to eliminate all cats and owls throughout England for over a century.

Chapter 25
Showdown

Ryan woke up early the next morning and went to work before Christine had a chance to confront him. He knew she would be upset so he left her a note and told her she was welcome to stay in the house. He told her he had things he needed to take care of before he could just drop off the radar and would be back as soon as possible. But mostly, he wanted to get a way for a while to clear his head. Between Christine and her father, he was overwhelmed with information, most of it sounding completely unbelievable, and yet, somehow, he knew it was all true. He'd experienced the proof and had met Roger-the Society's number one assassin according to Christine. Roger did attack him and tried to drain his life force. This Ryan was certain despite Christine's insistence to the contrary. He understood the seriousness of the situation, but he was having trouble believing his life could really be in any danger.

"Damn owl! It's all his fault. If it hadn't fucked me up that night, I'd never be in the mess I'm in now!" Ryan said to himself out loud as he sat in his office thinking about all the recent events. He knew his situation was extraordinary. But even being hunted, he felt so alive. The ability to tap into living life energy and renew himself was incredible. Ryan had never felt so good. He thought over and over about what Christine told him. The incredible story of his distant ancestor, Dr. Wolchek's tragic execution and his desperate quest to find and protect the bloodline, was just all so unbelievable. But he could not deny the reality of his situation. So much about him had changed over the past six months. Each day revealed new discoveries and he knew there was so much more to come.

Ryan felt like an eager student on his first day of school. Was he special? Was he on the verge of becoming more? He did not know the answers to those questions, but for whatever reason Dr. Wolchek seemed to believe he was capable of becoming something unprecedented if given the chance. Ryan took a deep breath. "You know what you need to do," he said out loud to himself. "Dr. Wolchek gave his life for me, and Christine has risked hers for my protection. I need to see this thing through to its end, whatever that may be or wherever it leads." Picking up his phone, Ryan hesitated for a minute before calling David Peterson. "David. I need a few minutes can I come down?"

A few minutes later Ryan was meeting with David, the most senior partner. Ryan told David that he would be taking a leave of absence; that he had emergency personal business he needed to attend to and was not sure how long it would take to resolve. Needless to say David was floored. Ryan and his team were the top earners. Losing either could be devastating to the firm. Knowing David's concerns, Ryan eased his worries by telling him that he would inform his team of his emergency leave then designate someone to be in charge and lead them while he was away. He also told him that Stan was not to have anything to do with his people or his accounts. Ryan had confidence in his people and felt comfortable turning over the reins. He strongly recommended David accept his choice in this matter because not doing so would surely cost the firm. Understanding what Ryan was telling him, David assured him that his wishes would be honored.

"How long will you be away?" David asked with obvious concern.

"I don't know, could be a few months, could be a year." Ryan said. He tried to make light of the situation. "Don't worry David, I trust my team. They know what to do and, of course, I'll check in from time to time," he said. He did his best to ease David's concern knowing all the while that it might be the last time he saw any of these people ever again.

Ryan called his team to an emergency meeting and told them he had urgent family matters to attend to that would require him to be away for some time. The announcement caused much commotion and concern. Ryan assured them he would return when everything was sorted out, but in the meantime he needed everyone to hold down the fort while he was away.

Then he created a leadership structure and spent the remainder of the afternoon tying up loose ends.

The day passed with lightning speed. Fortunately, the suddenness of his announcement helped to diffuse the situation. Ryan and his team were like a big family. Assuring them that he would return was the only way he felt he could get out of there without creating mass panic and an emotional disaster. He was confident in his choice to lead the department, yet he also felt a great sadness that he struggled to hide throughout the afternoon.

As the day wound down, his team sporadically filed in to express their gratitude and wish him a speedy return. Cindy was the last to approach him. Standing in the doorway unnoticed she stood looking at Ryan wondering what was really going on. He sat at his desk with his back to her staring out the window lost in thought. She had known him for several years and knew something was not right. Finally she walked up behind him and put her hands on his shoulders. Leaning down she whispered in his ear. "What's really going on Boss? You can't fool me with this family emergency stuff."

Smiling and looking at her reflection in the window, he reached up and held her hands. "I knew you'd never buy it. You're too smart for that."

"You know I am. Are you going to tell me the truth?"

Ryan turned to look at her. "The truth is, I'm not entirely sure what the truth is. But I know I have something I must do," he said.

Cindy smiled and tried to hold back her emotions. "Are you really going to come back?" she asked.

Ryan stood and hugged her tightly. "I honestly don't know."

No longer able to control herself, Cindy burst into tears and buried her head in his chest.

Ryan felt a surge of anger. Anger toward Dr. Wolchek, Christine, and that bullshit Society. Having to leave his life and the people he knew and cared about infuriated him. As he held Cindy, he silently promised himself that he would return. Somehow he would get his life back.

After they said their goodbyes, Ryan returned to his office to take care of a few last minute items. It was 7:00pm. The day had passed quickly. Knowing it might be the last time he laid eyes on his office, he took one last long look before turning off the lights and heading for the elevator.

# # #

Even with the extraordinary recent events, Christine's beauty did not escaped Ryan. Her crystal blue eyes, sandy blond hair and perfectly shaped body had not gone unnoticed despite the tragic circumstances leading to their meeting. He was still a man after all and she was a very attractive woman. As the elevator came to a stop at his parking garage level, he realized he was excited about getting home and seeing her. When the elevator doors opened he stepped out. At once he noticed a strange darkness in the garage and could barely make out the outline of his car 10 parking spaces away. He also felt a presence. His senses were alerted to danger. Something was there in the darkness with him. Something strange, but also familiar. He was not alone. Remembering what Christine said about the Society sending someone to kill him, he prepared himself for a confrontation. He continued to his car as if nothing was wrong. When he approached, he pushed the unlock button on his key chain causing the car's lights to flash as it disarmed and unlocked. As the light flashed, Ryan caught the glimpse of someone standing by a column next to his car. As he approached, the person stepped out.

"Good evening, Mr. Anderson."

Ryan recognized the voice immediately. "Roger?" he said.

"I think we have some unfinished business."

"Do we?" Ryan asked.

"My boss wants me to invite you to join our organization."

"That's very kind, but please inform your boss that I'm really not the joiner type. But do thank him for the invitation," Ryan said combining fake politeness with obvious sarcasm.

"You don't know how happy I am to hear you say that," Roger said.

"Why is that?" Ryan asked. He prepared himself for an attack.

"Because my orders were to either get you to join us or kill you."

Before the last word left Roger's lips his eyes erupted in a fiery yellow glow. Ryan felt the punch of his energy as it locked onto him and began draining his life force. But expecting something, Ryan was not caught by surprise. He knew if he did not act immediately, Roger would over power him. His strength was impressive. In one sweeping motion, driven mostly by survival instincts, Ryan leapt toward Roger and grabbed him by his neck. The second he made contact, Roger's connection was cut off. Ryan's speed and strength caught Roger completely off guard. He quickly opened his mind and threw off all restraints. Ryan had the upper hand and Roger knew it. There was no way for him to recover. His face contorted in pain and disbelief. "How could this be?" he thought as he felt his life slipping away. He and Lord Malcolm were the strongest and deadliest of the Society's assassins and he was being drained with relative ease by this nobody.

As Roger's eyes grew dark, Ryan sensed his weakness and released his grip allowing him to fall to the ground in a weakened crumpled state.

"Why are you trying to kill me?" Ryan demanded. He stared down at Roger with blazing white glowing eyes.

"I'll tell you nothing you bloody bastard!" Roger hissed looking at Ryan with raging hate in his eyes.

He pulled a gun from his coat, but his movements were slow and clumsy. Ryan's eyes flashed and locked onto him with such force that it knocked his arm back sending the gun flying across the garage floor. The impact was more than Roger could handle. He fell back limp and lifeless. Taking in the last of Roger's energy, Ryan shut his eyes as if he was savoring the flavor of a delicious piece of perfectly cooked steak. Immediately, he felt Roger's energy coursing through his body. What a feeling! He'd never absorbed so much living energy at once. It felt great. Like a tremendous rush.

"Wow!" Ryan said out loud. He leaned against his car trying to calm the energy raging within him. "That was intense."

Knowing this would need some kind of explanation, Ryan called 911. When the police arrived, he told them the man attacked him. They fought and then he just dropped dead. Ryan said he thought the guy might have had a heart attack or something. Having no reason to doubt his story, the police told Ryan he was lucky and was free to go.

As he drove out of the parking garage, Ryan continued to feel Roger's energy. It was unlike anything he'd ever encountered when feeding. Then suddenly the realization that an attempt on his life had occurred filled him with dread. "Christine!" he shouted. What if Roger had already gotten to her? He drove home as fast as he could not knowing what he would find when he got there.

Speeding like a mad man, it took only minutes for him to make it home. As the car screeched to a stop in the driveway, Ryan sprang out and ran into the house calling Christine's name. He yelled again as he ran from room to room looking for her.

Running in from the pool deck she met him in the living room.

"What's the matter? Are you okay?" she asked.

Not saying a word he walked up to her and embraced her tightly.

She held him at arm's length and looked him in the eyes. "What's happened?"

"I killed Roger" he said.

"You did what?" Christine asked stunned. "How? Where?" she demanded. The reality of what he said became clear.

"At my office. He was waiting for me in the parking garage. He said he was sent here by his boss to invite me to join their organization. When I declined, he tried to kill me," Ryan replied. "I killed him instead."

Christine was speechless, shocked by the news. But she was also impressed.

"Incredible." she said. "Roger was one of the strongest of our kind. He's been killing for centuries."

"I could feel his strength. And I could also feel his hate. He loathed me

Christine. He wanted me dead. Why?" he asked.

"Because they fear you. They fear what you might become," she said. "My father was right. You're the one we've been looking for all these long years." She noticed he was trembling. His muscles were tense and she could see the veins bulging from under his skin.

"I feel strange Christine. I've never consumed so much living energy at once. I feel so alive. So strong. Like I could lift a car or jump over a house," Ryan said. He curled his arm up and made a fist. "I feel over charged. Is that possible?" Ryan asked fascinated. The strange new sensations were causing him to tremble and shake.

"You're out of balance," she said and reached out and took his hands. Upon contact with his skin, she felt his body trembling as it fought to try and control the excess energy. "Focus on me. Look into my eyes," she commanded. As he did, her eyes glowed a soft yellow-green. He could feel her pulling the excess energy from him. It was soothing-not painful or invasive. Calming. Little by little, he felt his body relax as it became more balanced. He was also aware of another building sensation. The longer Christine stayed connected, the more sexually aroused he was becoming. His primal sexual instincts were heightened like never before. Exchanging so much energy was erotic. His desire to have her was over powering. He couldn't control himself any longer and pulled her into him kissing her passionately. She kissed him back. Without saying a word but exchanging their feelings in energy, Ryan reached down and scooped Christine off her feet. He carried her down the hall to his bedroom. The need to consume the other boiled within them. They stripped off their clothes and embraced, exchanging energy through touch and physical contact. As he ran his hands along her soft silky body he charged her with energy causing her to erupt with sensation. Christine passionately caressed him both exchanging and receiving energy as she ran her hands over his body causing it to tense and tremble in uncontrollable spasms. Roger's energy was freely flowing between them in an erotic orgy of desire and sensations. The sex was wild and uncontrolled, both craving the embrace of the other. Exchanging energy allowed each to experience what the other was feeling, only enhancing the act for both. At the height of climax, both felt an orgasmic explosion of release. The feeling was so powerful it almost caused them to pass out with pleasure.

They laid motionless for a few minutes so they could catch their breath.

"I've never felt anything like that before," Ryan said.

"It was the energy. I was feeling what you were feeling and you were feeling what I was feeling," she said breathlessly.

"So you're saying we had a double orgasm," Ryan joked.

"You could say that," Christine said as she smiled and took his hand.

It wasn't long before both were lost in a deep sleep.

Chapter 26
Time to go

As Christine awoke the next morning, she stretched out her arm expecting to find Ryan lying next to her, but felt nothing. She lifted her head and through half open eyes looked for him but the bed was empty. Sitting up, she found him. He was sitting on the floor with his legs crossed in front of a large picture window. His eyes were closed and he looked as if he was in a state of deep meditation; he sat perfectly straight with his hands resting on his knees. Christine ran her eyes up and down his chiseled back. When she noticed her fingernail marks on one of his shoulders, she smiled with satisfaction.

Christine continued watching Ryan, entranced by his stillness. It was as if he was not in his body, almost like he was a statue. If it wasn't for his occasional breathing, she would have thought he was dead. Looking past him and out into the garden, she focused on the waterfall cascading down large rocks and into a pond.

She suddenly realized not all of the rocks were rocks. One was a large owl. It was nearly two feet tall. Then she noticed another smaller owl and another. There were owls all over the rocks facing the window. They, too, had their eyes shut. Panic filled Christine. She instinctively jumped back and pressed herself against the headboard of the bed with such force that it made a loud noise as it banged against the wall.

Hearing this, Ryan snapped out of his trance and looked back at her.

"Are you okay?" he asked smiling.

"Those are owls," she said fearfully as she pointed to the window.

"I know. They're always there. They're my neighbors," he joked.

"But how can this be? Don't they affect you?"

"Yes, but I affect them too."

"Don't they drain you? Do you feel weak when you're around them?"

she asked confused and yet infatuated.

"No," Ryan said still smiling. He stood up and walked back to the bed.

"How can this be?" she asked puzzled. She nervously looked back and forth from Ryan to the owls while attempting to hide behind the sheet she was holding in front of her.

"I don't know," Ryan said. He sat down on the edge of the bed. "We seem to have reached a balance."

"A balance?"

"It's strange, but it's like we're all tapping into and sharing this, well, for lack of a better explanation, a river of energy. Alone I'm aware that it's there, but just out of my reach. But together we're able to tap into it and pull its energy in."

"Incredible," she mumbled. "So you don't need to feed on people in public through casual contact?"

"Yes and no. I can get a direct infusion by touch or close proximity, but this is different," he said pointing toward the window and yard beyond. "It's like a free flowing effect. I feel energy going in and out-like its washing through me."

"So you gain nothing? Like a neutral balance?"

"No, I do get energized. Incredibly so, but it's more like a cleansing effect. Take this morning for example. When I woke up I still felt out of balance with Roger's energy, but after sharing his energy with you and tapping the field with the owls, it helped me find a natural balance again."

"You're not worried that they might turn on you and drain you?"

"No, not at all."

"How can you be so sure?" she asked.

"I know it sounds strange, but I trust them. It's like we're all connected somehow."

"I saw Tor lying on your chest the other night. I couldn't believe it."

"I know. He told me," Ryan said.

She shot him a confused look. Ryan laughed.

"He didn't tell me with words. I could feel it in his energy."

"So you two can communicate?"

"Through shared energy, yes. To a point. I know that he knew you were outside the door."

"Unbelievable. And you're not concerned he might take too much from you while you sleep? Cats can do that you know. They don't know how to stop."

"Has it ever occurred to you that maybe they're trying to protect themselves, or that they can sense people with our gift. Maybe it's us who are a danger to them."

"We just assumed they couldn't turn it off because they were lower life forms," she said.

"Maybe they figured this out a long time ago?"

Christine sat lost in thought pondering what Ryan just said. Everything she thought she knew was being turned upside down.

"You could be right. Our arrogance never allowed us to conceive of that possibility."

"All things considered Christine, I feel humans are relatively new to whatever this thing is. We are only now just evolving this ability and only a few of us at that. But what if some animals have long since arrived at this point. Still, I feel you are not entirely wrong either about them being lower life forms. After all, we are the only species who are aware of our own mortality. Given that, we may be the only organism capable of beating or at least postponing our death. We know for example that we need to keep a balance of food and energy. Yet, I suspect at some point the absorption of energy by lower life forms dominates their cravings. They stop eating food and their bodies die. Humans however, understand the need to sustain the organic side of this and therefore can prevent starvation. I've observed this with several of the older owls that I share energy with. They feed off the field, but I've noticed their bodies withering away until one day they don't come around anymore. I assume they pass on when their bodies fail."

"To think we were so wrong about the abilities of other organisms, especially cats and owls," said Christine.

"If it wasn't for Tor, I would not have lived long enough to meet your father. Tor was keeping me alive all those months."

"How can you say this?"

"Because if Tor wanted me dead, when I was at my weakest he could have killed me. Instead, he stayed by my side the entire time. Being in his presence was the only thing that seemed to relieve the pain. I told your father this and he agreed. He also told me of the Society's feelings toward cats and owls. We figured Tor somehow sensed my condition and was trying to help. Unfortunately, he was just too small to give me what I needed."

"But why you Ryan? Why do you think he helped you?"

"I don't know. Your father thought it may be connected to the owl I rescued. Tor had been hanging around my house for weeks but it was on that night that he actually approached me. He seemed friendly enough so I let him come in to get out of the weather and he's been hanging around ever since. Maybe when the owl fed off me it changed me somehow and it was something Tor could sense; something he was familiar with and was not threatening to him. I don't know. I do know that it was the encounter with the owl that set my transformation into motion and without Tor's constant infusion of energy I would have died. I know it sounds strange but neither Tor nor the owls would ever hurt me. It's like we're all connected somehow."

"My father was right about you. You are a unique case Ryan. But your life is still in great danger. We need to get you out of here and go someplace safe. A place where I can study you and you can explore and develop your powers in safety. I fear the Society will make another attempt to stop you before you can develop into whatever it is you are going to develop into. Ryan, this river, this connection with animals, this could all just be the tip of the iceberg. There could still be so much more to come. I know my father felt this way. That's why it's so important we get out of here and go someplace the Society will never find us. And now that Roger has been killed, I'm sure

Lord Malcolm will stop at nothing to see to your elimination. You are a threat. Killing Roger only proves that. They'll do everything possible to eliminate you now."

"But why? Why are they so threatened by me. I don't want anything to do with their damn Society."

"I know Ryan, but it's what you could do to them that's the problem. Lord Malcolm has very ambitious plans to get more involved in mankind's future. He envisions himself and his kind as gods and man is beneath him and needs to be ruled. You are something he cannot control. Therefore you and any others like you represent a threat to him and his plans. I'm afraid your existence is a risk he is just not willing to take."

Taking a deep breath, Ryan carefully chose his next words.

"Until now I really couldn't care less about the Society or Lord Malcolm, but having had an attempt made on my life and learning of your father's death, the gloves are off. Who the hell is he to decide who gets this ability and who doesn't?" Ryan paused to catch his breath. "There could be others capable of far greater things if only given the chance. Lord Malcolm cannot install himself as the sole authority," he said looking out the window. "Hunting down and destroying others like us while they are still developing is cowardly." Turning back to face Christine he looked her squarely in the eyes. "This ability, whatever it is, is obviously a part of mankind's evolutionary path and needs to be allowed to develop on its own and in due time."

This is exactly what Christine and her father had been fighting for. They knew there were hundreds, maybe even thousands, of people with their abilities. And now with the fall of the council and Lord Malcolm's assassins dispatched at his will, not only would these people never be discovered, Christine and Ryan were in grave danger.

"Our only option now is to go into hiding," Christine said. She was desperate for him to believe her.

"So run and hide is the strategy. That's the plan?" he asked shaking his head and looking away.

"The Society has an enormous amount of resources at its disposal. Their hit teams will eliminate any threat they perceive to its existence. They carry out assassinations on prominent people, even world leaders. They've been doing it for centuries and they are very good at it."

Ryan hated the idea of running away. But he also knew he was out matched. At least for now. Maybe going into hiding and allowing himself to fully explore and develop his new powers and abilities was the smart move. "Who knows what I might be capable if given enough time," he thought to himself.

"Okay," he said.

Ryan paused and looked up at the ceiling as if he was thinking about something.

Christine sat up in bed.

"But with one nonnegotiable condition," he said.

"And what is that?"

He looked Christine in the eye and smiled. "Tor comes with us wherever we go."

Christine was relieved, but somewhat hesitant. A cat accompanying them? "I'm okay with that, but you may need to talk it over with him. He doesn't seem to care much for me."

"I'm sure once you two get to know each other, you'll become lifelong friends," Ryan said as he leaned down to give her a kiss. "Besides, we may need him for protection."

"Oh Ryan. How little you know about me. I'm not completely defenseless," she said giving him a sly smile.

Ryan reached up with his hand and felt over the marks she made on his shoulder. "No, you aren't."

Christine pulled him toward her.

"No I'm not." She kissed him while slowly pulling him down on top of her.

# # #

That afternoon Christine, Ryan, and Tor were ready to go. They took Christine's car to the airport where her plane was waiting. As the sun set she guided the plane into the western sky. Looking out the window as they ascended, Ryan felt sad. The only life he had ever really known was disappearing behind them. Still, as he settled into his seat and closed his eyes he tried to remain positive while pondering what the future might have in store for them all.

Chapter 27
London

"Why am I just now finding out about this?" Lord Malcolm said slamming his fist down on his desk. "Are they sure it's Roger?"

"Yes, your Lordship. His identity has been confirmed," said Captain Donald Blythe, second in command of the Society's elite assassin squad. "Roger last reported that he was going to make contact with Ryan Anderson Monday evening. That was the last we heard from him. We intercepted a police report and learned that the local police were called to the building where Mr. Anderson works. Mr. Anderson reported a man with a gun attacked him in the parking garage. It went on to say that they struggled and then the attacker suffered a fatal heart attack."

"That damn fool! I told Roger not to confront him alone." Lord Malcolm said. He stood up from his desk and walked around to face Donald.

"Are you implying that Roger was killed by Mr. Anderson?" asked Donald.

"That is exactly what I'm implying."

"With all due respect, that is not possible. Not Roger."

"But it is, Captain. It appears we have another Wellington bastard on our hands."

"Even so, how could Mr. Anderson possess the strength to kill someone like Roger? Roger was the most highly trained member of our team. There is no way a new convert, Wellington bastard or not, could kill one as strong as Roger. It's just not possible."

Captain Blythe was confused. The concept of someone besting Roger was too incomprehensible for him to believe.

"I suggest we send a team immediately, your Lordship, to deal with this Mr. Anderson. I'll see to it personally."

"I agree. Ryan Anderson must be eliminated at all costs. But, first tell me what have you learned of Christine?" Lord Malcolm asked.

"Nothing yet, sir. She has disappeared. We have a team going through the rubble of her and her father's apartments for any clues, but the fire was very thorough. Not much remains to give us any help."

"That was the idea, Captain. I'm afraid we're too late. I believe they've gone into hiding. Send your team to America anyway and see what you can find. If you discover that Mr. Anderson has gone missing, then we can only assume she is with him. Use all our resources to track them down. Everything Captain. Spare no expense. We need to find Mr. Anderson and Christine Wolchek as soon as possible."

"Yes, my Lord."

After Captain Blithe left his office, Lord Malcolm walked to the window and looked out. He looked into the distance. "So Alistair, you finally found one. Congratulations. Too bad you'll never get the chance to see what becomes of him," he said out loud to no one.

Lord Malcolm's stated goal was to eventually dominate mankind. But this was not his real objective when he took control of the Society. Appearing to be a compassionate humanitarian, concerned about mankind's future and the well-being of the planet, generated far more support than stating his true intentions. Truth be told, Lord Malcolm couldn't care less about mankind. The more dysfunctional and divided they were, the easier it would be to manipulate and control them. Lord Malcolm knew Ryan Anderson and others like him possessing strengths and abilities greater than his own could jeopardize his plans. By controlling the Society, its members, and its resources, he and his hit team could find and eliminate new converts that appeared to pose a threat to him and his ambitions. Lord Malcolm's takeover of the council was only the first step. With council opposition successfully silenced, he could dispatch his assassins at will. All threats to his control would be eliminated before they ever had a chance to become dangerous.

# # #

Weeks passed with no trace of Ryan or Christine. The Society's reach was vast. Their intelligence division had access to worldwide banking records, security systems, traffic cameras, military satellites, cell phones, and more. By using special software developed to look for and identify specific people by vocal, facial mapping, and other physical characteristics, the Society knew it was only a matter of time before Christine or Ryan used a cell phone or wandered in front of a camera somewhere in the world. The software would identify possible matches and assign a probability rating. If the rating was high enough, a team would be dispatched anywhere in the world within hours. However, weeks into the search and nothing had been found. Lord Malcolm was becoming frustrated. Even with all the resources he had at his disposal, Ryan and Christine remained elusive.

PART SIX

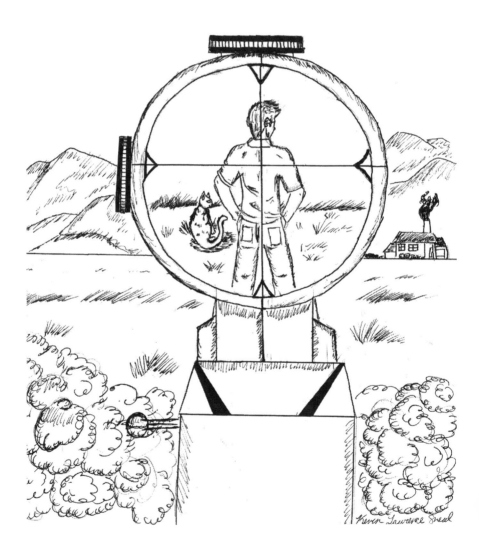

Chapter 28
Hiding Out

Two days after leaving Jacksonville, Ryan and Christine caught up with Danny in Denver. Danny had gone on to the first of many safe house locations. While waiting for Christine and Ryan, he purchased supplies and prepared for the next destination.

Christine and Ryan met him at a private airfield outside the city. It had a grass runway with no tower and was used mostly by local pilots and crop-dusters. Christine had a voice altering device attached to her plane's radio, but she still needed to limit all chances of detection. The airfield was first-come-first serve and the runway was just long enough to accommodate her jet. At one end were several old hangers large enough to hide the plane from satellites. As she taxied to a stop just inside one of the hangers, Danny walked toward it. When the door opened, Christine emerged and spotted him immediately. She ran to him and gave him a big hug.

"I was so relieved to get your message last night. I was beginning to worry," he said.

Danny noticed Ryan walking toward them. "Holy shit!" he said unable to contain his surprise.

Ryan wasn't quite sure how to take Danny's comment. He did not say anything as he stopped next to Christine.

"Danny, this is Ryan Anderson," Christine said.

"He looks just like the picture that hung in your father's office..., please forgive me. You look like someone," Danny said as he studied Ryan's facial features.

"I'm getting that a lot lately," Ryan said. He smiled and extended his hand to shake Danny's.

Tor came down the stairs of the plane and stretched before walking over to an area in the dirt and started rolling. Shaking off the dirt, he casually walked toward them.

"What's a cat doing on the plane with you?" Danny asked. He had a terrified look and tried to hide behind Christine.

"It's okay, Danny. He's a friend," Christine said laughing.

"A friend? How's that even possible?" he asked.

"That's a long story. I'll tell you all about it later. Right now maybe you two should meet." She turned to Ryan. "Would you please make the introductions?"

Tor walked up and stood next to Ryan. Ryan squatted down and scratched his head. "Danny this is Tor. Tor, Danny."

Danny stood motionless. Tor, however, walked over and rubbed his head and body against Danny's legs and purred loudly.

"Looks like he likes you," Ryan said.

Still frozen with fear, Danny tried to smile. "Great...I think."

Christine laughed as she pat Danny on his shoulder. "Trust me. That's a much better response than I got when we first met." She started back into the plane to get her things. "Okay, guys lets go. I'm tired of traveling. We need to get something to eat and get some rest. We have a long day tomorrow."

Christine and her father had rehearsed escape strategies for years. She knew what they would be up against if and when the time came for them to go on the run. She knew how to avoid cameras and did not use cell phones without a voice-altering device. Since she did not have an alternate ID for Ryan yet, she decided the United States would have to be where they hid until she had time to put the proper documentation together for him. Fortunately, the United States is a huge country and offered many off the grid places to hide.

Chapter 29
Settling In

Isolated deep in the mountains of Colorado, Danny, Christine, and Ryan began to feel relaxed and safe. The cabin they rented was ideal. Its seclusion was perfect; not another soul for miles. Danny did a good job finding the off-the-beaten-path hide out.

Several miles away was the small town of Rochester which was also ideal. It's residents loathed the modern world. Though the latest technology was widely available, the town's people chose to keep things simple. Outsiders wanting to change things were not welcome. The trio of refugees tried to make it a point not to go into Rochester often, but when they did, they felt somewhat safe. There were no traffic cameras or elaborate security systems because there was no crime. Even store transactions were carried out by old-fashioned cash registers. The town appeared trapped in the 1950s and was in no hurry to move into the future. Christine knew technology was a constant danger. Cell phones and internet connections were being monitored by the Society. She knew their reach was global and that Lord Malcolm would stop at nothing to find them. Staying off the grid was their only chance and secluded mountain communities like Rochester were the perfect places to buy time.

Having been on the run for months, they finally settled into somewhat normal routines. Ryan was accustomed to waking early and the crisp fall mornings were too good to pass up. The mountains were beautiful, especially at daybreak.

After feeding Tor and drinking a cup of coffee, Ryan and Tor began their day as they often did by going outside to take in the morning air and enjoy the scenery. As had become routine, they walked down a short path to a rocky bluff over-looking the valley below. Taking up their normal sitting positions, it wasn't long before both settled into a deep state of meditation.

Christine was also an early riser. Knowing Ryan and Tor were probably already out of the cabin, she sat in the kitchen enjoying her morning coffee. Looking out the window she saw the two of them sitting on the bluff. Though Tor seemed to be tolerating her presence, her relationship with him had only improved slightly since they began traveling together. Tor made it clear that he was willing to put up with her, but that was about as good as it would get. Christine remained guarded in his presence, but they seemed to have settled on an uneasy truce. Still, she knew the bond Ryan and Tor shared was special and that somehow Tor would play a big role in helping Ryan grow into whatever it is he would become.

Christine often joined the two of them in their morning meditation. Ryan had gotten much better at tapping the ever present undercurrent of energy. He was capable of drawing from it on his own but preferred the company of others when doing so. Alone, he found it difficult to direct and focus. Other lifeforms present made controlling it easier. He also knew if he could harness this power and draw from it at will, he would have an endless supply of energy when needed.

In the months that they had been on the run, Ryan discovered that he could move objects by manipulating their energy signatures. Even inanimate objects could be moved using the energy of the undercurrent. The size of the object did not matter. Drawing in just the right amount of energy and focusing it on what he desired was the key. Learning to do it was more a feeling than anything else. The more he practiced the better he got but controlling and focusing the power was exhausting and required considerable concentration, yet he knew it was possible. He could feel that this ability was natural. He just had to find the right combination of concentration and control. Tor and the others helped here. They gave him the ability to focus. By using them to draw off some of the energy, Ryan found it easier to manipulate. With Tor, Christine, and Danny at his side, Ryan was able to channel the energy into extraordinary abilities. These months of discovery had been exciting for all of them.

Christine was just about to turn away from the window when she caught a glimpse of something moving in the woods not far from where Ryan and Tor were sitting. Watching the shape get closer she realized what it was, a mountain lion. Panic filled her. She didn't know what to do. It emerged from the woods and headed across the small clearing directly toward Ryan and Tor. Desperate to warn them, she was about to beat on the window to scare it away, but something about the way it was moving made her stop. It didn't look like it was going to attack. Instead, it looked more like it was joining them. As it got closer Christine noticed Tor turn to face the approaching predator without alarm. Christine knew if Tor saw the mountain lion then Ryan had to know it was there. The big cat walked up next to Ryan. Tor was on Ryan's right side and the large cat was on his left. The mountain lion laid down and assumed the position of a sphinx within an arm's length of Ryan. Fascinated, Christine watched as the three of them sat motionless for what seemed like an eternity. She knew Ryan was tapping the energy field. She knew he knew the Lion was there. The three of them were all feeding on the energy. *Amazing* she thought to herself. *This is truly incredible.* Captivated by the scene before her she did not notice Danny approach.

"Is that a mountain lion lying next to Ryan and Tor?" he asked amazed.

"That's exactly what it is," Christine replied. She could not take her eyes off what she was seeing.

"Uh... Should we do something?" he asked.

Before she could reply they saw Ryan extend his arm and pet the large cat on its neck and back. Tor walked over and rubbed affectionately along its side and under its chin. For a few seconds the three of them looked like long lost friends recently reunited. Then, the big cat stood up and stretched before walking back into the woods and disappearing into the underbrush. Ryan also stood and stretched. "Okay, boy. Let's get some chow."

When they walked in Christine's eyes were huge.

"That was amazing! You knew he was there? You petted him! Tor..." she was unable to continue.

Ryan smiled. "She was there and yes. I've been feeling her presence for a few days. But today was the first time she approached. She's a mother with two cubs around here somewhere so be careful on your walks," Ryan said.

"Great. Just my luck I escape the Society only to be eaten by a mother mountain lion defending her cubs. It just doesn't get better than this," Danny mumbled as he took a cup of coffee and walked out of the kitchen.

"At first I thought she was going to have the two of you for breakfast."

"Not this morning anyway," Ryan said. He reached around Christine and hugged her good morning. "And speaking of breakfast, what do we have to eat around here, I'm starving." He continued to hold Christine in a warm embrace.

# # #

As the weeks and months passed, Christine and Danny were constantly amazed by Ryan's progress. With each passing day, Ryan made new discoveries. Not having a gym, he used the natural landscape for exercise and conditioning. He drew from the undercurrent and used the energy for strength and endurance when exercising in the rugged terrain. He could run faster and jump farther than he'd ever been able to do before. He use to hate to run. Now he looked forward to it. During his runs he would often push himself, sometimes jumping huge rocky gorges and climbing steep rock walls with only his hands and feet. The natural environment provided many physical challenges and using energy from the undercurrent Ryan eagerly tackled them all. Christine and Danny frequently commented to each other about how proud her father would be by Ryan's developments.

It had become routine for Christine to record Ryan's daily progress in her journal. Since his case was unprecedented, she and Danny thoroughly and carefully documented everything. Ryan's case was unusual enough and having the ability to be a part of his growth and discovery was a rare privilege. Being on the front lines of discovery was always exciting, but actually being a part of the process was a dream come true for them. And

Ryan was also happy to have them there. It was comforting to him to have the support and encouragement of his friends.

As she recorded the day's notes in her journal, Christine paused and looked out the window. Letting her mind drift she entertained thoughts of her father and his excitement when telling her about Ryan. She remembered her father's enthusiasm the night she picked him up from the airport. Recalling him chuckle and slap his knee as he told her about his experience with Ryan made her smile. "I wish you could see this Dad, you would be so proud."

Chapter 30
The Cub

Late one night several weeks after sharing energy with the mountain lion Ryan was abruptly awakened from a deep sleep. Sitting bolt upright in bed he felt something was wrong. He looked over at Christine who had been awakened by his sudden movement.

"What's wrong?" she asked still sleepy.

"I don't know." Ryan replied. He paused and then shut his eyes trying to focus on the feeling. "Oh no!" He threw the sheet off and jumped out of bed.

"What is it? What's the matter?" Christine asked now completely awake.

"It's the mountain lion. She's very upset. Her energy is wild and panicked. I think something's happened to one of her cubs." Ryan quickly put on his jeans and boots.

"Where are you going?" Christine was dressing, too.

"To find her if I can. Her energy is screaming for help. We need to hurry!"

By the time they made their way to the back door, Tor was already waiting.

"You feel it too, don't you boy?" Ryan asked, looking down at him. Grabbing a flashlight off the counter and opening the door he motioned for everyone to go out.

"Lead the way, buddy."

Tor, led them to a small clearing over looking a cliff with several deep jagged and eroded gullies descending hundreds of feet to the valley floor below. They noticed at once the mother mountain lion pacing excitedly along the top of one of the jagged openings. Looking around Ryan saw a cub anxiously waiting next to some bushes on the edge of the clearing. Its eyes were huge as it looked on.

"The cub!" Ryan said.

"What cub?" Christine asked.

"The other cub must have fallen into that ravine and she can't get to it."

"Is it still alive?" Christine asked.

Closing his eyes and concentrating on the cub's energy Ryan could feel its faint heartbeat. "Yes, but just barely. We need to get to it fast if we're going to have any chance of saving it."

Cautiously approaching the mother lion, Ryan made his way to the edge of the cliff. He had to lean far over the edge to see. He shined the flashlight down into the narrow ravine and located the cub. Seeing a way to climb down Ryan descended about twenty feet to where the cub was laying. The small cub had fallen over the cliff and down in between a narrow outcropping of rocks. The mother lion could not reach into the rocks to get the cub out. But Ryan could just position himself to reach in between the rocks and gently pick up the cub's limp body. Ryan quickly made his way back up the cliff. Once he reached the top, he carried the cub to the clearing and gently laid it on the ground.

Christine covered her mouth to try and hide her emotions.

"Oh, God. The poor baby."

Ryan felt the mother mountain lion's concern. She gently licked her small cub causing it to quietly whimper, but its condition was rapidly deteriorating. Ryan could feel its life force fading. The mother lion looked at Ryan with desperation. Reading her emotions, he nodded to her and put one hand on the cub's broken body. At the same time he closed his eyes and connected with the undercurrent.

Knowing what he was attempting to do, Christine, Tor and the mother mountain lion all focused and helped Ryan control the energy. He channeled it through himself and into the cub. Being physically connected to the cub, Ryan was able to assess the damage in the cub's body. He then focused the energy to the damaged areas and repaired them.

After a few minutes the cub began to regain consciousness. Once he felt all the damage had been repaired, Ryan removed his hand from the cub's body. Almost at once the small cub was on his feet. The other cub came running over and tackled her brother with a loving playful embrace. Their mother joined the playful duo and bathed both cubs with motherly affection. Ryan, Christine and Tor watched the reunited family frolic before them.

"Amazing. You were able to bond with the cub and channel energy to heal its injuries. How did you know to do that?" Christine asked.

"I have no idea. It just felt like I needed to touch him to establish a better connection. Once I had hold of him it was as if we were one being. I could feel his injuries so I treated them as if they were my own and it worked," he said. "It really wasn't that hard once you guys joined in and helped me control the flow."

Christine was speechless. Having the ability to heal oneself was not uncommon with their kind but having the ability to heal another was unheard of. This had never been witnessed before.

Ryan put his arm around Christine and gently hugged her as they watched the happy family play. They could hear Tor purring loudly. He looked up at Ryan with wide excited eyes.

After a few minutes of playful relief, the mother lion walked over to Ryan. She gently nudged his leg with her head. Ryan reached down and rubbed her on the back of her neck.

"My pleasure, old girl. Any time," he said.

She turned and walked down a narrow path with both cubs following closely behind her.

"Did she actually thank you?" Christine asked.

"In her own way, yes."

"I guess we've discovered yet another talent you possess."

"Yeah? And what's that?" Ryan asked putting his arm around her. They walked back toward the cabin with Tor leading the way.

"Healer," she replied.

"In all fairness, I did have help," he said. He paused for a moment. "Thanks Tor. I couldn't have done it without you, buddy."

"Aren't you forgetting someone?" Christine asked. She gave him a teasing smile.

Ryan pulled her into him. "I was going to thank you privately once we got back inside," he whispered in her ear.

Chapter 31

A night out

As Christine sat curled up in a large chair next to the fireplace covered in a blanket reading a book, she looked at Ryan and Tor lying on the couch across the room taking a late afternoon nap. It had been seven months since Ryan agreed to leave Jacksonville and go into hiding with Christine. Even though he did his best to try and hide how much he missed going out and interacting with the public, Christine could feel that he was getting bored with the daily routine. She knew Ryan was a social person and enjoyed being with people.

Prior to meeting Ryan, Christine knew little about him. Her father's file only contained generic information about his medical condition. But after meeting him and getting to know him she was impressed. Not only was he developing unprecedented powers and abilities, but he was also both fascinating and well rounded. He was young in years, but his intellect and quick wit gave him the persona of a man of experience. Christine often remarked to Danny how natural Ryan was with his powers. He was finding new ways to grow and expand his abilities daily. Tapping into the undercurrent was getting easier with every connection. It was obvious that Ryan was stronger and far more evolved than any of the other members in the Society, even the elders. A fact Christine knew Lord Malcolm was also well aware of. A fact she knew would certainly have gotten Ryan killed if they had stayed in Jacksonville.

This was exactly what she and her father had wanted. Both knew that others like Ryan were out there. They knew this stage of mankind's development was just at the beginning. They wanted to follow and document the evolution of someone such as Ryan and had been searching for years. Unfortunately, Lord Malcolm was also aware of this and would stop at nothing to prevent others like Ryan from ever coming into existence. His fear and selfish desire to monopolize this ability led to the creation of his hit squads. By using and controlling the Society's resources, Lord Malcolm now had the power to seek out and eliminate those who might one day be a threat to him.

Christine knew it was just a matter of time before the Society caught up with them. But she was determined to help Ryan grow and become all he could before it was too late. She hoped he might be able to reach a state of existence where the Society could not or would not dare try and harm him.

Watching Ryan and Tor nap, Christine smiled. She looked over at Danny who was deeply engrossed in a book.

"Okay everyone. Get up. Enough of this loafing around. Let's go into town and make a night of it," she said.

"And what brought this on may I ask?" Danny said looking up from his book.

"Let's just say I'm tired of looking at the same faces all the time. The last snow of the season has melted and spring is here. Besides, not killing each other after being cooped up together for seven whole months deserves some kind of celebration," she responded with a big smile.

Ryan sat up yawning and stretching. Tor jumped off him to the floor yawning and stretching as well. Christine and Danny laughed at the sight of their simultaneous yawning and stretching.

"I agree. I think we deserve to treat ourselves to a night out. And I think I deserve a break from being your science project for at least one night," Ryan said with a wink and a smile.

"Well, I certainly have no objections. I'm tired of feeling like the third wheel around here," Danny said grinning.

"It's settled then. Let's get cleaned up and head into town for drinks," Christine said removing her blanket and standing up. She made a run for the only full bathroom in the cabin. "I call first dibs on the shower!" she said. Before Ryan or Danny had time to react she had darted into the bathroom and shut the door.

"It'll be cold showers for us," Ryan said to Danny. He laid back down on the couch to continue his nap.

Danny stood and stretched then made his way down the hall to a small half bath under the stairs. He flushed the toilet which was immediately followed by a scream from the bathroom.

As Danny passed by the sofa on his way to his chair, Ryan held up his hand for a high five.

"Nice job."

Danny smacked his hand grinning from ear-to-ear.

Chapter 32
Rochester

Rochester was a small town of about 800 people that catered mostly to tourists. The entire area was rich in natural beauty. Rocky mountain formations, stunning waterfalls, crystal clear lakes and streams, and numerous winding trails made for breathtaking scenic vistas. The locals had successfully kept resort developers from ruining the peace and tranquility of the area by passing strict zoning measures. The outskirts of the town offered a few select campground sites for tourists to enjoy and experience nature. In town there were two small hotels and numerous bed and breakfast establishments, but nothing large scale. Chain stores, international hotels, and other types of large commercial businesses were not permitted. In many ways, Rochester was a time capsule of a distant past. Only small, locally-owned establishments were allowed. The town's residents were determined to maintain the unique atmosphere of the area. And this is what attracted tourists to Rochester. Fortunately, the local residents were on board with this plan. Presenting a united front to outside pressures helped deter such influences. Not only did the locals resist growth and development, they also loathed technology adding to the town's charm. Many privately enjoyed connecting to the internet, using computers, cell phones, iPads and the like on a personal basis, but business wise, they were frowned on.

These were the reasons Christine and her father determined this community was a possible hideout in the event they ever had to go on the run. Not having time or the immediate resources at first to generate the proper paperwork for Ryan to leave the United States, Christine opted to temporarily hide out in this secluded remote mountain wilderness. Knowing the Society's capabilities, she felt they would be safer in a town with as little technology as possible.

Rochester also had a great saloon called The Station which was frequented by locals and tourists alike. Located just off Main Street, the three story building was one of the largest buildings in town. The Station had a colorful history. Built in the late 1880s along one of only a handful of westward railroad routes, its original purpose was to be a saloon, casino, and brothel for the hordes of people who came to the area in search of gold and silver. For several decades, it served its customers well in all capacities until prostitution was outlawed. Still, the building continued to thrive as one of the town's more popular local saloons.

Rochester was a tough frontier mining town in its early days and The Station was at the center of many tales of gunfights, murders, and vigilante justice. Though the town had gone through many transformations over the years, The Station, and other prominent buildings along its main street, looked almost unchanged. Knowing its history and having heard some interesting stories about the wild and lawless early frontier days, Ryan, Christine, and Danny were looking forward to visiting The Station and getting a taste of Rochester's local folklore.

Located eight miles from their secluded mountain cabin, driving to Rochester to buy provisions had become routine. The area was heavily forested with breath-taking mountain views uncloaked along the winding two-lane road into town. Each of them looked forward to the drive when a trip for supplies was necessary.

After arriving and parking their car in a public parking lot, they decided to walk up and down the main street before heading to The Station. It had been a long time since the three of them had been out in public so they decided to make the most of this rare outing. Most of the shops were closed since it was early evening but they still enjoyed window shopping and playing tourist.

The cool spring night air felt nice as they walked the town streets. Christine put her arm around Ryan and pulled him close to her.

"Do you think Tor will be mad at us for not bringing him?" she asked half joking, half serious.

"Naw. I doubt he'll even realize we've left the cabin. Last I saw him he was crashed out on a pile of your clean clothes," Ryan said causing Christine to playfully smack his arm.

When they reached The Station they walked up three steps to a beautiful 12-foot wide wooden porch that completely surrounded the outside of the saloon's ground floor. It had floor-to-ceiling windows which were open so people could walk in and out through them at will. The porch also had tables and chairs spread evenly about next to the railing.

Upon entering the saloon through the ornate leaded-glass front doors, the trio was stopped in their tracks by what they saw before them. The room was huge. There was an elegant wooden curved staircase immediately to their right which led to an open landing running all the way around the inside of the room on the second floor. Each room upstairs had the original room number on its door left over from The Station's inn and brothel days. Downstairs, along the wall beyond the staircase, were several booths with slightly raised partitions between them. To the left was the original intricately carved wooden and glass saloon bar that stretched almost the entire length of this side of the room. Three bartenders were busy working behind the bar. Directly in front of them on the far wall was a sizable stage set up for live music later in the evening. And located throughout the room were tables and chairs sparsely filled at the moment. Spotting an empty booth about midway down the wall Christine led the way.

They ordered a round of drinks.

"Very neat place. It's like we time-traveled back to the days of the early American wild west," Danny said.

"You almost feel like a gunfight might break out at any minute," Ryan said jokingly as he gazed around the saloon.

After several drinks and feeling more relaxed, the group made their way to empty bar stools at the far end of the long bar. They were fortunate to get the stools-the rest of the bar was standing room only Wild West style. From this position they could see the entire room. It was a great vantage point for people watching.

Around 9:00pm, three guys walked up next to where they were sitting and ordered beers. They reminded Ryan of his band. He knew they were musicians; they just had that look about them. He didn't even have to read their energy to know.

"Are you guys the entertainment tonight?" Ryan asked striking up a conversation.

"Yep. If that's what you want to call it. I'm afraid it's just acoustics tonight. Our singer is in the National Guard and is on assignment for the next couple of weeks."

"What kind of music do you play?"

"Mostly we're a cover band and do a variety of songs, classics, current and everything in between."

At this point an intoxicated Christine joined the conversation. "Why don't you see if you know any of their songs? If you do, maybe you can help them out."

Smiling at Christine's drunken demeanor, Ryan laughed. "It doesn't really work that way. You can't just drop one singer in to replace another," he said.

"You sing?" one of the guys asked.

"I use to. I worked with a group of guys who performed on the weekends. I also helped them make demos from time to time, stuff like that."

"Don't be so modest. The first time I saw you, you guys had packed that building out. It was standing room only! There were probably 3000 people there just to see you!" Christine blurted out trying to push the point.

"You sing? Really?" Danny asked surprised. "Are you any good?"

"He has a great voice!" Christine blurted out again.

"Well this I have to see!" said a somewhat drunk Danny.

Ryan laughed at the two of them. "I guess I know who'll be driving us home tonight, he said."

"Hey Fred, do you have a list of tonight's line up?" a band member asked.

Fred handed him a folded piece of paper. The guy handed it to Ryan.

"Know any of these songs?" he asked.

Ryan looked at the list nodding his head. "I'm, pretty familiar with most of them. We performed many of these songs ourselves."

"Great! Then we have our singer boys!" Fred said.

"Hold on guys. It's been months since I've sung anything. I mean I'd hate to damage your local reputation."

"No worries man, our singer sucks most of the time anyway so unless you're really really bad, I doubt you'll be any worse," a member said laughing as he put his hand on Ryan's shoulder. "My name is Brad, by the way, and this is Scott and Fred."

"Ryan. And these two drunks are Christine and Danny."

"Well nice to meet you all. Now ma'am, if you'll excuse Ryan, we need to get him to the stage and get ready."

"Have fun," said Christine as she waved them off.

Ryan shook his head and pointed at Christine. "You'll get yours later," he yelled over the growing crowd.

"I'm looking forward to it! Now go show Danny what you can do," she yelled back as he headed to the stage with the others.

Though Christine pretended to be drunk, she knew what she was doing. She felt this situation provided the perfect opportunity for Ryan to let loose and do something he loved. She knew it had been hard for him to give up everything and go on the run with the two of them. Yet he never once complained. He had done everything she and Danny had asked of him over the past many months without so much as a peep. At times, she felt he kept his regrets to himself on purpose since her father had made the ultimate sacrifice. She appreciated his compliance and knew it was risky to be so publicly visible, but she felt okay with him performing this one time.

"So he's really going to do it?" Danny asked surprised.

"Order another drink and get comfortable. I have a feeling we are going to be here for a while," she replied.

At 9:30, the lights blinked a few times and Brad took the microphone to introduce the band.

"Tonight we have a special guest preforming with us. Since Carl is on duty this weekend this kind stranger from the crowd has volunteered to step in for the evening and cover. So everyone please give it up for Ryan. The tourist from out of town!"

Immediately the band plunged into the first song of the evening. The music was fast and to Ryan's surprise sounded good. He found it easy to improvise as he performed. After the first few songs, Ryan had found the band's rhythm and was performing to his standards. The guys were impressed. After the first set the crowd erupted with applause and cheers. Taking a quick break, Ryan and the band planned a new song line up and went back out to perform. The crowd filled the inside of the saloon and spilled out onto the porch. Christine smiled. "What did I tell you?" she asked. "He's pretty good isn't he?"

Danny tried to remain nonchalant. "Not bad. Not bad at all," Danny said as he patted the bar in rhythm with the beat and attempting to sing along.

After several sets, followed by more collaboration over drinks about what to perform next, they finally wrapped up around midnight. The band members were delighted to find that Ryan knew most of their cover songs. Ryan's voice and ability to keep up with the rhythm made for one of their best performances ever.

After helping the band break the stage down and pack up, Ryan, Christine, Danny and the band members met for drinks at the bar.

"Thanks for helping out tonight," Brad said holding up his glass.

"It was an honor gentlemen," Ryan said clinking his glass into Brad's.

The group drank and hung out until closing. This evening was exactly what the three of them needed. The months on the run had been hard, but tonight they put that all behind them for a few hours and attempted to act like normal people enjoying a much deserved vacation.

# # #

Angie Simmons Facebook Post:

"Spent the evening listening to a local band in Rochester, Colorado. The music was awesome and the band members were hot, I'm posting a picture. Check out the lead singer!

Tomorrow we're moving on to the next family experience. Can't wait to get home..."

Posted 1:33am Sunday.

Chapter 33
Capture

Spring had been in full bloom for over a month. The snow had melted and Ryan and Tor got back into the routine of waking early and taking a long, meandering walk. They followed a path through the woods to a stream and small lake then returned following a different winding path leading them back to the cabin. Walking with Tor was quite the challenge. He was not a dog, after all, and had a mind of his own. He had to investigate every smell and curiosity he discovered along their journey. Ryan found it easier to walk and not wait for him. Eventually Tor would come running at full speed to catch up. Even when he lost sight of Tor, he stayed connected through his mind. He could scan the area to make sure no predators were waiting to jump either one of them. Ryan felt better about leaving Tor to his investigations knowing the area was safe.

Ryan enjoyed his morning walks. Though he appreciated Christine and Danny's company, getting away for a while allowed him to think and clear his head. It had been two days since performing at The Station. The euphoric high had not worn off yet. He loved singing and did not realize how much he missed it until he was on stage again.

These months of growth and discovery had been exciting, but it wasn't the same. He always enjoyed being the center of attention. Maybe it was because he didn't have a warm, loving environment growing up. Performing through sports and academics as a child and through competition at work and entertaining by singing as an adult provided the outlet he needed to fill an ever present void. He often wondered about his real parents. On occasion he asked Mr. Blake about them, but never got much information. Having been adopted as an infant and then orphaned so soon didn't give him a chance to know his adoptive parents either.

After graduating from college Ryan attempted to find out who his real parents were, but immediately hit a dead end. Mr. Blake knew very little about the situation. Ryan's adoptive parents left for an extended trip one weekend and when they returned they had Ryan with them. They told friends and family that he had been adopted out of state, but never revealed anything more. In settling his parents' estate Mr. Blake had to clarify some aspects of Ryan's adoption. He traced what paperwork he could to a Catholic organization in Virginia. When he tried to contact the organization he learned it closed after a devastating fire destroyed the orphanage. Many children were killed and all records were lost. Ryan frequently wondered about his biological parents. For years he believed getting such information was hopeless. But then with Dr. Wolchek and Christine entering his life he was again encouraged. Knowing Christine's father had been following his bloodline Ryan hoped she would be able to help him learn more but this was not the case. Christine explained to Ryan that after the council ordered all of Robert Wellington's descendants terminated, her father altered documents to hide the bloodline. But, after saving countless offspring he lost track of many others. It wasn't until his first meeting with Ryan that Dr. Wolchek knew with certainty who and what he was. His physical resemblance to his distant ancestor convinced him immediately. As for records and other information, Christine was as much in the dark as he was.

On his walks, Ryan often reflected on various aspects of his life. Had there been clues along the way? Were there signs giving him hints about what he was to become? He did not remember anything specific. Until his encounter with the owl he couldn't recall anything that would have led him to believe any of his new life was possible. He thought to himself how unbelievable the whole experience has been. Sometimes even asking himself if this was really happening. But, then the reality would hit him. He was on the run. He'd been forced to leave the only life he knew behind in order to try and become whatever it is he was to become. He knew an attempt had been made on his life and that he was being hunted. Fortunately, he had the help of three good friends to see him through all that lay ahead.

Walking ahead of Tor, Ryan couldn't shake an uneasy feeling he'd had since starting their walk. Something didn't feel right. It's not that he sensed danger, it was more that he wasn't sensing much of anything at all. There was a storm building to the west of their location which was supposed to be moving their way by early afternoon so he figured maybe that was why he felt strange. He kept his guard up just in case.

#

"I have him in range, sir. Your orders?"

"When you have a clear shot, shoot to kill. I repeat shoot to kill. This one is not to be captured."

"Yes, sir. Shoot to kill, sir"

#

As Ryan was rounding the last corner of the winding trail he felt a sudden impact to his chest, followed by two more. It felt as if the air had been punched out of his lungs. He stood for a moment then fell to his knees. Clutching his chest with his hands he saw blood. It hit him. He'd been shot. His mind was very aware. Everything was suddenly very clear. There was a sniper in the woods. The Society found them! His mind was sharp, but his body was severely injured and dying.

Tor came running up the Path having sensed Ryan's condition. Focusing all the power Ryan could manage to gather given his dwindling state, he pushed Tor into some nearby brush with the power of his mind just in time to save him from two more rounds that hit the ground where Tor had been standing. Through a large burst of energy, he told Tor to RUN! Unable to remain focused and conscious, he fell to the ground, eyes open, staring out with an empty, lifeless gaze.

A moment later a man appeared in camouflage and reached down to check his pulse placing his fingers on his neck. Ryan was lying on his back looking into the sky with empty eyes. The man examined the grouping of the shots on Ryan's chest.

"Not bad," he said out loud. "Not bad at all. All fatal," He pushed the call button on his headset. "Subject one is terminated," he said.

"Is the kill confirmed?" a voice asked through the headphones.

"Yes, sir. I'm standing over subject one now. Some of my better work if I say so myself."

"Good work, soldier. Report back to your position. If any of the other subjects manage to escape from the cabin I want you to be able to see where they go," said the headphone voice.

"Yes, sir. What about the body sir?"

"Let it rot."

"Understood."

# # #

Standing at the kitchen window Christine did not see Ryan or Tor on their usual perch of out cropped rocks. Figuring they were still on their walk she did not think much of it and turned away from the window to focus on preparing breakfast. When she turned, a man was standing in the kitchen opposite her dressed in full camouflage and pointing a gun at her. Christine froze in panic.

"Morning, Miss Wolchek. Good to see you again," said an arrogant and cocky voice.

Christine gained her composure quickly.

"Captain Blythe. I should have known. Still doing your master's bidding I see. What do you want from us?" she asked already knowing the answer.

He gave her a twisted smile. "I've been sent here to eliminate Mr. Anderson and return the lost sheep to their rightful flock. Lord Malcolm was very clear that he did not want you harmed. Not yet anyway."

"Bastard! I'll never go with you," Christine threw the coffee, cup and all at the Captain and tried to make a run for the back door. As soon as she opened it, she was blocked by another soldier. When she turned to try another way out, Blythe cut her off and smashed her in the head with the butt of his weapon. Christine felt the violent impact then fell to the floor unconscious.

Bending over to check her, Blythe suddenly felt a tremendous burst of pain come from his neck and shoulders causing him to loose balance and fall to the floor next to Christine in a dazed state. When the other soldier turned to see what had happened, a large iron frying pan caught him under his chin with such force that it sent him flying across the kitchen.

"Christine!" Danny shouted. But, before he had time to go to her another soldier appeared in the kitchen from the dining room with his weapon drawn.

"Freeze!" The soldier said pointing his gun at Danny.

Out of nowhere, Tor jumped onto a nearby counter- his eyes blazing yellow green. The soldier panicked and recoiled in fright stumbling back into the dining area where he tripped and fell to the floor.

Danny heard other soldiers entering the house. He grabbed Tor and took off out the now unguarded back door. Within seconds he and Tor disappeared into the nearby underbrush.

"Lookout come in," Captain Blythe said into the microphone of his headset.

"Here sir," the lookout's voice crackled back.

"We lost Overstreet. Do you have his location?"

"Affirmative sir. He and the cat are..." the soldier stopped talking in mid-sentence. Staring through his scope, lying on his stomach looking at Danny and Tor the lookout became aware of hot, steamy air on the back of his neck in repeated hard bursts. In one rapid turning motion, the soldier flipped over to be confronted by the mother mountain lion. Before he could react, she had his entire neck in her mouth. He managed to scream before she ripped the soldier's neck from his body.

Hearing the commotion over the radio, Blythe ordered the soldier to report, but got nothing but static. "We have a man down, lets go," said Blythe. They ran to the back door only to be stopped in their tracks.

The four soldiers could not believe what they were seeing. The trees, rocks, and lawn furniture were covered by owls, hawks, and eagles. The sight was surreal. Frozen with fear, and also amazement, the soldiers did not know what to do. Blythe finally came to his senses and with a calm voice ordered the men back inside the cabin. They picked up Christine and left through the front door. They jumped into their waiting truck and sped away.

Danny and Tor made it to another hidden out cropping of rocks and were trying to catch their breath.

"Thanks, old man," Danny managed to say between deep breaths as he looked at Tor and steadied himself against one of the large rocks. Tor looked up at him and screeched excitedly as he looked at Danny with big wide eyes.

"What is it, old man? Remember I'm not Ryan. I have no idea what you want," Danny said.

Screeching, Tor stood up on Danny pawing at his legs then pushing off and running a little down a path before stopping to look back at Danny.

"You want me to follow you?" he asked.

Screeching again, Tor ran off down a trail with Danny doing his best to keep up. Moments later Danny and Tor entered the small clearing where Ryan's lifeless body was still lying.

"No!" Danny cried. "This can't be." Tor took a position next to Ryan's head looking at Danny with a pleading look to help him.

Danny knelt down to check Ryan's pulse. He could not find one. He looked at Tor as he felt tears welling. Out of nowhere the mother mountain lion appeared from the underbrush and also took a position next to Ryan. She sat as still as an Egyptian Sphinx and stared at him. Tor also assumed a focused state. The sky began to darken. Danny looked up to see flocks of owls and other birds landing in the trees above them. "Amazing," he mumbled out loud. He was bewildered but not afraid by what he saw. Then, as if a switch turned on, all the eyes of the animals and birds began to glow. Feeling the energy flowing Danny knew what they were attempting to do. He felt it all around him. He sat down next to Ryan and went into a state of meditation finding it easy to join the animals. In a burst of excitement, Danny could feel Ryan's energy. He was alive, but just barely. He was hanging on, but did not have the ability to heal himself. The damage was too great. Understanding this, Danny was able to be a conduit of sorts. Being human helped focus the energy given by the animals so Ryan could use it to repair his wounds. The animals knew how to generate the power and Danny enabled Ryan to focus it to where he needed to heal his body. Danny watched in stunned amazement as Ryan's wounds were healing and closing right before his eyes. Suddenly, Ryan's body convulsed in a massive spasm as he gulped in a large breath of air. It was a violent reaction and was followed by another. Then another. Soon, he was breathing normally. His eyes blinked open and Danny could see life had returned.

"Welcome back. You have some friends here who were very worried about you," Danny said.

Ryan pulled himself up and rested on his elbows.

"Thanks guys," he said in a raspy voice. Tor was beside himself. He excitedly rubbed against Ryan and purred loudly. The mother mountain lion nudged him with her head. Ryan pet her neck in gratitude before she turned and disappeared into the underbrush. Within a few minutes, the owls and other birds flew away leaving just the three of them.

"I thought you were dead," Danny said as he sat next to Ryan petting Tor who was now rubbing against his knees.

"It was close. After I realized I'd been shot, I tapped the undercurrent. It was strange. I felt weak, but I also felt incredibly strong. I found the mother lion and asked her to take care of the sniper, then sent Tor to the cabin to warn you guys."

"Did you call the birds and lion to help you?"

"No, they did that themselves and Tor brought you here on his own too. I was fading fast at that point and was barely able to keep a connection with my body. If you hadn't shown up when you did I don't think I would have been able to come back."

"Come back?"

"My body was dying, but I still had a presence. I was still me just in a different state," he said. He paused a moment taking it all in. "It was an interesting experience my friend."

"They have Christine," he said broken-hearted.

Ryan finally stood and brushed off the leaves and dirt from his blood-soaked clothes. He looked at Danny. "Not for long. It's time I finally meet this Lord Malcolm face-to-face."

They made their way back up the trail. "Great, the fun never ends," Danny said sarcastically.

"Thanks for helping save my life by the way," Ryan responded. He put his hand on Danny's shoulder as they walked.

"You're welcome. But we'll probably both end up getting killed in England," Danny said.

"Probably."

When they returned to the cabin, Ryan cleaned himself up while Danny finalized all the necessary documentation they would need for the trip. Creating new ID's had been Christine's first priority after leaving Jacksonville. She knew it might be necessary to leave again in a hurry and wanted to have more options. After retrieving the new ID's as well as packing any other items they would need for the trip, they were on their way. It turned out that Danny was also an accomplished pilot. After fueling the plane and making it ready for the flight, Danny, Ryan and Tor boarded and took off down the bumpy runway.

"Hold on Christine, help is on the way," Ryan said as the plane ascended into the darkening eastbound sky.

PART SEVEN

Kevin Laurence Sneed

Chapter 34
England

Christine felt her senses returning to her. She laid still trying to gather her thoughts through the pounding pain in her head. Dazed and confused she remembered trying to escape from Captain Blythe in the kitchen before feeling a powerful blow. As her eyes blinked open all she could see was the glare of a bright light shining above her. When her vision cleared, she realized she was staring into the reflective crystals of a brilliant chandelier hanging high overhead. Reaching out with her hands she could feel she was lying on fine linen. Holding her head to try and quiet the pain, Christine sat up slowly and realized she was in a large, beautifully furnished bedroom. She wondered where she was.

"It's nice to see that you're awake. We were beginning to worry about you," a familiar voice said from behind her.

Recognizing the voice, Christine felt a chill run down her spine. She turned around. "I should have known. What do you want from me?"

"I thought that would be obvious by now," Lord Malcolm said. He smiled a disturbing smile stood up from his chair and walked over to her bed. "You Christine. I want you, my dear."

Looking at him with pure disgust Christine laughed. "That will never happen."

"Oh, but I think it will. That is, if you ever want to see your father again."

"You killed my father."

"Did I? Or did I just drain him to the point of death. No young lady, your father is very much alive and my prisoner."

Christine was shocked and not sure if she believed him. "You're lying. You killed my father. I know you did."

"Captain," Lord Malcolm called out.

Captain Blythe entered the bedroom.

"Sir."

"Yes, be a good man and retrieve Miss Wolchek's father for her will you?" Lord Malcolm asked.

"It will be my pleasure," he said smugly. He turned and walked out of the room.

"And what of Ryan and Danny? Are you holding them prisoner here as well?" she asked. She was desperate to know if they were still alive.

Lord Malcolm laughed and looked at her with cold and empty eyes.

"They are dead," he said. "A pity really. I would very much liked to have met this Ryan Anderson. I hear he was...unique."

"Dead?" Christine said unable to hide her shock. She turned away from Lord Malcolm and looked out across the room not believing what she was just told. "That's not possible. Not Ryan! There is no way this can be true" she mumbled to herself in disbelief.

"Oh, but it is. I can assure you Ryan Anderson is very dead. Three nicely grouped shots to his heart took care of him most effectively."

"Bastard! You bloody bastard!" Christine snapped as she fixed Lord Malcolm with a look of pure hatred.

"Come now Christine, enough of this foolishness. Did you really think I would let a Wellington bastard live? You and your father have engaged in this foolishness for far too long. Nothing can come of that bloodline but trouble. The sooner we track down and eliminate any remaining Wellingtons, the better off the Society will be."

This sent Christine over the edge.

"It's not to better the Society. It's to better you! You don't want others to exist that might challenge you or your claim to the Society's wealth and power! Your ego and pride won't accept that there are others out there stronger than you!"

Just then there was a knock on the door and Captain Blythe walked in. Looking past him, Christine was stunned to see her father being lead into the room at gun point by another guard.

"Father!" She jumped from the bed, ran to him and embraced him.

Dr. Wolchek was weak and tired. "Christine, my child..." he said in a low raspy voice as he held her. Tears rolled down his cheeks.

"What have they done to you?" she asked as she held him tightly with both relief and dread for she knew that they were both Lord Malcolm's prisoners. Their lives were in his hands now.

"How touching. Father and daughter reunited after all these long months," Lord Malcolm said to Captain Blythe with false sincerity.

"What are you going to do with us?" Christine demanded.

"That depends entirely on the two of you. You agree to accept me as the undisputed leader of the Society and promise to obey me, then I will let you live."

Christine did not believe him for a second. "What else?"

Lord Malcolm looked directly at her. "What a smart girl you are, but why spoil all the surprises at once. We have plenty of time to discuss the terms of this arrangement later. People like us have all the time in the world." He turned to Captain Blythe. "Escort the good doctor and his lovely daughter to their new living quarters."

Blythe pulled a gun form his shoulder holster and pointed it at them motioning for them to move in the direction he was indicating.

Chapter 35
The Rescue

After arriving in England, Danny drove them to the small village of Devonshire not far from the Society's headquarters where they rented a remote cottage to plan their next move. Danny's knowledge of the Manor House and its daily activities would be useful in devising a way for rescuing Christine. Knowing that the Manor had multiple daily deliveries, they decided this would be the best chance they would have to sneak into the compound undetected. Once they were in, they would create some kind of diversion in order to buy enough time to find and rescue Christine. But what would cause enough of a distraction to create such a diversion?

"I got it!" Danny cried out.

"What?" Ryan asked.

"The generator room! It has 12,000 gallons of emergency fuel stored in huge tanks under the west wing of the house. It's not far from the main food storage facility. The trucks practically back right up to the underground entrance next to it when they deliver supplies. We just need to sneak into the room, plant the explosives and wait for the show. That much fuel will require several fire services to come from nearby villages. This should cause enough mass panic for us to get in and pretend to be helping rescue people from the burning building."

"That's a good plan, but how do we make sure Christine is not injured or even killed in the explosion?" Ryan asked.

"I'm pretty sure they'll be keeping her in one of the dungeon holding cells located several stories underground and far from the generator room. If she is there, she'll be safe. If she's not, then Lord Malcolm is likely keeping her close to his apartments which are also located at the other end of the house in the north wing. Either location should shield her from any danger."

Ryan thought about it for a few moments. "We're going to have to chance it. At this point we don't have any other options." He stood up from his chair and walked to the window ledge where Tor was lying and rubbed Tor's head. "Where are we going to find the explosives we need to blow up the generator room?"

With a cunning smile, Danny said, "Leave that to me." He grabbed the car keys off a nearby table. "I'll be back in a few hours with everything we'll need."

After Danny left, Ryan decided to go for a walk with Tor. The cottage was located on a small river deep in the country. Ryan was unaware it was the same river that ran next to the Manor House about four miles away. The area outside the village was mostly agricultural mixed with large expanses of new growth forest and numerous nature trails built by the locals for recreation.

The walk was relaxing. The tranquility of the woods and the gentle flowing of the water helped Ryan calm his mind and body. The last twenty-four hours had been hectic. The rush to leave Colorado, the long flight and refueling stops, and the constant worry about Christine was all weighing heavy on his mind.

After walking for about twenty minutes, Ryan and Tor found a small clearing not far off the main trail next to the river. Ryan sat on the ground facing the water. It was about 3:00pm and the spring air smelled delightfully fresh and clean. Allowing his body to relax, Ryan sat there taking in the area's beauty. Tor found the scenery exciting. His senses were heightened by new smells and places to explore. Sensing Ryan's concerns, Tor rubbed against him. "Thanks buddy, I needed that," Ryan said as he scratched behind his ears.

Tor laid down and rolled over on his back. Ryan smiled and rubbed his belly. "What an adventure we've had wouldn't you say, bud? If you hadn't saved my life I would be long dead by now. Thanks, my friend." Ryan was thoughtful for a moment. "I'm not sure where we go from here. But I do know I have to try and save Christine and maybe finally deal with this Lord Malcolm character. If I don't take care of him now, we'll be running for the rest of our lives and I don't know about you buddy, but that's not acceptable. I want my life back." After sitting by the river and tapping the undercurrent for a while, Ryan and Tor made their way back to the cottage to wait for Danny.

Danny did not disappoint. He returned not only with the explosives, but also several small incendiary devices and uniforms for a particular delivery company. If the idea was to start a fire, then Danny had the right equipment to do just that. He had acquired four blocks of C-4 along with detonators and timing devices. He also had six grenade-like incendiary devices that when detonated, cast a flammable sticky napalm-like substance in a 10-to-15 foot radius. Such devices are often used by arsonists for maximum effectiveness.

"What are these for?" Ryan asked holding one of the incendiary units.

"Insurance. If the C-4 isn't enough, then we can toss these into other rooms as we pretend to help rescue people from the burning house. They'll help us spread the fire and keep the panic and confusion going until we find Christine. Once you push the button on the top you have 10 seconds to throw it. To be honest Ryan, I'm willing to burn down the whole damn place and everyone in it if it helps us find Christine."

Ryan knew Danny wasn't kidding. He admired Danny's devotion to Christine. Having lived with the two of them for months, Ryan knew him well. Dr. Wolchek had taken Danny under his wing many years ago. In need of an assistant and capitalizing on Danny's medical background, Dr. Wolchek found him to be invaluable in helping with research and medical evaluations. Danny was like a brother to Christine and a son to Dr. Wolchek. They spent many decades together and developed a close bond over the years. Danny's love and devotion to Christine and her father touched Ryan. He could see the pain in Danny's eyes when he recounted the events of the coup and the doctor's murder. Ryan knew Danny wanted to get Christine back as badly as he did. And Ryan knew Danny was serious about burning the whole place to the ground if it was necessary to find Christine.

For the remainder of the evening, Ryan and Danny finalized the details of their plan. Knowing they had to get an early start to intercept the delivery truck they needed, both decided to turn in early. They knew the next day would be long and dangerous. Though neither one of them said it out loud, both were aware that it could also be their last. Lying in his bed staring at the dimly lit ceiling with Tor on his chest, a strange feeling of calmness came over Ryan. He felt at peace. Like everything would be okay. He drifted into a deep, restful sleep.

# # #

Sitting in the Security and Surveillance Center at the Society's headquarters, Adam Locksley noticed his computer flashing a possible likeness match. Since Captain Blythe had been searching for Christine, Ryan and Danny for many months, likeness notices were not uncommon. Adam would often see them pop up during his shift as he monitored surveillance systems from around the world. This particular notice got his attention because of the 70% likeness match. Because a high percentage was rare, Adam decided to inform his supervisor.

"Sir, is Captain Blythe still interested in surveillance searches for those three on the run?" Adam asked his supervisor.

"What? Haven't you heard Captain Blythe's account of the matter?" asked an irritated supervisor.

"Well, yes sir. Of course I have," Adam replied.

"Then why do you ask?"

"Because the computer claims to have found a 70% possible match for Overstreet."

The supervisor gave Locksley a disinterested look over his reading glasses.

"And practically in our own back yard, sir. The computer says the possible match is in Devonshire. Should we inform Captain Blythe?"

"Absolutely not! He took care of Overstreet when he assassinated the Wellington bastard and captured Miss Wolchek. He would not be happy if we brought this to his attention now. It would look as if we were questioning his report. Besides, Overstreet is a redhead. You know all those people look alike. The computer was probably confused," the supervisor answered.

"Yes, sir," Adam replied. He crumbled up the report and grainy black and white picture that accompanied it. "Far be it for me to question the Captain's credibility," he said as he threw the ball of paper into a nearby trash can.

Chapter 36
Putting the Plan in Action

Feeling Tor's paw patting his face, Ryan tried to ignore him by changing position and shielding his face with his arm. Tor was an early riser, but Ryan was determined to get a few more minutes of sleep. Tor had other ideas. Since he failed to wake Ryan with gentle nudging, he resorted to more violent tactics.

"Ouch!" Ryan hollered as Tor smacked his arm with his claws fully extended.

"I'm up, I'm up! What's so urgent?" Ryan asked. He stretched before getting out of bed.

Tor jumped down and paced the floor while meowing repeatedly. As Ryan made his way to the main living room, Tor ran to the front door and started pawing at it.

"Oh, I see. You want to go out. Okay old man, I'll turn you loose on England but stay close to the house. When we return we may need to get out of here in a hurry," Ryan said as he opened the door. Ryan knew Tor did not understand what he was saying and tried to express his wishes through energy. As Tor shot outside he ran about half way down a small stone path before stopping and looking back at Ryan. Feeling his energy, Ryan could tell Tor was on a mission.

"You okay buddy?" Ryan asked feeling Tor's urgency.

Tor meowed softly then turned and ran at full speed down the path and out the gate.

Puzzled by Tor's behavior, Ryan closed the door and headed to the kitchen to get something to eat.

"Morning," Danny said. He was wide awake and already dressed sitting at the kitchen table.

"Morning," Ryan responded. "You're dressed? When did you get up?"

"About an hour ago. I wanted to go over the details of the plan one more time."

Ryan poured a cup of coffee for himself and sat down across form Danny. "Relax. We've been over this a hundred times. What could possibly go wrong?" Ryan asked smiling at a nervous Danny.

Danny looked at Ryan with a blank stare frozen in his chair. "You're right. What could possibly go wrong?" He shrugged his shoulders and shook his head laughing along with Ryan. "God help us!"

After breakfast, Ryan and Danny packed the uniforms matching the delivery company truck they were going to highjack into a duffèl bag along with the explosives and loaded it in their car. The plan was to pretend to be stranded motorists and flag down the delivery truck for help. They would use their power to knockout its occupants long enough to allow them to take the truck and get away. In theory it all sounded pretty clear cut, but both had deeper concerns.

At 8:30am, Ryan and Danny positioned themselves along a wooded section of road not far from the turn leading to the Manor House driveway and began their wait.

They did not have to wait long. Deliveries to the Manor were tightly controlled. Danny knew this particular truck arrived at the Manor about 9:15am every Thursday. He could see it from the window in his former office.

"Here it comes," Danny said.

"Showtime," Ryan said.

Ryan walked into the road waving his arms. When the truck slowed to a stop, Ryan asked if he could borrow some tools so they could change a flat tire. The driver said that they had a delivery to make, but could loan them the tools and pick them up on the way back. Ryan thanked them and acted grateful for their help. After pulling off the road in front of them, the occupants got out and walked around to the back of the truck to meet Ryan and Danny. Again thanking them Ryan and Danny extended their hands to shake. When they gripped hands, Ryan and Danny pulled a huge amount of energy from them causing them to cringe in pain before passing out.

"Get them into the woods and out of sight," Danny said looking around.

After dragging the men into the woods, Ryan recharged their energy and put their minds in a deep sleep; one they would not wake from for hours. Danny and Ryan quickly changed into the uniforms and loaded the explosives in the truck. In a matter of a few minutes they were on their way.

"So far so good," Ryan said. He adjusted his hat and pulled the truck out onto the road.

10 minutes later they were approaching the main gates of the Manor House. Recognizing the truck, the guard simply motioned them through.

"That was easy," Ryan said. He looked at Danny and shrugged his shoulders.

"They've become complacent. Their arrogance would never let them think they might one day be attacked. Remember Ryan, they believe they are above man on all levels and in all things. They have no idea what's about to happen," Danny said confidently.

Ryan positioned the truck to Danny's instructions in the delivery area. They got out, opened the roll up door on the back of the truck and began unloading supplies. Security was around, but seemed uninterested in what was happening. It was routine. Following Danny into the supply corridor, Ryan learned where the supplies were to be taken. Given the quantity, the unloading process would take some time. Fortunately, the Manor House staff were only involved in showing them where to put the bulk of the supplies. Once they were in the storage room, other house staff would organize them. There was virtually no supervision. On the third trip in, Danny disappeared into a side corridor and entered the generator room. Once inside, he quickly planted the C-4 explosives on the emergency fuel tanks. Knowing it would take another 20 minutes to unload the truck, Danny set the timers. The explosions would start while they were still on the grounds so they could pretend to help evacuate people.

10 minutes later, Danny rejoined Ryan and continued helping unload the truck. They anxiously counted down the minutes.

Standing in the storage room, Danny tapped his watch. "9:37. Two minutes until the first explosion. Let's get back to the truck."

Two minutes later, pretending to be getting supplies from deep inside the truck, Danny and Ryan were rocked by a huge blast as the first explosive went off. The truck rocked violently and was pelted by bricks and stone from the house.

"Here, take a few of these," Danny said as he pulled a few incendiary devices about the size of a hockey puck from his back pack and handed them to Ryan. "Just push the button and throw."

Kitchen staff ran out of the delivery exit as well as other doors leading out of the house. The fuel had ignited and was burning red hot throughout the bottom floor where the kitchen and storage areas were located. Suddenly there was another violent explosion which caved in part of the kitchen ceiling causing even more fire to erupt out of the second floor windows above the kitchen. Black smoke and burning debris scattered over the delivery area and into some of the formal gardens that surrounded this wing of the house. People were running in all directions scared and confused. The Security detail was busy trying to help people get out of the burning building. Alarms could be heard going off throughout the Manor House prompting people in all sections to evacuate.

"It's now or never," Ryan said.

Danny nodded in agreement. "Follow me and stay close."

They took off running across the smoke filled compound and made their way through another emergency exit door left open for people to escape.

"Lets check the dungeons first. That's likely where they're keeping her," Danny said. By now smoke was making its way through the house. People were panicking and hurriedly trying to find avenues of escape.

The door they entered led them through a series of servant passages.

Danny knew the most direct path to the dungeon holding area would require them to exit the passageway next to the formal dining room, then cut through the library to another large hall where the dungeon entrance was located. Hoping there would be enough smoke obscuring security cameras, Danny looked out from the passage way and saw that the smoke was light. He tossed an incendiary device into the formal dining room. The room was 100 feet long by 30 feet wide with ceilings three stories high. As beautiful as it was, Danny thought nothing of turning the entire thing into a raging inferno if it helped to get Christine back. After the ten second delay there was a powerful explosion and then the room erupted in fire. The centuries' old wood ignited at once and fire engulfed the room.

"Come on," Danny yelled to Ryan as they ran out the door making their way to the library. Danny threw another incendiary device into the center of the room as they passed through.

They ran down another hallway to a door leading to a crude, modern set of stairs descending under the Manor House. This was a much later addition and had been built with reinforced cinder block. The lower floors of the Manor House were built after World War II and further strengthened during the Cold War era. The chance of the fire raging above reaching the lower levels was slim. Still, it was the diversion they needed. After descending several flights below ground, Danny and Ryan emerged into another large hall. On both sides were doors that resembled those found in a prison with slots at the bottom for delivering meals and a small window at the top.

"You take the left and I'll take the right," Ryan said, as he motioned to Danny to start looking.

# # #

"What the hell is going on?" Captain Blythe said as he entered the Manor's main security center located in one of the out buildings.

"Explosions in the generator room, sir,"

Just then a monitor flashed bright and turned to static.

"What was that? Where was that? Blythe shouted.

"The dining hall sir. There's been another explosion. It must be a gas leak."

Blythe pointed to another officer. "You. Play back the video of the dining room right before the monitor went dead. Now!" Before the officer had a chance to play it back, the library camera flashed and went dead.

The security officer played back the footage of the dining hall the explosion was captured on film.

"How can the fire get from the generator room to the dining hall so fast?" Blythe asked out loud. When the library camera went out he was really confused. "How can this be?"

"Did you order the prisoners evacuated, Sir?" asked another security officer as he looked at one of the monitors.

"No, why?"

"Someone's in the holding area."

Looking at the monitor, Blythe gasped when he recognized the two men. "Overstreet and that Wellington bastard are here," he yelled.

Shocked by what he was seeing, Blythe quickly regained his composure and turned to the nearest officer.

"Order two officers to meet me by the south staircase. Tell them to wait for me to join them. They are not to engage the intruders. Is that clear? I want the honor of capturing these two myself." He quickly exited the security floor and headed to the main house to join the other officers.

# # #

Looking through a small window five doors down Ryan yelled out, "Christine!"

Having heard the explosions, Christine was standing by the door trying to look out the window when Ryan's face suddenly appeared. Both immediately broke into smiles.

"Danny, she's here."

Danny ran over to Ryan and looked through the window. "Hello, old girl. Good to see you again," he said.

Ryan grabbed the release lever and opened the door. Christine jumped into his arms and kissed him passionately while reaching out and grabbing Danny and pulling him into them.

"I'm so happy to see you both. Now let's get my father and get out of here."

Danny gasped. "Your father?"

"Yes. Lord Malcolm is holding him here, too. We must find him!"

"Look in all the cells," Ryan ordered. "And be quick about it."

"Here, here, he's here," Danny yelled out as he opened a door at the far end of the hall.

"Danny my boy! What are you doing here?" Dr. Wolchek asked.

"We came to rescue Christine. You're a bonus," Danny said, as he grabbed the doctor by his shoulders and hugged him tightly.

Christine called out to her father as she and Ryan ran over to him and buried herself in his arms.

"My sweet child," Dr. Wolchek said. He noticed Ryan. "Mr. Anderson. Good to see you again."

"And you, sir. Now if you don't mind we need to get out of here. Now."

They made their way back to the staircase with Danny leading the way. Abruptly stopping on the stairs, Danny motioned for the others to hold. He could see under the door from his position and noticed two pairs of boots standing on the opposite side. He put his finger to his lips and motioned for them to go back down one level. Danny pulled a grenade from his backpack and pulled the pin. He rolled it next to the door and took cover with the others. Within seconds, pieces of the door and walls rained down the stairwell.

"Follow me," Danny said. They made their way through the smoldering doorway and out into the large open hall only to be confronted by Captain Blythe and two security officers with their guns drawn.

"Going somewhere?" Blythe asked with a cocky tone.

Ryan's eyes immediately flashed white but Blythe was not startled. He turned his gun on Christine. "That will be enough," he said threatening.

Ryan's eyes returned to normal, but the intensity was no less diminished.

Blythe put his finger to his ear to better hear his ear mike.

"Yes, sir. I'll bring him to you now." With a cocky smile, Blythe turned to one of his guards.

"Mr. Anderson will be coming with me. Take the others to the dungeon. If they resist, kill them."

"Yes, sir." The guard pointed his gun at Christine and the others, motioning for them to move.

Chapter 37
Victoria

Blythe turned to Ryan. "I don't know how you survived being shot, but I can guarantee you will not survive what's waiting for you next." Ordering the remaining guard to pick up Danny's backpack with the explosives and bring it with them, Captain Blythe led Ryan to the grand staircase in the main foyer at the base of the north wing of the Manor. The building was filling with smoke ranging from dense to light, but the fire was only burning out of control in the west wing. Manor security and other staff were manning fire hoses trying to keep it from spreading to the rest of the house. The decision was made to let the fire burn, containing it to the already damaged wing of the house. Per Lord Malcolm's order, nobody in the compound had called any of the local fire services. Guards were even sent to the end of the quarter mile driveway to secure the entrance. The entire estate was on lock down. No one was allowed in or out. They did not want an investigation or an inspection of the compound. Sacrificing this part of the building would be a heavy price, but one worth paying in order to avoid any outside involvement.

As Ryan was led up the stairs, he thought of Tor. That look Tor had when he turned back on the path and stared at him weighed heavy in his thoughts. Did Tor know this was the end? The last day of his life? He thought it was strange that came to mind at this particular time. But, Ryan was not willing to go down without a fight. Knowing he was being led to Lord Malcolm, he actually welcomed the encounter. Finally he was going to meet the man who for whatever reason wanted him dead. If nothing else, Ryan was hoping to finally understand why.

They reached Lord Malcolm's office located on the second floor in the far corner of the north wing. Lord Malcolm had not evacuated. Instead, he ordered the rest of the house secured and had all available personnel report to help the Society's fire service contain the fire in the west wing. Blythe knocked on one of the double doors leading to Lord Malcolm's office.

"After you," he said to Ryan as he opened one door and motioned for him to enter. Ryan walked through without hesitation.

Lord Malcolm rose to his feet from behind a large desk.

"Mr. Anderson. We finally meet. I take it this commotion is all your doing?" he asked as he gestured toward the window where the entire west wing of the Manor house could be seen burning out of control.

Not answering, Ryan looked at Lord Malcolm with a mix of disgust and curiosity. He looked to be a man in his late forties or early fifties. Distinguished looking, like a man who expected and required others to serve him. Nobility, Ryan thought. And someone who was not accustomed to being told no.

"Yes, your Lordship. He and Overstreet are responsible for the commotion. We found this backpack with C-4 and other explosives in it," Captain Blythe answered. He leaned the backpack against the side of Lord Malcolm's desk.

"Overstreet? The same Overstreet you said you took care of in Colorado?"

Humbled and out of character, Blythe lowered his head in shame. "Yes, your Lordship. It appears that I was mistaken about Overstreet's condition." In an attempt to try and save face, he apologized. "I apologize my Lord for misleading you, but I was convinced he..."

"Enough! It's too late for an explanation now. It also appears Mr. Anderson has somehow made a miraculous recovery as well."

"Mr. Anderson was confirmed dead! Three shots to his chest! I..." he couldn't finish his sentence.

"Look at what your incompetence has caused! Our home is on fire. Leave me. I want to speak with Mr. Anderson alone."

"But, your Lordship. Do you think that's wise? He's dangerous. I request you keep one of us in here with you," Captain Blythe said as he motioned to himself and the other guard.

"Leave us," Lord Malcolm ordered with a tone not to be questioned again.

"Yes, your Lordship," Captain Blythe replied. He partly bowed then nodded to the other guard to leave the room.

As the door shut Lord Malcolm stood looking at Ryan studying his facial features with great interest. "So it's true. You do look like your distant ancestor. How fascinating," he said.

"That's what people keep telling me."

"Do they now? Alistair believes you are destined to become something special. I wonder...what do you think?" Lord Malcolm asked.

"I have no idea. And I take it you have no intention of finding out, either."

"I have no intention of letting you leave this room alive."

"I kind of figured that. But before you kill me can you at least tell me why you're so afraid of me?" Ryan knew this would provoke a response. A man with Lord Malcolm's ego would never admit to being afraid of anything. Ryan knew his only chance was to buy time and hopefully find an opportunity to attack.

"Afraid of you? Hardly. It's not fear. Far from it actually," Lord Malcolm said amused. "I'm not afraid of you at all, my boy." Lord Malcolm got right up in Ryan's face. "I loathe you. You and your entire bloodline. I have made it my life's quest to eliminate you and any others like you."

Ryan was shocked. The depth of his hatred was deep. He was consumed by it and Ryan wanted to know why.

"What have I done to offend you so?" Ryan asked with genuine interest.

Lord Malcolm sat down at his desk. He took his time responding to Ryan's question. "Nothing you've done Mr. Anderson, but your distant ancestor. When Lord Wellington evolved into one of our kind, the Society did not exist as it does today. It was a loose association of like-minded people such as ourselves. I had already reinvented myself and obtained a position of nobility. I took a mortal wife and had a daughter as part of my cover. We were active members in London Society and enjoyed all the benefits such a position afforded us. My wife and I loved each other deeply and spoiled our daughter, Victoria, to no end. We wanted only the best for Victoria and had planned that she marry into society. Victoria had a future, responsibilities, obligations to her family. But she was bewitched by the young Lord Wellington. I did not know he was what he was at the time. It's possible he did not know it yet either. Nevertheless, he relentlessly pursued my daughter against my express wishes. They began meeting secretly. I later learned they went to great lengths to conceal their encounters."

"Why did you disapprove? He came from nobility?"

"Because I saw him for what he was! My daughter was a conquest. A game. He did not love her as she loved him."

"But how do you know?"

Irritated by the question, Lord Malcolm rose to his feet and walked around the desk toward Ryan. "Because I had him followed. I knew he frequented brothels, opium dens and other unacceptable establishments. When I confronted Victoria she did not believe it and insisted that I had fabricated the information. This only made matters worse." Lord Malcolm paused. His eyes burned with rage as he stared through Ryan remembering past events. "One evening after I forbid her to have contact with Wellington, she left the house and did not return. She was gone for weeks before we heard from her. She had been with Wellington. They left the city and embarked on a wild love affair on the run. Three weeks later I got a message from her." He looked at Ryan with a mix of deep sadness and intense hatred as the memory of it burned in his mind. "He had abandoned her in a small town far north of here. I went to bring her home immediately. Victoria was devastated. She felt shamed and humiliated. I knew her reputation in London society could never be salvaged, but she was my daughter and I loved her."

Lord Malcolm paused and looked toward a portrait of a young woman hanging over the fireplace.

"Shortly after arriving home Victoria became deathly ill. We later discovered she was pregnant. Over the next several months it became obvious that the pregnancy would be difficult. Despite the problems she was experiencing, Victoria insisted on having the child," Lord Malcolm said shaking his head.

"She died in childbirth didn't she?" Ryan asked.

"Yes. But that was not the end of this tragedy. Not only did I lose my only daughter, but also the child. My wife was so distraught she became ill and died two days later. So you see Mr. Anderson, in the short span of a few days, I lost my daughter, grandchild, and wife. Do you have any idea what that kind of pain is like? Do you Mr. Anderson? No I don't think you do."

Neither one of them said anything. The silence in the room was deafening. Both stared at each other incapable of finding the right words.

"I'm sorry for your loss. I truly am. But I am not that man," Ryan said.

"Maybe not, but it changes nothing. Your ancestor wasn't content with only destroying my daughter, he continued creating monsters and addicts of good people. When he finally resorted to murder, the time came to put an end to him."

"But it wasn't so easy was it?" Ryan asked.

"No. Alistair was right about one thing. Wellington was strong. He had developed his gift into a powerful weapon. We tried for months to catch him. Finally after bribing one of his servants were we able to get into his house and ambush him. Though it almost cost me my life, killing your ancestor was probably the most satisfying experience I have ever had. I decided then and there that I would eliminate every bastard child he spawned no matter how long it took." Lord Malcolm got right in Ryan's face. "You, sir, are simply unfinished business from a night long ago."

Ryan knew it was now or never. He had to strike while he had some element of surprise. Ryan lunged for Lord Malcolm and managed to grab his neck, eyes blazing a brilliant blue-white. He opened his mind to draw in Lord Malcolm's life force, but it did not happen. Lord Malcolm smiled an evil smile then his eyes ignited into a fiery, reddish-yellow glow. Before Ryan realized what was happening he was flying through the air. He hit the far wall with such force it knocked the air from his lungs. Gasping for breath as he fell to the floor in a heap, Ryan was dazed and confused. He heard Lord Malcolm laughing across the room.

"Oh come now, boy. You have to do better than that if you want to defeat me. Get up and try again."

Knowing he was clearly out matched, Ryan's mind raced to come up with a plan. But, it was too late. He felt himself being picked up by energy. He knew Lord Malcolm had mastered drawing from the undercurrent and was using it against him. The energy held him suspended in the air. Then, just as before, Lord Malcolm threw him across the room smashing into the side of the desk and spilling the contents of Danny's backpack on to the floor. Laying there, with his body screaming in pain, Ryan saw one of the incendiary units under the desk out of sight. From his present position, he was unable to reach it, but given the chance, he would use it to create a diversion allowing him time to escape. Forcing himself to stand, Ryan connected to the undercurrent but could only draw enough power to repair himself before he was once again sent flying across the office crashing into furniture. Lying on the floor Ryan pulled in more energy and tried to repair himself. This time, he stayed connected. He focused on a nearby chair and threw it at Lord Malcolm. The movement was clumsy, but it partly worked. He could feel what he needed to do. Controlling the energy without help was difficult. He had always had Tor, Christine or Danny to help, but he was on his own now and it was do or die.

Ducking to avoid the chair, Lord Malcolm did not miss the attempt. "Very good Mr. Anderson, but not good enough" He pushed Ryan against the far wall. Then with a huge surge of power, Lord Malcolm picked Ryan up and pulled him toward him only to smash him into the front of his desk. As Ryan fell to the floor, he reached under the desk and pressed the button on the incendiary unit. With as much energy as he could muster he pushed the incendiary unit toward Lord Malcolm. Simultaneously focusing energy to push himself across the room toward the door. He did it with such force he threw himself against the far wall by the door.

Lord Malcolm laughed out loud.

"What was that? If poor Alistair could only see you now, he would be so disappointed! But enough of this foolishness. It's time to say good bye, Mr. Anderson."

Just as Lord Malcolm's eyes blazed with intent to kill, there was a huge explosion from under his desk. Liquid fire covered him in a sheet of flames. Ryan dove for the door and managed to escape the inferno before the fire reached him. The desk deflected the explosion and afforded him just enough time to escape. He heard Lord Malcolm screaming. It was a terrible sound. While he was glad to be alive, some part of him felt sorry for the man. Ryan quickly tapped the undercurrent and used its energy to repair his injuries. Knowing someone would soon be coming, he stood up and ran down the wide hallway to the staircase determined to rescue Christine and the others.

Chapter 38

Just as Ryan reached the top of the stairs, Captain Blythe appeared.

"And where do you think you are going?" he asked arrogantly.

Without thinking, Ryan's eyes blazed the brilliant blue-white. The force knocked Blythe over the staircase railing sending him to his death on the marble floor below.

Feeling confident, Ryan stayed connected to the current. As he made his way to the landing midway down the stairs, another guard appeared at the bottom of the staircase. Using the energy, Ryan slammed him into the far wall of the foyer, knocking him unconscious.

Ryan made his way to the stairs leading to the holding area. He knockout two more guards by throwing them into opposite walls. The ability to draw on the power and project it at will became easier with every attempt.

When Ryan reached the holding block, he noticed at once that smoke was beginning to fill the corridor. He quickly located Christine and freed her, then Danny and Dr. Wolchek.

"How did you escape?" Christine asked.

Danny saw the two unconscious guards. "What happened to them?" he asked.

"Let's just say my powers just took a huge evolutionary leap forward."

"What did I tell you? He is the one," Dr. Wolchek said.

"Not now, Father! Ryan, I don't know what you did, but do you think you can use it to get us out of here?" Christine asked.

"I think so. Follow me," he replied. He led them back to the servants' corridors where they made their way to another emergency exit that opened to a side courtyard. Most of the staff and household residents were either fighting the fires in the west wing or had been evacuated to a courtyard far from the fires on the south side opposite from their present location. Looking out the door, they saw the courtyard was empty with the exception of a few parked security vehicles. As soon as they entered the courtyard they were immediately spotted by two guards who ordered them to stop. Ryan effortlessly disarmed the men and then threw them as far as he could.

"Wow!" Christine said.

"Nice work," Danny added.

"I learned it from Lord Malcolm before I blew him up," Ryan said shrugging his shoulders. He was answered by a barrage of questions.

"What?"

"You blew him up?"

"How?"

"With one of Danny's explosives."

"I would like to have seen that," Danny said shaking his head with approval.

"Me too," Dr. Wolchek said with a slight chuckle.

A hail of gunfire suddenly rained down on their position. They had just enough time to take refuge between the two parked security vehicles. The vehicles' armored siding offered them protection.

"Can you see where it's coming from?" Ryan asked. He looked around one truck only forced to pull back when additional rounds hit the ground in front of him.

"From the roof of those buildings. They have us pinned down in a crossfire," Dr. Wolchek said.

"What can we do?" Christine asked.

"I have an idea. I'll pretend to surrender and then when they reveal themselves, use your power Ryan to knock them off the roofs," Dr. Wolchek said.

"Wait, Doc. I just learned this. I'm not sure what the range is," Ryan replied.

"Nonsense, my boy. Just focus and do it."

Before Ryan had time to object, Dr. Wolchek stood up and was waving his hands. Unknown to them, the guards were not taking prisoners. They had orders to shoot to kill.

Suddenly Dr. Wolchek was blown to the ground by a bullet smashing into his right shoulder.

Christine screamed in horror.

Danny was able to drag him back behind the vehicle before the next shot was fired.

"Bad plan, Doc," Ryan said, with a disapproving look.

"Worth a try, anyway," Dr. Wolchek said. He winced in pain after attempting to shrug his shoulders.

Ryan put his hand on the doctor's injured shoulder and used the energy to heal it like he did with the mountain lion cub in Colorado. After a few seconds the wound was closed. Ryan patted his shoulder then moved back to another position so he could try and get a better view of the courtyard.

"He healed my shoulder! How did you do that?" Dr. Wolchek asked as he repeatedly extended his right arm bursting with excitement. "Christine. Look. He healed me!"

"I know, Father. That's old news. Right now we need to figure out how we're going to get out of here."

"We need some kind of distraction," Ryan said looking around.

Additional security guards arrived and took up positions across the courtyard blocking their access to the main gate.

"Damn it! There's at least twenty guards blocking the gate, Ryan. What are we going to do?" Danny asked as he studied the situation trying to come up with some kind of plan.

"Lets see if this really works," Ryan said. He was about to step out from between the trucks, when they heard gun fire erupting from everywhere.

"What the hell are they shooting at?" Danny asked.

"Look!" Christine shouted pointing skyward.

"Reinforcements!" Danny said.

"Tor!" Ryan shouted. He could feel Tor's energy.

A gigantic flock of large birds filled the sky above almost causing a total eclipse. Owls, hawks and other birds swarmed the compound. The guards panicked and tried desperately to stop the advancing wave. Eyes blazing, the birds swooped in causing the guards to break ranks.

At the same time, Tor came running through the main gates followed by countless other cats. The guards were under assault from both the ground and sky. As the cats advanced, their eyes glowed a brilliant yellow-green, terrifying the guards and causing mass panic.

Ryan took advantage of the distraction to come out from between the trucks and tap the undercurrent. It was so much easier now. He thought that maybe the animals were making it possible. He knew he only had a limited window so he focused and slammed energy into the guards. It was as easy as throwing a baseball. One by one he picked them off. First ripping their guns away, then smashing them into the compound walls and knocking them out. Hearing other guards firing their weapons, he spotted their locations on the roof tops. He grabbed the guards, lifted them high into the air before releasing and letting them crash to the ground in a bloody heap. As more guards approached, he disarmed them and knocked them aside effortlessly. Tor ran over to Ryan and stood beside him as calm as ever.

"Thanks, old man. I owe you big," Ryan said. He continued to disarm and smash approaching security details as they emerged from other buildings. Manor residents and staff were joining in the mass panic and confusion as the birds and cats drove them form their evacuation sites. Mayhem filled the smoky compound.

Looking at Dr. Wolchek, Ryan said, "Your call, Doc. I can level this entire place if you want. I think I have the hang of it now," he added with a wink and a smile.

Lowering his head for a minute then saying, "No...no, I don't think that will be necessary. Call off the animals, please. It's over." Watching Ryan wield his new found power at first excited Dr. Wolchek. But after witnessing the devastation brought about by the conflict, he felt an overwhelming sadness. This is not what he wanted. He was not Lord Malcolm and did not want to become the kind of leader who led by fear and intimidation.

Nodding to the doctor, Ryan raised his hands and slammed them together creating what sounded like a deafening thunder clap. In an instant, both people and animals froze. "Enough!" Ryan's voice boomed out amplified by the energy. His eyes blazed their brilliant blue-white.

No one moved. "The floor is yours, Doc," Ryan said.

Dr. Wolchek climbed on to the tailgate of one of the security trucks. "Lord Malcolm is dead, so is Captain Blythe. At this very moment the Society as we once knew it is also dead." Dr. Wolchek paused to let what he said sink in. He looked out over the stunned group of people before him. "But together we can rebuild the Society into something great-something positive. We have the resources and wisdom to make this organization into something unprecedented. I'm willing to concede that maybe it's time we assume a more proactive role in humanity's future. And why not? We share this planet too. I believe together we can accomplish much, but we cannot abuse what we have. We all have been given a very special gift, no, a responsibility. A responsibility to help each other and the human race. I believe in the Society. I believe together we can make it strong again. Make it an organization that we are all proud to belong to. If you agree with me then let me hear you!" Dr. Wolchek shouted pumping his fist into the air.

Without hesitation, the crowd cheered in agreement. The fact that Ryan was still standing next to the doctor with his eyes blazing and the crowd was surrounded by hundreds of cats and birds all acting as sentries may have had a little to do with their level of enthusiasm. Still, for the most part, the majority of the people supported Dr. Wolchek.

Ryan helped Dr. Wolcheck down from the tailgate of the truck.

"So, I guess it's safe to assume you're going to stay?" Ryan asked as his eyes returned to normal.

Dr. Wolchek listened as the excited crowd continued to cheer before answering. After a few moments he looked at Ryan and smiled. "There is much work to be done here," he said.

"Well if you're determined to stay, I guess the least I could do is put out the fires Danny started," Ryan said smiling.

Danny's eyes got big and his mouth hung open with surprise.

"You are just as much to blame for this mess as I am my friend. And remember, it was you who blew up Lord Malcolm," Danny replied.

"I don't care who did what you two, just put out the fires before there is no Society left," Dr. Wolchek said trying to express the urgency as he watched more of the Manor go up in smoke.

All watched in stunned amazement as Ryan focused the energy and used it to extinguish the flames. In a matter of minutes the fires were all out and the grounds' staff were back at their stations spraying water on the smoldering embers.

The damage to the west wing of the Manor was considerable, but the majority of the house had been spared. The underground levels were also untouched. Still, much work would need to be done to repair the damage-both to the structure and the organization.

"And what about you Ryan? You know there is a place here for you if you want it," the doctor asked. But he already knew the answer.

"I appreciate that Doc, but I'm not ready to give up my life just yet. I still have at least one lifetime to live first. Maybe I'll catch up with you in a decade or two, but for now, I want to go back to a normal and quiet life, whatever that is."

Nodding his head Dr. Wolchek turned to Christine. "And you my dear? The Society could use someone like you on the council. Interested?" he said enticing her with the idea.

Looking at Ryan and then her father, Christine did not immediately answer. Torn between the two men she loved, she remained silent.

Danny cleared his throat. "I think Christine deserves some time off, Doctor. Maybe take a long vacation; a decade or two herself," he said. He lowered his voice as he said to her, "Leaving me here with your father is going to cost you big. You'll owe me."

Dr. Wolchek looked at Danny and smirked.

"Hmm. Rebuilding the Society or a nice quiet life in America...why can't a girl have both?"

"Why not indeed?" Ryan asked as he put his arms around her.

PART EIGHT

Kevin Sneed

Chapter 39
Back in the US six months later

Walking out of his house to the pool deck carrying two rum runners, Ryan handed one to Christine who was lying on a lounge chair in a very flattering two piece bikini.

"You have to admit, Jacksonville, Florida is much nicer than dreary old England. And besides, you deserve some time to yourself. You've been a very busy girl over the past six months."

Christine smiled and sipped her drink. "A girl could get use to this. Thanks."

Christine, Dr. Wolchek, and Danny had indeed been busy over the last six months. Rebuilding the Society demanded a considerable amount of their time. One of their first objectives was restoring the council. She, Dr. Wolchek, and Danny were among those newly elected. After a series of internal debates and lengthy discussions among the members, new directives were drafted spelling out what the Society's roll would be in world affairs. No longer would they stand on the sidelines and watch as the world tore itself apart. Where appropriate, intervention would be allowed but only after serious debate. Events would be studied and judged by all members. If it was decided some kind of action was needed, then a proposal would be put before the full council. The council still had the final word. It was not their intention to dominate or control mankind, they saw themselves more as its guardians. This was a new direction for the Society and everyone knew it was best to begin with small steps. The members were excited about this new direction and had high hopes not only for their future, but for the future of the entire human race.

Christine threw herself into the role with everything she had, and although she loved Ryan very much, she was not about to pass on an opportunity to participate in reshaping the Society. This had been her and her father's dream for many years and now she was finally in a position to make it happen. Ryan understood how important this was to Christine and supported her. When they could make the time, they visited each other. Christine enjoyed spending time in the U.S. Ryan occasionally traveled to England, but mostly he shied away from Society politics. This was not something he wanted to be a part of, at least not yet. She loved Ryan and he loved her but he was still young in years and Christine understood this. She wanted Ryan to enjoy his life and those he shared it with. She had seen so many people come and go in her many years. This was the unfortunate part of being immortal. Watching mortal friends age and eventually die was difficult. She knew Ryan still had a lot to learn about the emotional side of their condition. Over time, immortality can be taxing and she wanted to be there for him when he needed her. And she knew he would as the reality of his immortality became clear. Even though both were leading somewhat separate lives, they still looked forward to their visits and when they were together nothing else seemed important.

Holding hands Christine and Ryan basked in the Florida sun enjoying their drinks happy to be together. Ryan had also been busy over the last six months. Once he returned to Jacksonville he threw himself back into his work and band performances. He loved what he did and more importantly, he missed the people he worked with. He found performing and his advertising work rewarding and challenging on many levels. In some ways having the power he had and not using it was not much different from the way he had chosen to live his life prior to developing his abilities. He always had access to considerable wealth, but chose not to take the easy road. Instead, he preferred to work for what he wanted. Having his unique powers and keeping them to himself was very much the same thing. He knew he could draw on and use them at any time, but chose not to. Instead, preferring to let life and luck dictate the outcome of his daily activities. In this way he felt normal, human.

Tor found it easy to adjust back to his normal routines. The local wildlife lived in constant terror as Tor had proven to be an avid hunter. Ryan disapproved of his murderous tendencies, but he respected that Tor was a cat.

Ryan heard Tor cry out as he approached the two of them lying by the pool. "Hey buddy, where have you been all morning. I assume you're hungry?" he asked.

Tor meowed in agreement.

"Let's see what I can find for you," Ryan said. He was getting up when Christine volunteered.

"You stay right here. I'll get him something to eat. And I want to top off my drink. Can I get you another one?" she asked.

Ryan was surprised. He looked at Tor and shrugged then looked back at Christine. "I see what you're trying to do. You're trying to bribe your way into his good graces with food."

"You know it and I think it's working too," Christine replied.

She stood up then leaned down to kiss Ryan. "I'll be right back." She took his glass and looked at Tor. "Come on boy. I'll take care of you."

Tor meowed and trotted behind her into the house.

Smiling and shaking his head, Ryan settled back into a comfortable position in the lounge chair as he soaked up the warm rays of the afternoon sun. Noticing something reflecting brightly on the ground in the bushes off the deck, he decided to investigate. The sun was casting light on a densely overgrown section of the yard. Since Ryan had let the trees and bushes grow wild in this area for privacy, he had to push his way through the overgrowth to get to whatever it was reflecting so brightly on the ground. It was a small brass name tag still attached to a broken black collar. When he flipped it over to read it, he was dumbstruck. "Well I'll be damned."

After leaving Tor with a plate of food in the kitchen, Christine walked back to the bedroom to retrieve a gift she had brought for Ryan. When she rounded the corner to the room she suddenly felt herself get lifted off her feet then slammed to the floor. Stunned and dazed by the impact, she laid there on the verge of drifting into unconsciousness.

"Did you miss me?" asked a familiar voice. Christine immediately recognized the voice. She saw a grotesque face and gasped in shock.

"Lord Malcolm!"

"I'm here to take back what's mine," he hissed. "First, I'm going to kill Ryan then I'm going to take you. Now sleep." He put his hand on her head and drained enough energy to put her in to a deep sleep.

Standing, Lord Malcolm caught a glimpse of himself in a mirror. He had managed to survive the fire, but his burns were severe. He was only partly successful in healing himself. His reflection further ignited the burning hate he felt for Ryan and all of his bloodline. Quietly walking through the house, he snuck up on Tor who was gorging himself on the turkey snack Christine had given him. Grabbing him with energy, Lord Malcolm tossed him effortlessly into the laundry room adjacent to the kitchen and closed the door trapping him. "It's just you and me now, Mr. Anderson."

Feeling something was wrong, Ryan emerged from the bushes still holding the broken collar. He felt a sudden disturbance in Tor's energy pattern and he felt his distress. Turning in the direction of the house Ryan abruptly stopped. He was frozen in place by the familiar, grotesque figure that stood before him. Not believing what he was seeing he lost valuable time in drawing on the undercurrent. Lord Malcolm did not hesitate. He raised his hand, pointed a gun with a silencer on it directly at Ryan and fired. The impact was violent and tore through Ryan's left shoulder, knocking him back, but he did not go to the ground. When he righted himself and faced Lord Malcolm he heard and felt two more impacts in his chest and stomach. Ryan fell to his knees. Feeling his energy wildly flowing out of the damaged areas of his body, all he could do was tap and hold on to the undercurrent. He knew he was too damaged to fight back, repairing himself was his only hope but he doubted he would have the time.

# # #

Tor recovered quickly and ran to the door. Unknown to Lord Malcolm, Tor knew how to open doors with lever handles. Because of this, Ryan had all the door knobs replaced in the house just for him. Tor stood up and pulled on the handle then pushed the door open. His eyes blazed that brilliant yellow-green. Looking out the open patio door he saw Lord Malcolm standing over Ryan who was bleeding profusely and barely upright on his knees. He ran down the hall to the bedroom where Christine was lying on the floor and pawed her face, but got no response. He stood on her chest and leaned close to her face and forced energy into her. He could only give small amounts because of his size. It was enough to awaken her. Crying loudly, Tor pawed her again, but this time with force and she immediately woke up. "Lord Malcolm!" she said as she jumped to her feet and raced down the hall with Tor.

# # #

Savoring the moment, Lord Malcolm stood over Ryan.

"I've been dreaming of this every minute of every day since our last encounter. Goodbye, Mr. Anderson." His eyes burst into a frightening reddish-yellow glow as he grabbed Ryan by the neck and began to drain his life force.

Christine ran from the house screaming for him to stop. Lord Malcolm was startled and turned to look at her. Christine froze when she saw his blazing eyes and distorted face. He looked like a crazed monster.

Lord Malcolm pointed his gun at her severing his connection with Ryan. Free from his control, but very weak, Ryan lunged at him and managed to knock the gun from his hand and into the pool. Christine also ran at him, but he had already recovered enough to knock her back with energy into the side of the house, dazing her, but not completely knocking her out. Tor ran in and threw off all restraints, allowing him to feed at will. Tor's ability to draw off energy was amazing, especially for such a small creature. Lord

Malcolm knew he only had one option. Facing Tor, Lord Malcolm charged at him taking him by surprise with his sudden move in his direction. Without hesitation, Lord Malcolm kicked Tor with all the force he could manage sending Tor tumbling across the patio and into a planter knocking him unconscious.

Christine and Tor's distractions allowed Ryan to focus and rapidly repair most of the critical damage to his body.

After kicking Tor, Lord Malcolm quickly assessed Christine's condition and felt comfortable in seeing that she was incapacitated. Then turning back to face Ryan, it was his turn to be startled by the sight standing before him.

Ryan was standing fully erect with his head lowered. His muscular physic was even more imposing by the bright red blood covering his body. Frozen in place by both fear and bewilderment, he watched as Ryan slowly raised his head and fixed Lord Malcolm directly in his sights. Then, as if the sun had exploded before him, Ryan's eyes blazed forth in a blinding blue-white light. Lord Malcolm's eyes erupted in a fiery glow. Both determined to destroy the other. Ryan, however, was still weak. He could hold Lord Malcolm off, but he could not over power him. Lord Malcolm was able to hold Ryan off, but was not able to inflict a killing blow. Both were locked in a deadly stalemate.

Out of nowhere, a small owl appeared and landed on Ryan's damaged shoulder. When it landed it gripped him with its talons and sunk them deep into his flesh. Feeling the puncture Ryan was surprised he did not feel pain. Instead he felt an infusion of energy as if he had been plugged into an extra undercurrent. Feeling the owl's power coursing through him Ryan felt his body repairing itself. As he healed, he felt his strength return. He became aware of another presence at his feet. It was Tor. Tor had awakened and walked over to Ryan taking up his Egyptian statue position facing Lord Malcolm. Feeling renewed strength coupled with the power of the owl and Tor, Ryan smiled a wicked smile directly at Lord Malcolm.

"You're done asshole. For all the innocent lives you've taken I sentence you to death!"

Facing Lord Malcolm, Ryan was a frightening sight. His blood covered muscular frame and fierce, glowing eyes as well as the owl attached to his shoulder and Tor at his feet, together made Ryan a sight to behold. Realizing the end was near, Lord Malcolm hissed between clenched teeth, "Bastard! Bloody Bastard!"

Just as Ryan aligned his power with the owl and Tor, they simultaneously unleashed a huge surge of energy at Lord Malcolm. The blast was so big it broke his defense against Ryan and knocked him to the ground. Before he could reconnect to the undercurrent, the owl and Tor had him locked in their deadly stare. Together they unleashed another massive amount of energy at Lord Malcolm but this time focused and held it directly on him. Ryan was doing all he could to stay connected to the undercurrent. The owl and Tor were using Ryan as a ground. He was their connection to the energy but they were converting it into a powerful weapon. He could actually see the energy as it flowed from their eyes like a white-hot laser straight at Lord Malcolm. But this was not energy he could use.

Lord Malcolm screamed in pain as his eyes were burned out of his skull leaving only hollow glowing white sockets. The sight was horrible. Ryan couldn't look away. Within seconds his screaming was muted. Bright light began bursting out of thousands of rapidly expanding holes burning from within his body. In a sudden flash, a blinding white flame completely consumed him. Ryan could feel the heat as Lord Malcolm combusted in front of him. Burning form the inside out Tor and the owl used the converted energy to totally incinerate him and within seconds it was over. Nothing was left of Lord Malcolm but a scattered pile of ashes being blown about the backyard in a light breeze.

Closing his eyes, Ryan slowly felt them return to normal. The small owl released its grip on his shoulder and retracted its talons. Feeling the owl disconnect, Ryan cringed in both pain and relief. Pausing for a moment, the owl looked at Ryan then down to Tor before spreading his wings and flying off. Tor watched with excitement as the bird flew out of sight.

Ryan looked at Tor. "Don't even think about it." He felt the puncture holes. "Ouch," he said out loud and then used the excess energy still coursing through his body to repair the small wounds. He saw Christine trying to stand and ran over to help her. "Are you okay?" he asked helping her to her feet.

"Where did the owl come from?" she said trying to steady herself.

"I don't know but I'm glad she showed up when she did. That extra boost of energy saved my life. I could hold Lord Malcolm off but couldn't do much more than that until she connected with me."

"Did you tell Tor and the owl to kill him like that?" Christine asked.

"No, they did that on their own. They used me to connect to the undercurrent but they somehow used the energy to fry him. Personally, I think Tor was pissed off about being kicked," Ryan said.

"I told you cats and owls were dangerous," she said.

Ryan rolled his eyes.

"Did you and your father know Lord Malcolm was as strong as he was?" he asked.

"No. And those eyes. I've never seen that in any of our kind. But I've never seen the color of your eyes in any of our kind, either."

Noticing her holding her head and still trying to shake off a dizzy feeling, Ryan took her hand and slowly let some of the excess energy drain into her. Feeling the power, Christine felt better. She looked at Ryan and smiled.

"What is it?" he asked.

"Remember the last time you were so overcharged?"

"Smiling and leaning over to kiss her, Ryan said, "Would you like to help bring me back into balance again?"

Kissing him back then pulling away a little Christine said, "Of course, but you need to clean yourself up first." She pushed him causing him to fall into the pool. Immediately the water turned red as the blood washed from his body.

Ryan swam back over to the edge and pulled himself up and out of the pool. "You're next."

Christine smiled back and ran past him jumping into the water. When she surfaced, she stood in the shallow end looking at him. Water glistened on her perfect body. "What are you waiting for?" she asked.

Without hesitation Ryan dove in and surfaced next to her. He put his arms around her and pulled her close. "I love you," he whispered.

"I love you, too." They kissed. A long passionate kiss. When they separated, Christine laughed.

"What is it now?"

"I was just thinking what my father will say when I tell him about this."

In his best English accent, "Child, I told you he's the one!"

The End.

###

This book is dedicated to

Tor

The coolest cat I've ever known

Made in the USA
Columbia, SC
30 August 2020